For Rob.
Without you, this book
would still be a dream.

Table of Contents

INTRODUCTIONS

I first met Susan York (always Sue to her face) in late 2014. She had attended the World Science Fiction Convention (Worldcon) which had taken place in London that August. The T Party Writers' Group had held a writing workshop during the convention. I was a member of the group and had several times taken part in their workshops at previous conventions but hadn't attended this one as it took place on a day I wasn't present. But as a result of that workshop, Sue came along to one of the group's meetings in London. She was about to workshop a story at a future meeting but had to cancel due to an operation. However, I did read that story, which is in this collection: "Happy Birthday". As Sue has said to me, clearly not everyone in the group "got" that story, but it seems I did.

Sue made her first story sale a few years later ("The Little Lighter Girl") and now, seven years on, we have her first collection.

What is noticeable about the stories is their range. The settings include the present day, the future or the recent or further past, in this country or in well-researched others (India in "The Little Lighter Girl", the trenches of World War I in "Remembrance Day"). While the collection is firmly rooted in horror, the stories vary to take in both psychological as well as supernatural darkness, and science fiction and fantastical scenarios. Often the story is one of someone (often but not always female, often but not always a younger adult or a child) striving to establish an identity for themselves, often in the face of opposition to or a threat to that identity. Sometimes this comes from within the family itself, for example from the father in "Taking Flight", a clearly very personal story and my favourite in this book. Sometimes that threat or those obstacles come from wider society, either here on Earth or another planet. In "Justica", that search for an identity is in someone of an alien species, and that quest leads her to break one of her people's taboos.

Starless and Bible Black is Susan York's first collection and its seventeen stories are a fine showcase for her talent and abilities. I recommend you read on.

Gary Couzens
Aldershot, July 2022

Introductions

Starless and Bible Black represents Susan York's full-length debut in the science fiction / fantasy / horror genre and showcases an exciting new voice as, in these tightly-plotted stories, she ranges through past, present and future. She is particularly strong on empathic female characters such as emotionally broken war correspondent Julia ("A Cup of Tea"), the young mother Kimea in "A Gambling Man" or Amy in "Where The Train Stops", who is undergoing therapy for night terrors that may in fact spring from a real-life trauma.

There are tales of forbidden love ("Justica"), atmospheric isolated landscapes ("Starless and Bible Black") and abusive childhoods ("Taking Flight"). The outstanding piece here is the horror novelette "Rhapsody" – a compellingly plausible and brilliantly paced account of a new threat to the safety and wellbeing of our teenagers, told from the up close and personal viewpoint of paramedic Amanda who is seemingly doomed, like Hellenic Cassandra, to tell the truth but not be believed. This memorable story will have you keeping the light on all night afterwards.

Susan York's collection *Starless and Bible Black* is a fulsome, wide-ranging and welcome publication from a British genre author who is certainly one to watch. And read. Heartily recommended.

Allen Ashley
London, July 2022

A CUP OF TEA

Each time she returns from an assignment, Julia brews a cup of tea. PG Tips, Tetley, the brand is unimportant – it is a ritual, one which serves to reinstate her "back home" identity. First Julia rinses out and fills the kettle, places it on the hob. Once it has boiled, she uses some of the water to warm the pot, then ceremoniously measures out the tea. Whilst she waits for it to brew, Julia wipes the work surface then washes away the dust coating her favourite porcelain cup and saucer. Milk and two sugars complete the preparatory process. As she pours the golden stream from the brown pot, a sigh always escapes her. It signifies the commencement of her journey from War Correspondent into a more relaxed personage. Drinking tea from a china cup is a rite of passage between the two. Now, for the first time, the ritual fails.

*

"You need a rest," says Dr Stanton. His eyes watch her response over the thin gold rim of his half-mast glasses. "Your body is telling you to stop, take a break. It's worn out." He smiles gently, this kindly man who has kept watch over Julia's physical fitness for the past twenty years. "You're fifty-one. Now might be a good time to step back, let someone else report on the war."

"No!" The protest emerges before she can stop it.

Dr Stanton holds his hands outwards as if to deflect the sound. It hits the surgery wall and rebounds back into her own ears. Julia wills her body to remain seated. She doesn't want to walk out, knows he means well.

"There must be plenty of jobs in broadcasting you're capable of," he says, removing his glasses and rubbing the bridge of his nose. Red pressure marks indicate the nose pads are too tight.

"And do something different? No thanks."

11

Her irritation is met with calm sympathy. Julia looks away. Her hands are shaking. She sits on them.

"If necessary. It wouldn't hurt to slow down." He indicates towards her hidden hands saying, "Physically, you're in pretty good shape, but your hands, your raised blood pressure and heart rate suggest you're stressed. I'll prescribe some tablets to help, but you need to take steps to deal with whatever is upsetting you." He scrawls on a prescription pad, tears the sheet off, hands it to her. "Your last assignment was tough. Counselling might help."

"But I don't want to slow down," Julia says as she takes the prescription, "I want things to be as they were before."

*

Steam explodes from the kettle's spout causing the whistle to scream. It jolts Julia out of her reverie. Heart racing and with fumbling fingers she turns the gas off, then stands trembling, waiting for her breathing to return to normal. At moments like this she is frightened, yet she felt no fear in the field. She has nerves of steel, everyone tells her so; the film crew, other journalists, members of the public who see her reporting on the news. Why this sudden change? Why now? At her blood pressure check-up, Dr Stanton again suggested counselling.

"It might be sensible to explore why you appear to resent change," he'd said.

"I don't resent change, I don't choose to change."

"Think about it. Phone me if you change your mind."

Julia looks out of the window. Her tenement flat is situated three floors up, giving an intimate yet panoramic perspective on the metropolitan scene below. She purchased the flat in the mid Seventies, just before the property boom. It was as close to the centre of London as she could afford at the time. Since then, the area has grown in popularity, become trendy. She used to love Camden, it's people, the markets, the hustle and bustle of it's streets. Yet, today, after only being home a month, she is stifled by its urbanity. People scurry past her building, heads low, shoulders hunched. They move faster than the cars, which are crawling due to the ever-present roadworks. Julia is certain this particular entrenchment is the same as the one she left behind six months ago. Once, Camden's bustle exhilarated her. Now, it feels tame, alien.

Her attention is drawn to a young woman pushing through the crowds, gaining ground, crying out, raising her hand and waving. She is such a solitary figure, isolated by her actions in a solid mass of moving flesh.

A memory bombards Julia, relentlessly showing images from a news item of a middle-aged woman wearing khaki. The cup shakes, slops hot tea into the saucer and over the fingers holding it. Julia doesn't notice.

The woman is dirty, her dusty face streaked by sweat. The clothes she wears look crumpled as if she has slept in them. She is pushing her way through those who block her path. They slow her desperate movements and once again, Julia feels resentment stirring inside. The white stone of the surrounding buildings is torn in places, crumbled into yellowed dust by the fierce, unrelenting blasts of targeted shells. Here and there, red/orange flames greedily lick the air. The woman waves and calls out. A man staggers towards her, clutching what remains of his arm. Blood is flowing freely between his fingers. Her arms reach out as if to enfold and support him, but he falls at her feet, stretching out a red hand. Blood drips off his fingers onto the dusty road, giving it substance. A reverent silence falls as the cameraman continues to film and the woman realises the injured man is dead.

The woman on the street below reaches her arms out, flings them around a smiling young man. He scoops her up in a bear-hug. The crowd parts around them, reforms further down the pavement. The couple laugh. The man kisses the woman whilst, three storeys above,

Julia smashes the cup and saucer down on the thick carpet. Tea flies everywhere as the cup cracks in two. Julia kicks and punches a wall. Holes appear in the ageing plaster. She digs her nails into the soft fabric of the sofa cushions, ripping them apart. Yet nothing gives within Julia. Treasured mementoes, gathered from war-torn countries, are flung and shattered. One, a small solid statue, is used to smash the glass-fronted cabinets set against one wall. Afterwards, Julia places the statue on the glass-strewn carpet, wraps her slender frame around it. Her breath comes in ragged gasps and her throat is sore. The wreckage around her is meaningless, her actions futile. Finally tears fall, but they harbour no relief.

*

Two months have passed. Julia continues to regard her re-acclimatisation into ordinary life, as a rite of passage. She has rituals to help her cope with the transition from cutting-edge war reporter into city-dweller. Her therapist encourages her to set achievable targets but, she suspects, frowns upon the ceremonial aspects she's introduced, considers them obsessive. *Tough*, thinks Julia, who finds being bloody-minded a coping mechanism. Today, she is visiting Camden Lock market.

August sunshine beats a fierce tattoo on the pavement beneath her feet. Traffic noise seems immense, overwhelming; she can feel the rumbling pulse of passing HGVs. It reminds her of how the impact of shells, pounding buildings into oblivion, registered in her body. She recalls the tension in the unearthly silence surrounding their blasts and shivers.

Julia crosses a busy Chalk Farm Road, copying the jaunty walk of a man who weaves his way through the cars with ease. His fluid movements make her think of how she dodged bullets, when working her way amongst the so-called security barriers, separating the Israeli farming communities from neighbouring Palestinian territories.

Once she's across the road, Julia smiles at how swiftly she's moving while weaving through the crowds. All's good until she bumps into a woman who shoots her a disapproving look.

"Sorry!" says Julia.

The lack of empathy in the woman's stare is familiar. The same emptiness was there in the eyes of her chief, on her return to the broadcasting studio.

"Your job will always be open to you," he said, but she'd known he was lying. After years of working with him, Julia knew his tendency was to offer the "stressed" individual a less demanding field. She'd overheard him telling Tom, her cameraman, "Your film shows she's lost her nerve. There's no way I can send her back."

Unable to stand the looks of pity from her colleagues, Julia went to the staff room. She drank a tasteless tea from the drinks machine.

Tom came in, slung his arm around her shoulders. "It'll do you good to have a break. Things don't get much tougher than the Green Line. None of us liked what happened. Take the time and get well."

The squeeze he'd given her felt meaningful and Julia considered his tears to be real, but misplaced. She wasn't unhappy about what happened during the crew's time at the Green Line. She was angry. Still is. If only memories could be turned off so they didn't impinge on the present, on her so called "recovery". Anger seems such a negative emotion, although her counsellor has told her it can be positive, when used constructively.

The stench of diesel from the narrow boats and the pressure of bodies crowding the market, threatens to overwhelm her. Although, over the years, she has returned to Camden between assignments, these visits have been infrequent and of short duration. The Camden Town of the nineties disorientates her, as does the memories of that fateful day. It resurfaces over and over again, the events shaping and controlling Julia's life, her emotions and others perceptions of her.

She stops before a stall selling oriental goods, is browsing when a boat at the quay side roars into life. Julia flings herself to one side. She rolls under some tightly woven rugs hanging next to the stall and curls into a ball, clasping her hands over her head. Her heart shunts adrenalin through her system and bile rises in her throat.

A rug lifts. A sunburnt face peers at her.

"Are you alright, luv?" the market trader asks. His expression is anxious. Julia's face becomes hot. Once, she was proud of her physical responses, but this? This is embarrassing.

"Yeah, I'm fine. Thanks."

He helps her up then returns to chanting his wares. The crowd has already moved on. If they ever stopped. No attention is paid to her as Julia brushes dirt off her jeans. From the thought she is invisible arises a strangely powerful sensation.

*

"What would you like to discuss today?" Mr Jordan asks.

Julia smiles.

"Has something amused you?" He smiles back, but is ever watchful.

"It's your name," Julia says, "and I can't help but wonder what your first name is."

This time, he smiles for real. "Moses."

Together they laugh at how ridiculous parents can be in the naming department.

What the hell, today I'll tell him.

"I'd like to talk about my last assignment. It's the reason why I wondered about your name."

"Go on."

"I assume you've seen me on the news."

Dr Jordan nods. "Yes, I have."

"Then you know I was reporting from the Green

16

Line. Near Jerusalem."

"I remember it well." His face is blank. It gives nothing away.

Julia begins. She tells her counsellor about the conditions, the difficulties the news crew encountered. The contrasts between the streets of Jerusalem and the broken, dusty remains of the agricultural settlements they passed through. She speaks about car bombs, of the ineffective galvanised steel rails and cement walls dividing Israel and Palestine. About the midday heat and the midnight chill. Finally, she tells him about Paul.

"He looked to be in his thirties, worked for a rival news crew. We shared a passion for the work, for reporting from the front line in times of war. It's dangerous, but exciting. You have to keep your wits about you, ride the thrill in a way that keeps you alive."

Moses leans forward. "Didn't you see Paul die?"

An obligatory plastic cup of water sits on the low table in front of her. Julia picks it up and slowly drinks – stalling for time. What is he expecting her response to be? He must have seen the footage on TV. It was played and replayed extensively. His prior knowledge of what happened, and her part in it, places her at a disadvantage.

"How do you feel about what happened?" he asks, watching her intently.

For a moment, Julia cannot breathe. The gates in her mind are pushed open and the past overturns the present, covers it with a red mist.

"The bastard! He died! How dare he! How dare he!"

She is out of her chair, throwing her plastic cup at the door, upturning the table. Her words and actions have slammed Moses back in the comfy chair he favours.

Julia sits down. Their positions are reversed. She is in control.

"What do you make of that?" she asks, watching her therapist carefully.

Moses gets up, replaces the table, puts the thrown cup in a bin, then sits back down. Throughout, he maintains a silence which deflates her. Julia resigns herself to surviving the usual questions and answers routine.

"What occurred had a deep emotional impact on you," says Moses.

Julia shrugs.

"How did you feel about Paul?"

"Good, I guess. Until he died."

"Did you get on well together?"

Julia recalls their moments of shared laughter and the sense of belonging she had. "Yeah, we got on great."

Moses nods in a wise and masterful manner.

"I'm pleased you shared your anger over his death with me, Julia. It shows you are making progress."

"So what?" she says.

"This man, Paul, the tabloids and news reports described him as a rising star. One showed a photo of you sitting together with the headline, 'Time To Go Home, Julia!'. Did this bother you?"

"No."

Her therapist raises an eyebrow then says, "When he was there on the front line with you, was it possible the assignment had a competitive edge? One you enjoyed?"

Her foot begins tapping the floor. Julia tries to control it, but can't.

"You were both passionate about the job and you had a strong connection." Moses leans forward in his chair.

Julia knows this move. His professional denouement regarding her anger will be next.

"You're a very private person, Julia, but I have seen many people who, when they lose a loved one, become angry. It could be useful to discuss your feelings for Paul when he was alive. And to accept your anger at his death as part of the grieving process."

Her foot stops tapping.

What a shallow man he has revealed himself to be.

"You're wrong," she says. "You're so wrong."

Julia stands, looks down at Moses who sits back in his chair. His fingers grip the armrests. "All you have done is to make the same presumption others have. You think that because I had a rapport with a man who was as passionate about his work as I am, I must have been in love with him." A wry laugh escapes her. "You're right about one thing. I am grieving, but not for him, not for Paul. The thing I've lost is far more important to me."

"And what is it you've lost?" asks Moses.

Julia taps the side of her nose. "Work it out."

His disappointment is tangible.

For the first time, Julia is smiling as she leaves.

*

A year has passed since Julia returned from the Green Line. She is much better now – all her colleagues tell her so. They began calling round after she recommenced work at the studio and appear thrilled by her first assignment.

"It's a great opportunity," they all say. "Yes, it's a change of focus, but it puts you back in front of the camera, gives you airtime. And you've got your old crew working with you. Just this once, but how great is that."

"Yeah, it's great," says Julia while envy eats away at her soul for those of her crew, like cameraman Tom, who've been away on exciting assignments in war-torn countries. He's just returned from one and Julia is expecting him round.

"How was it in Serbia?" she asks, once Tom stands in her newly decorated living room.

"This looks good," he says.

The room reflects Julia's love of her mid-eastern assignments with its palette of sandy-yellow, sun-bleached-white, shady olive green and burnt orange.

"Gosh, you can really relax in here." Tom plonks himself down on her plush sofa with its plump velvet cushions.

Julia thanks him and goes to make tea with her new automatic kettle. So far, every visitor has commented on how relaxing the room is.

While she waits for the kettle to boil, Julia finds herself thinking about Paul.

How thrilling it was to meet another reporter with the same perspective on social unrest and war as herself. She loved the time they spent in each others company, exchanging fast and furious tales of dodging sniper bullets. The thrill of being in the right spot and alive when a mine or grenade exploded. They'd both loved the tense and fraught atmosphere generated by war. Julia knew, when Paul winked at her from behind the barricades, he mirrored her excitement at being on the front line. Although they both spoke on camera about the human cost, in private they discussed how this aspect of warfare didn't really bother them.

Julia sighs as she spoons sugar into Tom's mug. Like so many of her news crew, he thought Julia was in love with Paul. Yet their connection hadn't arisen from sexual attraction: they'd been soulmates of the strangest kind. Paul's death was terrible. When Julia began running towards him, she was high on adrenaline, excited to tell him about the near misses and how the action had proceeded from her vantage point. She didn't give a damn about the people she shouldered and pushed out of the way. When she'd waved, Julia expected Paul to wave back, or wink. When he failed to do so, she realised he was injured, looked at him properly.

The terror on his face was horrific. Julia still doesn't know why she held her arms out, but she did. Paul stumbled towards her, fell to his knees and lifted his remaining hand, asking for help. Julia saw his fear of death, became aware how, one day, this bloody mess could be her. An innate sense of revulsion held her in place.

Stirring Tom's tea, Julia once more acknowledges her grief is not for Paul's death. It is born from the realisation she isn't invulnerable, or clever at making the right choices. She's just been lucky. Julia hates the feeling of vulnerability Paul's death bestowed upon her. This is the root of her anger, her rage. The difference between when she first arrived back in Camden and now, is in how she responds to it. A tight smile tilts her lips slightly upwards.

Readying herself for yet another congratulatory conversation, Julia carries the tea to Tom, turning her back to the spare bedroom door as she enters the living room. She keeps the door locked. It is her secret place, the source of her recovery. Inside it is sparsely furnished with a bed roll, a computer and one other item. Julia spends most of her time in there online, when she's not putting components together.

"Thanks, Julia," Tom, takes the delicate cup. He sips the hot tea then says, "I hear you're reporting on the Notting Hill Carnival. Congratulations. I'm looking forward to being there with you..."

He continues to make small talk, but Julia's mind is elsewhere.

She resented nothing Paul did in life, but when he died, the media immortalised him. This is what Julia wants. She doesn't fear death. Her new colleagues know this and have supplied what is needed to fulfil her desire.

Julia smiles at Tom, sips her tea. He deserves a shock. She'll never forgive him for filming her, in all her vulnerable glory, while Paul died. Tom's film is why she will never again be reporting from a war zone. After the carnival, Julia has no doubt she will become an invisible cog in the machinery of media. She's not ready for that, never will be, but she is ready to die. And if she happens to injure or kill Tom? So what. As long as her death is caught on film, Julia doesn't care.

TIME TO GO

After a moment's disorientation, Luna looks around and sees Cailin in the shade of the cliff. He's crouched by a rock pool, intent upon whatever lies within. She runs towards him, soft sand slowing her progress. Her limbs feel strangely heavy as if she were a dreamer struggling free of restraining sheets. Rising panic echoes back from the cliff face as she calls, "Cailin! Cailin!"

He stands, brushing grains of sand off his hands.

"Cailin!" She cries again, throwing herself against him, "You're here."

"Of course I am." He holds her tight.

Luna raises her head to marvel at the beauty of the man before her. Trembling fingers brush against his jaw, travel softly down his throat to rest against his chest.

She says, "I thought I'd never see you again."

As pent-up tears flow, he gently kisses her face and, turning her towards the sea, surrounds her with his arms.

"Look at the ocean," he commands. Together they watch the ceaseless breaking of waves upon the shore. "That's how my love is for you…eternal." His voice sounds like a rush of sea upon the sand. Leading her out from the shade Cailin says, "Come on, let's skinny dip." He's grinning and pulling his t-shirt off.

Luna shakes her head.

"Why not?"

Looking at the blue sea spread so invitingly before them, she shrugs, saying, "I've changed. My body is…well…time and gravity take their toll."

His laughter fills the air. "Oh Luna. Look at yourself, you're beautiful."

She glances down and begins to laugh with him, for her body is as upright and firm as it was when she was a girl. Ignoring a momentary sense of unease, she pulls her

23

dress over her head, removes her underwear, and calling, "Catch me if you can!" runs into the sea, her movement raising a cool spray in its wake.

*

Later, when Cailin lifts himself off the hot sand to trace the line of her spine, she asks, "Do you remember the beach on the Isle of Harris?"

"Good grief, that was years ago." He rolls on his back, facing the sky's brilliance.

"Yes, but do you *remember*?" She watches his face intently. No recognition lights his features, and a frown creases his unlined brow. A chill retraces the line his fingers recently drew.

"Hang on. It was like a pair of cupped hands. A small beach surrounded by low cliffs. The sea was the most amazing colour."

Luna sits up. Hugging her knees she says, "It was like blue crystal. So clear you could almost see the colour of the sand beneath."

"It was like here," Cailin notes, "but the cliffs were not as dramatic as these."

Luna recalls being on the beach waiting for Cailin to finish exploring the island's small stone church, her joy when he appeared, and of how that day cemented their love for each other. Something tugs at her mind and the fabric of the day momentarily ripples, instantly dispelling the suns warmth. Her body shudders, yet the days heat reinstates itself while soft waves lap the sand near their feet. *Enjoy the moment*, she tells herself. The man beside her means more than life itself.

*

Cailin builds and lights a fire from driftwood he says he gathered earlier. Luna is uneasy – she cannot remember him doing so – but her day has been idyllic and she doesn't want to question anything. It's as if the passage of time is effortless, with only the sunset and ascending moon to mark its journey. Luna watches Cailin throw wood on the flames. How taut his nakedness felt against her in the sea. He hasn't changed at all. Sitting beside her in the warm glow, Cailin places an arm around her shoulders. Luna rests her head against him and strokes the inside of his thigh. His skin feels cold.

"It's time we spoke of what you must do."

"What do you mean?" she asks.

"You must come with me."

"I will."

"Are you sure? You need to be sure."

A single tear begins to track down his cheek. Gently, Luna wipes it away, disturbed by his strange insistence. How long is it since she last saw Cailin? Images of an elderly man jitter like old film stock through her mind and Luna pulls back from the smooth, young face. Standing, she moves nearer the fire, holding her hands out to its warmth. She tries to think of how she got here and finds, apart from their conversation about the Isle of Harris, she has no clear recollection of anything.

"Where are we, Cailin?"

"On the beach."

"Yes, but where?" She listens but cannot hear the sea. The cliffs are now shrouded by night.

"Does it matter?"

Shivering uncontrollably, Luna wraps her arms about her body. "Of course it matters. Why are we here?"

"You chose this day," he states bluntly. "We've not got much time."

His words sink in and realisation hits Luna hard in the core of her being. She breathes sharply inwards, tasting wood smoke. A wail of fear projects from her mouth into darkness which smothers sound.

"Why make me feel as if I have a choice?"

Cailin flinches at the torment in her voice. "I had to be sure you're ready."

25

Sobs wrack her body. Once she is calm, Cailin takes her in his arms. Luna draws comfort from his quiet strength.

"I never stopped loving you."

"I know," he replies.

"All that time wondering if you'd be there for me."

He presses a finger firmly against her lips. "Hush. No more." He kisses her tenderly, then more insistently. After the waves of climax ebb, they lay entwined, close to the fire, watching flames swiftly dwindle into flickering embers until darkness threatens to eclipse what remains.

Standing, he reaches out to help her up. A memory surfaces. She's approaching an altar. Cailin turns towards her, holding out the same hand as the one he offers her now. Smiling, Luna takes it, allowing him to lead her to the empty blackness where once the sea had been. She falters.

"It won't hurt. Time to go."

Cailin is smiling at her with such love Luna is encompassed by the total joy of belonging. With an involuntary cry of release, she steps forward.

*

Luna's daughter sits by her mother's bed. They'd explained how the process worked. The memory used was the one Mum said was her happiest. Even though less than an hour has passed in the waiting room, apparently Mum was given an entire day with the man she loved. Caro smiles through her tears, hoping this was the case. She's refused to have a recording chip inserted into her own brain. Caro prefers to keep her memories private, doesn't want technicians trawling through them, tampering with one to ensure a happy end to her life. Plus, there's the cost. After saying a final goodbye, Caro makes to leave the room. On reaching the door she turns to look once more, still unsure if Mum is smiling, or grimacing. Pressing the exit buzzer, Caro wishes she could be certain.

A GAMBLING MAN

Summer sun roasts my back as I and other women from our tribe toil on arid earth. Each of us knows we're wasting our time; the fields are barren. I have seen fifteen summers, each one drier than the last, and rivers are but a trickle. Ditches, dug to collect rainwater and melting snow from the mountains, are so dry the earth at their base has cracked. Elders tell me the land was once vibrant with life: green trees, bushes overflowing with fruit, crops flourishing in fields. Our trade routes cut through vibrantly green plains. Now, trade routes are shrouded by dust when the wind blows. The boundary of trees between our homes and the mountains appears withered, the landscape surrounding them desiccated. Our shaman performs rain rituals daily, yet the relentless heat does not yield.

The maize I gather is pitted, shrivelled rather than plump, golden and meaty. Its dry husks rustle as I look amongst the leaves for more to place in the basket on my hip. My daughter begins to wail from the woven carrier on my back. I move amongst the limp-leafed maize to reach its edge. After placing the basket and carrier on the ground, I lift my daughter out, cradle her thin body in my arms, bare my breast. She feeds eagerly. Her tiny hands open and close against my skin.

One of the older women approaches me, her brown wrinkled face creasing into a smile. "She is hungry today," the woman says, reaching out to stroke the thick black hair covering my baby's head.

It takes me a moment to speak; I'm unaccustomed to kind words from members of my tribe. "She is, but she's not growing well, cries with hunger."

"You're not eating enough to produce what she needs."

"None of us are eating enough."

"That will change today." She presses a hand on my arm. "How? Our hunters tell us no game can be found."

"A sacrifice has been found. One which will put meat in our bellies." She nods towards my breast. "Tomorrow your milk will be richer. It will flow better."

As if on cue, my daughter lifts her mouth from my now-dry nipple, screams for more. I silence her with the other, praying it will give enough to calm her. The woman walks away, checks for cobs despite her talk of meat. I look to the sky, feel for a breeze hoping storm clouds are gathering. The sky is clear, air still. Heat shimmers upwards from the baked earth.

There is little relief from the heat as the sun dips down to slumber. Knives are being sharpened as I draw close to the tall dwellings carved out of the cliff. Homes honeycomb the rock, with additional rooms reaching into the mountain itself. I and the other women take what little we've been able to farm or forage into the store. Apart from what we place there, the store is almost empty.

Leaving the building, I enter the opening of the kiva and use the rope ladder to descend, under the ancient beams supporting its roof, into the ceremonial pit. I join those who, like me, have children too young to participate in the dancing. My daughter is sound asleep. I leave her on my back and wait for the ritual to start. What animal has been found to offer to our gods? Flames rise higher as more wood is piled on the fire in the centre of the kiva. The shaman begins the ceremonial chant and we join in where required. Harmonious voices and drums call dancers to a known rhythm. Legs, feet and arms move in a manner meant to appease angered deities. Those of us sitting with babes sway in time. The sacrifice is brought forward as our voices and drumbeats form a crescendo. A man stands before us. We fall silent. Those who were dancing still their limbs. His eyes search for mine and he gives an imperceptible nod. He does not sacrifice himself for the tribe, but for me, our daughter. Two hunters hold him as the shaman slices his willing throat. Blood sprays the ground, creates steam where it spurts into the flames. The shaman steps aside. Licks and sucks warm blood off his fingers while my cry is drowned by ululations and drums announcing the ritual of preparation.

One of the nearby women leans towards me saying, "The death of our lands and people is your ancestor's fault." She spits a wet, globular mass on the ground. If we were nearer the fire, it would sizzle with hatred. Others in our small group speak out.

"Your ancestor angered the gods, yet we are the ones paying for it."

"Once our tribe was many, look how few of us have children now."

"In the past our crops burst with goodness. Now we are starving."

I stand and face these women. "You know nothing of what you speak. The truth is not as you and your men tell." I walk away, climb out of the kiva and head home. I've no wish to watch the body of my lover skewered and placed above flames to roast as if he were a beast.

The full moon shines bright, revealing warnings carved into the cliff. They show men playing dice and other games using counters. I trace my fingers across those illustrating goods exchanging hands. Look at the depictions of enslaved men, women and children pickaxing rooms out of the rock before me. All because of a stranger. A stranger who was defeated by an ancestor of mine. I share my name with her: Kimea. Her story has been passed down to the first-born daughter by the mothers in my family. Kimea and I are linked, not just by ancestry. Despite the passing of many, many years, her story connects to mine.

Placing my feet on the hewn wood which

29

intersperses the rope ladder at regular intervals, I begin climbing. My home is in the middle of this structure, three storeys up. Each storey steps back into the cliff-face forming a shallow terrace on part of the roof below. As the tribe diminishes, we live further apart. The homes above and below mine are empty. Neither the height I climb to, nor the sway of the ladders, bothers me. I grew accustomed to both as a child. My daughter is waking. Her soft cries will soon grow in intensity and volume. It is cool in the dense rock. I remove her once more from the carrier, clean her as best I can and wrap her in a woven cloth. Place her to my breast hoping there is enough milk to keep her quiet while I tell her the true story of our ancestor.

*

Kimea is tired after a day foraging with her mother. The sun casts a red-orange glow across the land as they leave the pueblo storeroom to find her older brother. Pocano has yet to wash the blood from his arms and hands. This and the smile on his face proclaims the hunt was successful.

Mother cups his cheek. "You have done well, son. Go clean yourself before the meat is cooked. You also did well today, Kimea. Everyone will eat well tonight."

Quiet conversation, the warm arm around her and a full stomach lull Kimea towards sleep as she rests against her mother. Her eyelids are slipping shut when she notices a figure walking across the prairie, in the light of the full moon.

"Is that Oura?"

"No Kimea. Oura uses the trade roads. They fly straight like the arrow he is named for." Mother frowns. "I do not know this man. He does not move in a way I recognise."

When the man draws close, people rise to greet him, inviting the stranger to sit with them. Firelight shines off black plaited hair pulled back from a strong face. His eyes sweep over the people present, their pueblo homes and the mountains beyond the trees. A smile twists his mouth upwards. The stranger waves away the offer of food, notices a group of men playing dice. His smile deepens. When they invite him to play the man throws his head back and laughs.

"Ah! The gods are good. I will join you for a few games. Let us see if I can win myself a bed for the night."

Within moments dice are cast onto the ground. They roll, settle and the marks on their faces are counted. Despite her tiredness, Kimea wants to move nearer. Dice are a game of chance. One where numbers rule and the man whose throw is the highest wins, where men bet on their own and each other's luck. When he holds a large piece of turquoise up for all to see, it is clear this stranger is a gambling man.

The night air is warm, yet coldness touches Kimea's skin as her mother rises. "Come, it is time you slept," she says, placing rough hands under Kimea's armpits, lifting her to her feet. Kimea can't help but look back as she follows Mother towards their home. Her father and brother have joined those watching the men playing dice.

*

Once awake, Kimea climbs down the ladder leading from the family sleeping room to the ground. It rained as night passed. Air is fresh, sun barely risen. The ground feels cool and slick beneath her feet. Mother is spreading maize meal batter onto the hot greased rock sitting in the centre of the fire. A rich smell fills her nostrils as mother flips the unleavened bread over. Her mouth waters, stomach growls.

"We are walking quite the distance today, so eat well."

Maize bread is placed in an earthen bowl and passed to her. She can feel the heat of the cooked dough through the pottery. Blows to cool it, then tears a piece off.

The bread is still hot when she puts it in her mouth.

"Where are we going?" Kimea asks.

"Towards the west to pick chokecherries and berries. The prickly pears won't be ripe yet."

"Can I bring my flute?"

Mother smiles, reaches across, strokes Kimea's face. She nods.

Once she has eaten her fill, Kimea gets her flute and their baskets. Mother can carry two once full, Kimea just one. The sun has begun its journey across a clear blue sky as they join the other women. The path passing those tending fields of maize is well worn. Cobs will be ready for harvest after the moon has completed another cycle. Once they leave the fields behind, the short prairie grass brushes Kimea's legs just below her calf muscle, dampens her moccasins. Sunshine is hot against her skin by the time they reach the chokecherries. Ripe purple berries cluster along slim stems sprouting amidst thick green leaves. After putting her flute to one side, Kimea snaps the stem as shown and begins placing fruit in her basket. She eats some of the cherries as she picks, spitting pips on the ground. Sharp yet sweet juices run down her chin, stain her fingers. Next, she gently plucks delicate berries with bobbled red fruit off their stems. The colour reminds her of the poisonous red berries, with their clusters of creamy-white flowers, which grow during spring.

They seek shelter from the sun under some trees. Women are wrapping berries in their bread. Kimea copies them; finds the flavours enhance each other. Next time, she won't eat so many from the bushes or her basket. The women around her chat as they wait for the midday heat to pass before beginning their trek home.

"Did the stranger win his bed last night?" asks one.

"I'll offer him mine tonight if he had to sleep on the ground."

All the women laugh apart from one, who snorts

derisively, "Oh he won his bed all right. Thanks to my man's stupidity, he now owns our entire home and all its contents."

Mother stops leaning against the tree she's under, straightens her back. "What happened?"

"He kept gambling and losing. Told me he'll win our home back today." She looks down, pulls at the fabric of her skirt. "He'll lose. I'm certain of it."

"Foolish man," Mother says. "What is there left to gamble?"

The woman's fingers continue toying with her skirt. When she raises her eyes, Kimea can see worry is eating her. "Myself and our sons. His own body. That is what he has left."

The women fall silent. Their faces reflect each other's shock.

"Well, as the stranger doesn't need it, there's room for you in my bed," says the woman who spoke earlier.

Mother claps her hands. "Let's have some music." She nods to Kimea.

Lifting her flute to her lips, Kimea plays music of her own making. It represents the movement of the wind. Notes rise and fall, twist and turn. The wind blows soft then fierce across the land, building to a tempest. Lost in the flow of the music she creates, Kimea automatically counts the beats, increases the pace, then brings the flow of air back to earth where it rests. When the tune ends, the women thank her before rising. They make their way back to the village with brimming baskets.

*

Kimea stands a little way back while men gamble their homes, children, wives and bodies against the fall of dice from their and the stranger's hands. Beside her is Oura, who returned earlier loaded with goods from tribes to the south. Other girls are saying he has shell trumpets, copper bells and pottery to sell.

Shadows flicker when flames flare. Tension rises as yet another tribal member loses all he owns. The stranger throws his head back. Laughs uproariously.

"I now have ten homes to choose from! Which shall I sleep in tonight?"

The man who lost says, "You have the luck of a bad spirit."

The stranger's eyes narrow. "Be careful how you speak. Do not forget I own you and everything you hold dear." His mouth lifts in a fierce and challenging grin. "Will anyone dare to gamble with me? Try to win this man his life back?" The grin widens, revealing large, glistening teeth as another tribal member steps forward.

"I will, but we use dice I carved earlier today."

The stranger laughs. "Very well, if you win three out of five games, everything this man lost will be his again. If you lose three, you, your family and everything you own will be mine."

The man sits down, holds his palm flat so the stranger can view the new eight-sided dice, then puts his hands together and shakes. They roll across the ground to settle on the highest total possible: sixteen.

The stranger picks the dice up, weighs them in his hand and smiles. "Luck maybe with you for your first throw, but I doubt it will stay."

The dice fall. Kimea whispers as she counts the numbers and calculates the odds. She is aware Oura has moved closer to her, is listening. The fourth game ends on a tie. The fifth will decide the fate of two men and their families. The crowd tenses as the final round begins.

"You understand numbers," Oura says. "Do you think our tribesman will win?"

Kimea shakes her head. "I think each die is loaded and the stranger has adapted his throw." She nods towards the tribesman. "He is no longer calm. Will throw badly and lose."

34

"Then we shall leave."

Oura takes hold of her elbow, threads a way between those watching the game. The way bodies tumble into the space created behind them, reminds Kimea of a hunting tale her father once told, where a herd of bison plunged off a precipice.

A roar erupts as they reach where her mother sits with a group of women around a small fire. Kimea turns. The stranger stands, makes the same offer only now, one man can recover two. If they are brave enough to gamble everything they hold dear. Fear twists inside Kimea as yet another steps forward to accept the challenge.

"Your daughter has a gift for numbers," Oura says, "I would like to train her."

Mother stands. "Trading is not a position women hold in this tribe."

Oura indicates those gathered around the stranger, "Change is here. I suggest we embrace it in a way that may help your daughter."

The idea of becoming a trader, of travelling to and from other tribes, is exciting, but Kimea keeps quiet while Mother decides.

"I agree, change is here. Kimea already knows what plants to eat, how to live off the land. If she is to train with you, she sleeps with her family. You teach her during the day."

"She will be of age soon," one of the women listening from around the fire says. "Oura might want her for a wife."

"You are jealous because I rejected you, Chipeta. That was many moons ago, so hold your tongue," says Oura. His eyes remain on Mother.

Chipeta grins. "Perhaps it's your son he wants."

Mother raises a hand and Chipeta falls silent. "Apart from when you go to the mines, there will be no travel until Kimea comes of age. Once she is a woman,

Kimea can decide for herself if she wishes to accompany you to other parts of this land. The risk you take is that she may choose to stay."

"A risk I'm happy to take," says Oura.

Kimea hugs her mother.

"I will miss your flute when we gather berries, Kimea. You are gifted at music as well as numbers," says Chipeta.

"They go together, speak a similar language."

Oura gives her a curious look. "You named your daughter true," he says to Mother. "She is unique."

*

The autumn morning is mellow as Kimea follows Oura to a copper mine he owns. They walk towards the road cutting between the tall trees behind Oura's home. Leaf laden boughs give brief respite from the climbing heat of the day. Once through the trees, Oura sets a steady pace towards the mountains. A short distance before the road becomes a track up the mountainside, lies a fork in the road.

"This is new," Oura says, coming to a halt. "We shall see where it leads on our way back. Perhaps a new mine has been discovered." He resumes walking.

Soon they reach the entrance to the mine. Light filters through the opening to reveal wooden pickaxes, with copper points and blades, resting against rock in a roughly-hewn space. It is easy to stand upright here, but the tunnel Oura leads her down causes him to duck his head. Torches wedged into cracks in the rock flicker as they pass and the noise of metal hitting rock grows louder. Relief washes over Kimea when they reach a chamber high enough for fellow tribesmen to stand upright while they work. Oura greets each miner, then checks on the quantity of copper ore in the woven baskets placed at points around the chamber. He collects turquoise, carefully chipped from deposits found in and on the rock, into a pouch. When they return to the entrance, Oura shows Kimea the contents of his pouch. He spits on a small stone, rubs it on a cloth then places it in her hand.

"Hold it up to the sun," he says.

Kimea does as she is told and finds the blue-green stone shines with such luminosity, it takes her breath away.

"A stone of that size can purchase many beads." He takes a larger one out of his pouch. "With this I can buy a parrot."

Kimea catches the stone when Oura throws it, spits on it as he did, then polishes it on her clothing. "How do you know what each stone is worth?"

"You learn as you trade. I allocate each stone a number according to its size. The smaller one you hold I count as ten, the large stone, fifty. Not every trader works this way, but I do." He holds his hand out for the stones, places them back in his pouch, secures it within his clothing. "Come, let us see what lies down the road we passed."

The new road runs between the mountains and the trees they walked through this morning. An area beneath a section of cliff is full of people labouring. Some are climbing and descending the rock using rope ladders. Doors and rooms are being cut into the cliff. Many of the tribesmen, women and children can be seen carrying rocks in baskets on their backs, away from the hubbub of construction. Stumps from felled trees sit in an area where trunks are chopped into logs. An enormous pit is being dug into the ground a short distance before an area of homes already constructed. These rise upwards connected by ladders and terraces. They appear as huge steps with doorways tall enough for a man to walk through. Kimea counts five homes towering one above the other.

"I see you are admiring my work," the stranger says. "I chose well coming here. Your people work hard."

"What are the pits for?" Kimea asks.

"They will be used for ceremonial rituals. I call them kivas."

"Will there be a kiva for every twenty-nine homes, or will that be the only one?"

The stranger looks at her, "Why do you ask?"

"Because twenty-nine is a special number."

His eyes are whirlpools of darkness searching within, drawing her to him. They travel up and down Kimea's body before returning to her face. She covers her budding breasts and steps back.

"Perhaps I should gamble with your father to have you by my side," he says. "You would make an interesting companion and soon your body will be fruitful."

Oura steps between them. "She is promised to me. Come, we are leaving."

The stranger laughs as Oura leads her away.

*

The spring evening is drawing in fast when mother calls a meeting. Around the fire stand less than half of those who made up their tribe last summer. The majority are now slaves, their pueblos empty, falling into disrepair. They live in the cliff homes and the shaman has deserted those who remain in the settlement. Yet tonight, he walks towards them. Chipeta is with him. Her mother nods an acknowledgement as they draw close.

"We are here to represent the views of those living in the cliff," the shaman says.

"And I am to speak of the concerns those living here have with this situation," says Mother. "Our tribe is divided. We would be stronger as one."

"Come join us," Chipeta says, "The home I and my family live in is cool in the day, warm when night is cold."

"Surely you can see the kivas we hold ceremonies in offer protection from the weather too," says the shaman. "The wooden beams supporting the adobe roof are solid and the gods appear to smile on us each time a ritual is held. They have provided rain for our crops, for the ground and bushes women forage from. Our stores hold food for days to come."

"You are slaves," Mother says. "You belong to the stranger. Do you not resent this?"

Chipeta smiles. "It is a small price to pay for what we have gained and what you will gain, if you give your lives to him. My home is built. I am tending fields, gathering roots and onions. My man hunts again."

"And your sons, Chipeta? You speak as if your lives are your own, but is it not true your sons still work the rock while you and your man do as bid? I hear your man is gathering turkeys to tame and farm. He no longer hunts." Mother shakes her head. "You are not free. There is no honour in the way you live."

"You have no right to say I have no honour!" Chipeta steps forward. "I honour my tribe by accepting changes which better our tribe's position, while you refuse to."

The shaman quickly places himself between them. "This meeting is at an end. We have said what we came to say."

Her father stands with mother. Pocano joins them as the Shaman and Chipeta walk away. Her brother has the slim build and muscles of a young man who can run all day, is taller than a year ago.

"They are blinded by this man they serve," Father says. "When his luck runs out they will see him for what he is. I will play dice with him, win everyone back. They can continue living in their new homes, but they will be free."

"Only a fool would expect to win. You risk enslaving me, your son, and you forget he has expressed an interest in our daughter. No, there has to be another way." With a shake of her head, Mother leaves the fireside. Kimea follows her home.

Pocano returns much later. He wakes Mother, tells her something Kimea can't quite hear then begins crying. Throwing her cover off, Kimea gets up, goes to join Mother in comforting him.

"What happened?"

"Your father gambled his life away. Not ours, or our home and belongings, but he now belongs to the stranger."

*

Kimea is counting and checking the quality of Oura's dwindling stock, something she has been doing every day since Father was enslaved. Each morning she walks to the cliff face. Watches him cutting and trimming logs for the roof of the third kiva to be dug in the ground. The number of homes to each kiva remains twenty-nine. Kimea waves to let him know she is there, then plays her flute in the hope of lifting his spirits. He has yet to wave back.

"Concentrate child, you keep losing count!"

"Sorry, Oura," she tries again, but images of Father toiling instead of hunting and the song this makes scatters her thoughts. Tears prick her eyes.

"Come," Oura says, "we will take a break. I see you have your flute with you. Will you play me a song?"

He takes her into the living area and sits cross-legged on the beaten floor. Kimea places her flute to her mouth. The notes cascade up and down, expressing the joy of running and the thrill of hunting on the plains, culminating in a climactic kill. She then plays the same passage in a deeper tone reflecting her father's battle with the stranger, fingers flying across the instrument as dice are thrown, playing quietly to indicate loss. What follows next tells of enslavement and hard labour. Kimea's fingers falter. She cries while Oura comforts her. He hands her one of his gem cloths to wipe her eyes as the sobs subside.

"That is a sad song," he says. "I remember you telling Chipeta numbers and music speak a similar language. Can you tell me what you meant?"

"They both have patterns which form rhythms you can explore. They speak to me in the same way."

Oura frowns. "How does this work when you play?"

"I count beats, divide the music into equal sections so they have a pattern. Many songs have choruses which repeat. Numbers also have patterns. Some you can divide into equal sections, just like I do music. When I think of numbers, I hear music in my head."

"Ah, I see." Oura goes into his storeroom, brings back a long shallow pot half-full of dried earth which has been ground to dust. "I will draw some numbers and you play the music you hear."

Kimea gasps as the numbers appear. She has never seen them drawn, only knows them as marks on dice. Some have straight lines, others curve or are dots. Each one speaks to her.

"What numbers are they?"

Oura counts to ten.

Without hesitation, she lifts her flute and plays the notes she hears in her head.

"I don't need to see numbers to make music, Oura, but show me how to draw them. Can I draw them after you? Can I?"

"Patience child, patience," says Oura. "We have the rest of the day."

*

"You are quiet this evening," Mother says as they sit around a fire with other women and children. Pocano is with those hunters who remain, celebrating the deer they killed and ate. The smell of cooked flesh lingers and Kimea's fingers are greasy, even though she has licked them clean. She might wipe them on the blanket mother has put around her.

"I was thinking about numbers and the music they make. Most of the numbers have patterns within them, but not all. Some are special."

"Special numbers? Is this what Oura is teaching you?"

"No, he teaches me other things."

"Why are some special?"

Kimea holds up seven fingers. "Seven can be divided by itself, or by one. You cannot divide it by any other number."

Mother shrugs. "And why does this matter, Kimea?"

"The new homes being built number twenty-nine to every kiva. Twenty-nine is the same as seven. Between the numbers one and twenty-nine, there are ten which work the same way as seven." Kimea takes hold of her mother's hands, "I hear music when I think of the ten special numbers. It is different to anything I've ever played."

"Then I will tell Oura you are foraging with the women tomorrow. They enjoy your music, would like to hear a new tune."

*

Kimea walks with a small group of women across the plains to find wild strawberries. Damp prairie grass brushes against her legs while the sun rises overhead. They might find some onions and there may be early berries to pick. A different path is taken to any she is familiar with. Soon the women are busy plucking fruit and lifting the odd onion from amongst plants clustered in the ground. Kimea's hands are busy, her nostrils full of the scent of fresh vegetables and plump strawberries. They break at midday, gather under trees and eat.

"Kimea has a new tune for us," Mother says.

Some of the women clap in delight while others call her to play.

Kimea stands, lifts her flute and plays what she hears when thinking about the ten special numbers. The music has a fey sound which lifts and twists the notes in a spiral, then scatters them.

"Give us a different tune, girl," one woman says. "I feel as if I'm at a ceremony rather than enjoying a break from work."

Other voices rise in agreement, but Kimea cannot stop. She has to finish. Her mind and fingers will not let go until the swirling music is complete.

"What is that?" someone asks as Kimea lifts the flute away from her mouth.

Fingers point to an area under some nearby trees where sunlight seems to shimmer up and out of the land. The shimmering increases, becoming golden then brighter than the sun. Kimea shades her eyes. An elderly woman appears. Her back is curved and she leans on a wooden staff twined with green vines, which delve into the ground beneath her feet. The glow on her cheeks is akin to the bright red fruit in their baskets. Power radiates from her as she stares at those with Kimea. The women prostrate themselves. Their bodies are bathed by light so golden skin gleams like burnished copper.

"Why have you called me, child? What do you want with Earth's Grandmother?"

Kimea stands before the goddess of creation, her thoughts tumbling like dice thrown by the stranger.

She holds this image in her mind saying, "I was unaware the music I played would call you, Grandmother, but we are grateful you came. A stranger joined our tribe last summer. He gambles with our men, takes everything they own, enslaves them and their families. This stranger has changed how our people work, how they live and celebrate the gods. Some say his way of life is good, yet none of those living this life are free."

"Are these the only women whose men have not gambled?" Grandmother asks.

"Apart from a few who work the fields, yes. My father gambled only himself, so Mother remains free."

"Describe this stranger to me."

Kimea does so. She also tells of his laugh and of the way he looked at her body, how Oura protected her.

Grandmother listens carefully, her head to one side, both hands atop her staff.

"A god called The Gambler torments your tribe," she says, "not a man. And his wanting you, a mere mortal, as a mate is unacceptable. The Gambler left our realm a year ago. Until now, I did not know where to find him. Come here, child."

The rich smell of moist earth fills Kimea's nostrils, surrounds her as she draws close.

"I have a task for you. This god must return to our realm, but he will not wish to give up the power he has gained. I will send three gods to remove him. You need to play the music which brought me here, but differently. I will tell you how." She whispers instructions into Kimea's ear.

"I understand," Kimea says, although her stomach churns at the thought of what is to come. "Am I to do this alone?"

The goddess looks at her with eyes the colour of prairie grass just after it has rained. "There is one amongst you whose name means *the spirits are coming*. Find this person. They can help you."

Golden light flares causing Kimea to cover her eyes. When her sight returns to normal, the opening to the realm of the gods and Grandmother are gone. Her mother and the rest of the women no longer prostrate themselves; they sleep. Kimea sits pondering on the person she must find. Those sleeping awaken with no memory of the goddess. By the time everyone is ready to return, she knows who she needs to speak to.

Later, once everyone is fed and settled in their groups around various fires, Kimea searches for Pocano. She finds him sitting slightly apart from the other hunters sharpening arrow heads. His black hair has been plaited, a sign he is considered a man. Kimea cannot help but admire the surety of his movements as he brings the copper to a piercing point. She sits nearby.

"Will you help me free Father and our people?"

"You think there is a way, little sister?" Pocano picks up the next blunt head.

"I know of a way, but need to talk with you where we cannot be heard."

Gathering up the arrow heads, Pocano hands her those which have yet to be sharpened.

"Let us go home. You can tell me what we are to do while I sharpen the rest."

*

Kimea stands playing her flute while Father labours. The Gambler's eyes are on her. They rake her body over and over again and she wishes she had bound her breasts, even though they are still small. She knows when Pocano is speaking with the god as Father stops working. Fear shapes Father's mouth, causes him to down tools, but before he has a chance to move, his back is whipped. Kimea flinches, almost stops playing. Tears slide down her cheeks as he returns to work. Moments later The Gambler approaches her.

"Come," the god says, "your brother is gambling his life and yours for the freedom of your people. He wishes you to serenade him with music, says you will bring him luck." He leans in. Kimea can feel his breath on her face when soft fingers reach up to touch the dampness of her cheek. "Well might you cry, little one. No one has won against me yet and I am so looking forward to playing with you." He throws his head back and laughs. Fear twists her gut. Kimea gives a submissive nod, keeps her head down as she walks to where Pocano stands.

"Your father is working hard," says the god, pointing for Pocano's benefit. "Let us play here so he can see you both." The Gambler sits, leans forward and pats the earth. It is smooth as if games of dice are frequently played in this spot. Hope stirs in Kimea. This is where she wants them to play, not just in view of her father, but near where others working on the cliff homes can see them.

She watches as Pocano feels the weight of the dice offered by The Gambler in his right hand. Shakes and throws them to see how they spin in the air, roll and settle.

"These will do," he says. "We shall each throw eleven times so there can be no mistaking who has won. Make music and bring me luck, Kimea."

The god grins as he picks the dice up.

Kimea prays as she begins playing the music which bought the goddess to her but, as instructed, she plays it backwards. The sound is eerie, discordant in places as the notes spiral down.

"I dislike this tune, it distracts me," says The Gambler.

"I enjoy it and she is playing for me."

A hand reaches out to grasp Kimea's clothing. She swiftly steps aside then gives herself up to the sounds issuing forth, swaying and twisting, dancing out of the god's reach. She starts the strange melody for a second time, visualising the pattern contained within the special numbers when their order is reversed, hoping she hasn't made a mistake while moving. Eleven throws should be enough for her to complete the number of times she needs to play the melody, but Pocano has lost the first two games. Six losses in a row might be all the time she has.

Kimea begins to play the notes again, this time in the right order. The Grandmother told her to play the music five times; twice backwards and thrice correctly.

People are gathering around the trio. Sweat beads above Pocano's lips as he shakes the dice for the fifth time. The Gambler is smiling but his smile turns into a grimace as the throw is made.

"Tell your sister to stop playing or I will break her flute in two."

"Why? The music she plays is beautiful."

The god rises, steps away from the game. "Stop that noise, girl!"

Focusing on finishing the fourth iteration, Kimea dances out of reach, not missing a note.

"If you leave the game you will not have her, for I will have won," Pocano says, "and it seems you want her badly. As badly as she and I want freedom for our tribe."

Pocano is lifted off his feet. The Gambler's hands are around his throat. Her brother's legs thrash. He claws the god's fingers as his sun-kissed skin takes on a blueish tinge.

"Stop playing or I will kill him!"

They had discussed what to do if The Gambler became aware, if he threatened either of them. Kimea needs to hold her nerve as Pocano has held his. She plays on.

Behind the god, a patch of air is shimmering brighter than the sun on a hot summer's day. Those surrounding them shield their eyes. Some cry out for the gods to save them; others run. Kimea turns slightly so she's not blinded, keeping the flute to her mouth, playing the final notes.

"No!"

Pocano is thrust aside, his leg twisting as he lands heavily on the hard ground. There is a snapping sound. It reminds Kimea of dry twigs breaking under her feet. She would go to him, but The Gambler bars her way. Behind him, three figures enter the realm of men. These gods gleam as if passing through the doorway has coated them with ore. Their muscled forms advance while the errant god makes to grab her.

Kimea steps back, catches her foot on a rock and falls. She lifts her face until her eyes meet those of The Gambler towering above her. His hands are reaching for her exposed throat.

"Look behind you," she says. "You have lost."

He looks over his shoulder, cries out as his arms are taken by two of the golden figures. Kimea scurries backwards as the third steps in front of The Gambler, places both hands on the interloper's chest and begins to push. Muscles in his arms and legs tense as The Gambler fights to free himself. Those holding his arms strain to pull him towards the realm of the gods. With a twist of his body, The Gambler frees an arm. He waves his hand in an all-encompassing manner shouting, "I will kill you with lightning. I will send war and disease among you. May the cold freeze you, may the fire burn you. May the waters drown you."

Then he and the golden light are gone. Kimea and the tribe she belongs to, are finally free.

*

My daughter stirs against my breast. Her brown eyes gaze into mine as I continue. "Kimea went to her brother. He still breathed, but his leg was broken, he would never hunt again. So Kimea married Oura, stayed home caring for Pocano, when the trader travelled. In time they had a child and she was called Kimea. Our tribe was reunited. We lived in the cliff-face homes, held ceremonies in the kivas, honoured the gods. Even so, The Gambler's curse brought years of sun with little rain. No snow settled on the mountains to sustain crops planted in spring. People began roaming from place to place, taking what they could, killing those in their way. Our tribe dwindled. My people began to question the cost of returning the god to his own realm despite their freedom."

I stroke my baby's face, push the soft dark hair away from her forehead, kiss her gently. Her eyes shut and she sleeps. It is no longer safe here. We will leave in the morning, make our way south as others have done. I will forage and hopefully we can survive. My stomach rumbles as the smell of roasting meat wafts through the doorway cut through the rock. What little fat there was on my lover's body will be sizzling as it drops in the fire. The thought of this and how his flesh might taste makes my mouth water.

THE LITTLE LIGHTER GIRL

It is dark when Jiya wakens. The electric lights of Dharavi have kept the night's black stare at bay while she has slept, but they can do nothing to hold back the accusing look in her Father's eyes. At least he's left her curtain closed when he entered. Its faded fabric makes this part of the main living area her private space.

"Look at the time, Jiya. Get up. Get my breakfast ready and pack my lunchbox. Then there's the house to clean and work for you to do." He shakes his head angrily. "You need to change your ways. Come home with rupees today or I'll be speaking with Mr Basu." His hands, roughened by work, reach down and drag Jiya out from under her thin blanket. Jiya feels the calluses pressing into her skin as he grips her shoulders saying, "I mean it, Jiya, I mean it." She lands back on her bed when he gives her a hard shove. "Now get my food ready."

Jiya's stomach churns with fear as she begins to fulfil her father's orders. She knows his threat isn't an empty one. She has seen the way Mr Basu looks at her, hears tales about what happens to the young girls he buys. Were her mother alive, Jiya would feel safe. She wishes Father would remarry, but the torch he carries burns so bright she knows this will never happen. Before these thoughts overwhelm her, Jiya takes her distress out on the dough. Today, the chapattis are especially good.

Now he has gone and the house is as clean as a shack can be, Jiya gets ready for work. She washes using the last of their water. Collecting more is a job to be done later. Dressing in jeans and a t-shirt works best with the tourists, as does cleanliness. Her jet hair is brushed until it is gleaming. They are out of toothpaste, so Jiya makes do with water. Perhaps if she sells enough lighters today she can buy some. Surely Father would be pleased? The lighters are locked in a cupboard in Father's room. Jiya uses the key from the keyring tied to her belt loop. She fills her backpack then returns to her bed. Bending, she pulls from underneath the last remaining pair of her Mother's sandals. The leather has lost its suppleness, but her mother's jasmine perfume still lingers. By closing her eyes and breathing deeply, Jiya can almost see her mother, sense her presence, but the thread is now as tenuous as her scent. Sorrow flows through her as she carefully places the sandals on her feet. She wonders if this is how Mother felt when Grandma died. Jiya had only known her grandmother a short time, but she remembers her smiling face and the comfort of sitting on Grandma's lap, listening to tales of Hindu gods and goddesses. Which is strange, as recalling her mother is so hard. Lacing the sandals as tightly as she can, Jiya hopes they will protect her feet during her long walk to the High Street Phoenix. It is almost six miles, but it is time to re-try this territory.

Sunrise is just beginning to glint upon the horizon as Jiya locks their shack's frail wooden door. The walk to Tulsi Pipe Road takes her through some of the better residential areas of Dharavi. Although the streets remain narrow strips of compact dirt with open sewers, here houses are made from concrete blocks. They survive the monsoon flooding better than the wooden shack Jiya and her father live in. Hopefully the warmth of this day, together with the retreating south west monsoon winds, will finish drying the wood they haven't yet replaced.

As the sun rises Tulsi Pipe Road fills with people, cars and BEST buses. Jiya is accustomed to seeing other children carrying goods to sell. Most of them are boys and many have been stolen from their families. Jiya knows to avoid railway stations – they are full of men like Mr Basu – but she cannot afford to ride on the BEST service and so walks purposefully towards her goal, as if she had already been taken and employed. The sandals loosen making her scuff her feet clumsily so Jiya quickly tightens the laces. Is she drawing too much attention to herself? This thought makes Jiya uneasy. Avoiding eye contact with anyone, she continues towards the High Street Pheonix. Once she is working, no one will notice her shoes are too big.

Jiya's first stop is the coffee shop just beyond the Phoenix centre. The Phoenix is a tourist draw, so it's not unusual to find people exploring the area. Some enjoy a morning coffee before they begin shopping. Others, having been enticed by sizzling sounds and the aroma of pungent spices, are breakfasting on colourful food cooked by street vendors. From the number of people thronging the streets it appears many are visiting Mumbai to see in the New Year. A bold poster on the café wall advertises the firework party and countdown taking place this evening. Another, just inside the door, features a New Year's Eve feast at the city's legendary Seven Kitchens. As she removes a handful of the lighters from her backpack their colours gleam like jewels in the sun. Jiya thrusts them towards the first tourist sitting outside, giving him a beaming smile.

"Please sir, would you buy one of my lighters? It's only one hundred rupees." The man shakes his head. Next, the woman she approaches tells Jiya, "No thank you," then turns towards her husband muttering about Mumbai's "bloody beggars." This makes Jiya ashamed as she is trying to sell goods her father has bought, she's not begging. As Jiya walks the streets visiting coffee shop after coffee shop, on a route which brings her back to High Street Phoenix, the colourful lighters are constantly refused. No-one is buying and Jiya's feet are sore because her Mother's sandals have rubbed them raw.

When Jiya sits with her backpack against a wall to remove the sandals and rub her feet a small boy joins her. He looks to be about seven, his shorts are grubby and his hair sticks out in tufts. His wide brown eyes are anything but innocent. Jiya carefully draws her Mother's sandals closer.

"What are you doing?" The boy sits next to her, sticks his thumb in his mouth and begins sucking while waiting for her answer. Jiya remains cautious.

"What's it look like?" The boy slides towards her on his bottom, lessening the gap. "Sore feet?" Jiya nods. "Better you don't wear these then." He snatches them so fast that Jiya only manages to grasp the strap of one sandal.

"Hey! They're mine." But the boy is strong for his size. He jerks the leather out of Jiya's grasp and is off, running down the street with his prize held high.

"Thief! Thief!" Jiya yells, giving chase. No-one responds to her cries, they just part slightly to allow the children through. The boy is quicker on his feet than Jiya. To her horror, the last item she has to remind her of Mother is disappearing into the crowds. As bodies close behind the street urchin, Jiya stares in horror. She has no idea which way he went, where her mother's sandals are. A tear slips down her cheek as Jiya tries to recall her mother's scent and finds she can't. This morning's thin thread has been snapped.

*

At 1pm with the heat of the day rising to its zenith, Jiya enters the cool shopping centre hoping to find trade amongst the tourists who are lunching there. She walks past the security guards by blending in with the crowd then rides the escalator up to the food hall. Looking around she spots a pale faced, elderly gentleman sitting at a table alone. Pulling a few lighters out of her jeans pockets, Jiya approaches. She can see he is reading a newspaper on the table before him, but he holds a clear glass object over his eye. Fascinated, Jiya bends slightly to look closer. Suddenly a large blue eye is observing her. Jiya jumps back stuttering an apology.

"I'm so sorry sir, I… I didn't mean to stare." As he places the object on top of today's paper, the old man's face wrinkles into a broad smile.

"Yes you did, you were curious. Come on now, admit it." Jiya feels the hot blush rising and fidgets uncomfortably, realising he has noticed her bare feet and the lighters in her hands.

"Are you selling those?" Relief floods her. Embarrassment forgotten, Jiya beams,

"Yes sir." Her head nods vigorously. "Look, good quality lighters. Disposable, but very good quality. One hundred rupees each." Calmly the elderly man holds her eyes.

"I'm so sorry dear, I don't smoke. Neither does my wife." Crushed and starting to despair, Jiya turns away, gripping the lighters tightly. Will she manage to sell anything today? What little security she has left is unravelling. Stuffing the lighters back into her pockets, Jiya begins to walk towards another tourist with her shoulders bowed.

"Hang on." Jiya turns around and looks at the elderly man. An old lady is putting a tray of food and drinks on the table. "Are you hungry?" he asks. Looking at the food, Jiya realises she's starving. She nods then looks at the floor. A chair is pulled out; she hears it scrape against the floor.

"Sit. And eat. I can get more." It is a long time since Jiya experienced kindness. She doesn't know how to react, what to do. Afraid she might cry, Jiya keeps her eyes lowered and mutely shakes her head. "Okay, then take this. Perhaps you can sell it. It's called a magnifying glass."

"Henry! You need that to read the paper!"

Henry shakes his head at his wife's protest. "I've another one at home." Getting up, he presses the magnifying glass into Jiya's palm. His bony fingers gently fold over her hand and he creaks into a crouch so his clear blue eyes are on her level. When Jiya dares to raise her tear-streaked face, Henry pulls a handkerchief from his pocket and dabs at her eyes until Jiya begins to smile and then giggle. When he uses Jiya as a prop to straighten his legs, she places her hand under his arm for support. It is thin and trembles slightly. Sensing the man's legs are also trembling, Jiya helps him back to the table where Henry says, "I want you to have this also."

*

Jiya feels refreshed after eating the food Henry gave her and is ready to tackle the coffee houses on her way home. Surely things will get better. Her hand feels the magnifying glass that's tucked into her jeans under her t-shirt. Perhaps this gift will bring her luck. But the day is relentless. The final coffee shop is a Starbucks on Tulsi Pipe Road. It is busy, but everyone she approaches says, "No," despite the price drop to ninety rupees. They turn their backs and, just at the point where Jiya begins to plead, management tell her to go. The final part of her journey home is made in shame. Not only has she failed to sell any lighters, Jiya realises that apart from Henry, no one has cared about her. Perhaps if she'd told them what she was facing they might have done, but somehow Jiya doubts that. She will be eleven next March, an age which many traffickers see as perfect. Jiya is aware that amongst those tourists who have rejected her lighters, some will feel the same way.

*

The sun is curving downwards as Jiya fills the water jugs. Behind her the electric lights are not yet shining – they blend with what remains of the afternoon. In this light the water looks fairly clear. As she lifts each heavy jug out of the river Jiya feels the magnifying glass dig into her stomach. She couldn't bring herself to sell it, the gift is too precious to her, especially after losing Mother's sandals. Once both jugs are safely on the river bank, Jiya pulls the magnifier from her waistband and looks through it. First she examines the dirt. The detail both scares and amazes her. She can see huge bugs on the earth and in the earth when she digs it with her other hand. When she does this, they scurry away from her massive, prying fingers. Then she scans the scant grass which covers the foot-worn bank. Finally she lies on her front to examine the river's edge. Jiya gasps. There are so many tiny forms all moving independently upon the weeds at the edge of the river. Their barrel-shaped bodies have eight legs and they move slowly upon the greenery. Circular, tooth-filled maws move on and off the plant life. Jiya can see claws gripping, sense mouths masticating and she is filled with wonder. If only Henry was her father. How she would work to study and understand this world. Knowing Henry is so old he will die before she is fully grown, Jiya hastily pushes the longing aside shutting down the emotion. She stuffs her treasure safely back into hiding and carries the heavy water jugs steadily home. Jiya wishes she could remain by the river as every step weights her heart with dread. As Father comes into sight, it begins to pound.

*

That night, as celebratory music plays in the background and India begins to welcome in the New Year, Jiya is viciously beaten under the constant electric light of Dharavi. While the fireworks are readied and the countdown of hope begins, Jiya feels helpless and alone. Her Father has been very careful with how he beat her. He will be speaking to Mr Basu tomorrow and he doesn't want any bruises to show. But, it is hard to breathe. There is blood on her t-shirt from where glass has cut her skin and Jiya thinks he may have hurt her more than he realises. Hopefully she managed to get all of the glass out. Looking across the floor, Jiya can see the remains of the broken magnifying glass. Her Father's fury when he found it was such that he threatened to break her in himself. He'd not believed her when she'd told the truth, accusing Jiya of buying the magnifying glass with money stolen from selling lighters.

Jiya feels ashamed he didn't draw the curtain and beat her in private. She lies where Father left her on the floor while he snores from his room. Perhaps she should go to bed as she feels quite cold. It's a struggle, but Jiya manages to get up and pull the curtain so no one can see her. She stumbles to her bed where she finds her backpack. It's still full of lighters.

Pulling one out, Jiya flicks it so the flame burns bright. It glows orange and sweetly warms her face. Catching sight of movement near the closed curtain, she automatically thrusts it forward, as if to see better despite the electric lights. Pain shoots through her ribs. Jiya holds her breath with shock as Grandma steps through.

"Jiya, don't be frightened child. It's me."

"Grandma? What are you doing here?" Jiya's head is reeling. How can Grandma be here? She died at least four years before Mother. Jiya struggles to make sense of what is before her. It is Grandma though. Jiya remembers pulling at that dress with pudgy fingers, knows the feel of its fabric and the smile on Grandma's face, so full of love, is what she recalled earlier. In the flame, Grandma burns incandescently and Jiya is reminded of one of the tales she was told as a small child about the descendants of the Fire God Agni and the Goddess Agneya. "Have you become one of the Angiris, Grandma?" Her hand falters on the lighter and the flame goes out. Grandma fades with it. Quickly Jiya flicks it back on.

"Keep the flame burning Jiya, it will help us."

Filled with awe, Jiya cannot help but ask, "Are you an angel of Agneya?"

"No time to explain now. Come with me Jiya. We

must leave before your Father sells you to Basu. Basu will say he protects you while he transforms you and turns your world into a living hell. I am your guardian, Jiya. Let me guide you."

As she struggles to rise from her bed, the effort of keeping the flame alive makes Jiya's hand tremble. The lighter falls towards her blanket which flares into many flames. The sudden warmth gives Jiya the strength to stand and move away. Behind her the bed ignites and flames begin to lick the wooden walls of the shack. Grandma's form solidifies as the flames increase. She moves to meet Jiya who is making slow progress due to her injuries. While Jiya holds her side, Grandma takes the lighter from the flaming bed and throws it towards the curtain. The thin cotton blossoms as fireworks hiss, flare and cascade with the jewelled colours of unsold lighters in Mumbai's sky. As Grandma wraps her arms around Jiya saying, "You're safe now, Jiya. He can't hurt you anymore." the flames lick ever higher. A glow with the appearance of sunlight flowing through an orange gemstone fills the room as Jiya's haversack explodes. Finally, Jiya feels safe and she feels loved. There is no fear, for Jiya is coming home in her Grandmother's arms and has no doubt she will soon smell her Mother's scent again.

*

On New Year's Day, the residents of Dharavi who survived when their shacks burnt to the ground are wondering which fool started the fire. They watch as firemen continue dousing down their neighbours' homes.

"It's just as bad as a late monsoon," one of them comments.

Later, when they are able to approach the fire's epicentre, Jiya's neighbours stand and view what remains of her physical form. She appears to have been incinerated with her arms outstretched as if they held another.

"That poor girl," says the man whose shack had been just a street away. "She suffered so at the hands of her Father." The others nod in agreement.

"He gave her such a beating last night."

"Poor thing, she tried so hard to take her Mother's place."

"Yes, and she worked all hours to sell those damn lighters."

"He should have remarried," the woman from across the street observes. "She was only a child."

In solemn agreement this body of neighbours turn and begin searching for materials to rebuild their homes. Not one of them imagines how beautiful and glorious the flames had been for Jiya. Nor do they know of the amazement she felt in meeting a loving Grandma who had been lost for so many years, or her anticipated joy at being in her mother's arms.

JUSTICA

After a dry and dusty day amongst the library's archives, Justica enjoys being in the forest bordering the park just outside the city gates. The pleasure of slipping between the trees and walking through disorderly undergrowth, on a track shaped into the earth by her own feet, lifts her spirits. Bushes and vines flourish. Flowers burst through the foliage and sunlight dapples her path as she winds her way under branches covered with vibrant purple leaves. When she enters the clearing, a pool of light illuminates every blade of grass, every faceted flower. Reaching the centre, she spins, arms outstretched, dress swinging above her knees with the momentum, until joyfully dizzy. Stopping, Justica supports her hair with her hands and lifts her face to the late afternoon sun, allowing its warmth to penetrate her tawny skin. She breathes in the honeyed perfume of the blossoms. Justica's job is quiet, solitary, despite the other scholars who work alongside her, but here, in this beautiful space, she finds a different manner of solitude.

A cough disturbs her peace.

Slumped against one of the trees surrounding the clearing sits a creature. Nothing she has ever seen, or read of in books, prepares her for its appearance; it's not a species which is native to Orrack. Stranger still, it is clothed. An escaped pet maybe? Her mother has told her how some citizens of Hasalem import exotic species from distant continents, but she's never seen one. She approaches with caution. The creature regards her warily; its eyes flit upwards and stare at her hair. Has it come loose from the tower she coiled it into this morning? Justica quickly checks all is in place while she sniffs the creature before her. It smells ripe, unwashed; its clothing is dirty and in places torn. A section of its lower leg is bandaged, and a rusty stain has seeped through. As Justica slowly draws closer, she catches the putrid stench of pus. The creature coughs again, placing a hairless five-digit paw against its torso. Clearly, coughing hurts. Making soothing noises, Justica edges nearer, crouches down then tentatively places a hand on the bandage. The creature winces, but doesn't lash out. Gently she unwraps the injury, then rips the smooth fabric above it to examine the limb. The area around the wound is swollen and weeping, the skin hot. A red line runs from torn flesh towards the creature's groin and Justica knows that veins and vessels are carrying poison towards vital organs. Sitting back on her haunches, she considers her options.

She should report this creature to the Guards, let the authorities deal with it. As a responsible citizen, this is her duty, one which has been drummed into her since childhood. She hesitates, recalling play-time tales of what happens to unusual beasts once the authorities have them – even if they are lost pets. Then again, she could leave the creature to die and let nature dispose of its remains, or she could find herbs, make a salve, and treat the infection. The creature sits still, gazing at her. Its oval eyes are brown and most of its face has no hair. Strange. Looking into the creature's eyes, Justica decides what she will do and sets off deeper into the forest, taking care to ensure that her hair doesn't catch on the lower branches of the trees. There are plants nearby which the creature can chew to reduce temperature and inflammation, and those she can chew into a paste and place on the wound. This will have to do until she can get home. Mamin has plenty of dried herbs and ingredients in her workshop to make proper poultices. The trick will be to do this without her realising. Mamin is sharp, and will notice if Justica steps out of line.

Returning to the clearing, she sits near the creature, giving it the herb to ease pain after placing a small amount in her own mouth, chewing and swallowing. It copies, grimacing at the bitter taste. Once the other herb is on the wound, she wraps a purple leaf around the paste, then ties this in place using some vines she's gathered. Glancing at her patient, Justica can tell its pain has lessened. She indicates the creature should lift the cloth covering its body. It does so immediately, revealing an area where bruises shine purple, edged with a green-blue fading into yellow.

Justica can't breathe. The creature's torso is almost hairless. She's never seen anything like it before and longs to touch. Her fingertips tingle in anticipation. She glances at her own arms, at the back of her hands. They're covered with fine soft hair the colour of honey. The creature's head has dark hair, and some is present on the lower limb she examined, but its torso is...fascinating. Swallowing hard, she examines the bruised area. Underneath her fingers the skin is wonderfully smooth and soft, but the muscles are firm and its bones, oh so near the surface, are hard. Justica conveys her satisfaction at finding no breakages with a nod. She points at the path which leads out of the clearing, then at where the sun will rise in the sky, indicating how far it would journey before she would return. The creature's mouth twists strangely as she does this; it bares white teeth. As she rises to go, the creature points towards itself and utters a noise, then it points at her.

She responds instinctively saying, "Justica."

The creature stumbles a little over the pronunciation, but repeats her name back to her.

Oh holy Goddess, what has she got herself into? They said in school that any creature, other than themselves, that could talk must be reported to the authorities. She should have walked away, reported her find. Now she's helped it and, it can speak her name. Justica flees from the clearing on all fours, running out of the wildness into the orderly calm of the park like a panicked cub. Before her are the city gates, beyond them lies home. The setting sun causes Hasalem's famous towers to stand starkly silhouetted against the darkening sky. Years of painful training in stance and decorum kick in just in time and she stands upright. The action of smoothing her dress over her thighs calms her mind. She's later than usual. Mamin will question why she's been in the park so long and Justica needs to lie.

*

The following day Justica returns to the forest after work. She hasn't dared to alter her routine; that would be noticed. In the pockets of her dress she carries a poultice – made after Mamin fell asleep last night – a small bottle of antiseptic lotion, a cloth and most of her lunch. Her stomach churns with apprehension. Part of her prays the creature has died. The other part is excited to see what develops – if it still breathes. Ancient tomes, resting deep in the archives, detail such happenings, but she's always regarded these as merely stories. Justica knows of no other who has actually met a creature able to speak. Excitement made her steal a sheet of parchment and an ink pen from her work-station. Mamin is accustomed to seeing ink stains on her dresses, so it won't matter if the pen leaks a little. Once out of sight of the Guards, she breaks into an upright run.

  The creature is alert. It bares its teeth, raises a paw and once more says her name. Uncertainty swells like a storm cloud, then abates. Justica nods, crouches so she can check its wound and begins pulling the cloth and lotion from her pockets. She gives the cheese and rough grained bread to the creature. It rapidly devours Justica's leftovers. Some of her knots haven't held. The leaf holding the poultice in place has loosened and slipped a little. Justica removes both, pours some lotion onto the cloth and cleans the wound. It looks calmer and the red line is no higher than before. As she turns to the fresh leaf and vine she's already gathered, the creature places its paw on her arm, then points at the vine. Bemused, Justica hands it over. The creature shows her how to tie a different kind of knot. Softly hooting her pleasure, Justica uses this knot to tie the leaf to the creature's leg. It holds the dressing firmly. She claps her hands happily, then picks up the parchment and pen.

Pointing to herself, Justica says her name, then writes each letter. The creature bares its teeth then claps its paws. It must be happy. When it indicates the parchment and pen, Justica can hardly believe it. Pointing at itself, the creature says the word it uttered yesterday evening. It then writes four symbols or letters unlike any script Justica has ever seen. Brimming with excitement, she snatches the pen and parchment from the creature's paws. Pointing at a tree, Justica says the word then spells it out. She thrusts the parchment forward. The creature speaks then inscribes four more symbols under her letters.

Unable to contain her excitement, Justica springs up and spins. She doesn't care if her hair spills out of its carefully constructed tower, but she resists the urge to hoot loudly. That might draw unwanted attention. Justica's occupation, studying ancient tomes and deciphering strange languages, means every text she translates in the archives is old, written by those lost to time. This work has filled Justica with a longing to connect with an intelligent race other than her own. The creature might still die; she should use what time there is wisely and not get caught. Goddess knows what would happen if she was found conversing with an alien species. Justica stops spinning. Water is running down the creature's face. Softly hooting her concern, she kneels beside it, placing a hand upon one of its upper limbs. Picking up the discarded cloth, she finds a clean corner and gently wipes, making soothing noises as one would do to a cub. Brown eyes stare into hers. They shine wetly with an internal agony Justica doesn't understand. It tries to lift the corners of its mouth, she thinks to reassure her, and one of its paws begins stroking her arm.

*

In the days that follow, Justica soon begins to understand what is being said. She learns his name is Paul. He comes from a planet called Earth, a place called America. His ship crashed deep in the forest and those with him died. Paul teaches her many different ways of knotting vine. He used to be a Boy Scout. Justica finds this title confusing, but the knots are interesting – she's become good at them. Paul's leg is healing well. The red line is gone and with it the infection. He now has the strength to walk and Justica has shown him a nearby stream, so his clothes and skin are clean, and she no longer has to fetch him water. Justica repeatedly checks the bruising on Paul's torso. The smooth skin calls out to her, stirs unaccustomed feelings. When she strokes Paul's skin, he tends to begin stroking her arm.

"I love how soft your fur is," he says.

Justica has grown to understand what those words mean. She feels the same way about his bald skin.

"Can you let your hair down?" he asks, indicating her tower of braids. Justica shakes her head.

"Decorum," she replies, "I cannot be seen in Hasalem with my hair down." What she doesn't tell him is that, for a female of her race, the higher a tower of hair is, the more desirable they are. Justica is aware she's regarded as very desirable, has already received several proposals. But none of the males have engaged her the way Paul does.

*

Justica's deep in the archives when she hears whispering. Gathering up the tomes she's found so far, she sneaks towards the sound, peering around the edges of the wooden shelves holding records of ancient civilisations

66

and voices of the dead. The whispers are louder now. Soon she'll be close enough to hear whatever gossip currently has the city in its grip.

Mamin never gossips. "No good ever comes of listening to gossip. I never want to hear that you have engaged in spreading rumours."

But often those rumours are interesting, hold a grain of truth. Justica creeps close enough to hear yet not be seen.

"I tell you it's true!"

Justica knows the voice: it belongs to Arun, a trainee she's assisted on more than one occasion. He speaks on,

"They've found a crashed object deep in the forest, about twenty kiros from here. It was heavy enough to plough a line between the trees. Came to rest on its side, apparently."

"Enough of your nonsense, I'm going back to work."

Footsteps walk away from where Arun stands and Justica hides.

"Don't believe me then!"

Arun's exclamation is loud enough to warrant a response. Taking a deep breath, Justica steps around the corner cheerfully saying, "Don't believe what?"

"What did you hear?"

Justica shrugs. "Crashed spaceship, twenty kiros from here. Were there any bodies on board?"

"Hush!" Arun says, pressing a finger to his mouth, "Not so loud." He looks around to see if anyone in authority is nearby, then continues, "Yes, five in all, but they think there were six. A trail of blood led into the forest, heading towards Hasalem." He leans in closer whispering, "The Watchers and Guards are on high alert."

"Do you think that's true?"

Arun steps back holding his hands out in a *who knows* gesture, then returns to searching along the dusty shelves, leaving Justica to do the same.

*

Dread fills Justica as she hurries upright through city streets on her way to the gate. She thanks the Goddess that her habit of visiting the park is an established one. Less chance of any Watchers, who will be looking for changes in routines and behaviours, noticing her. She passes the Guards, then takes her normal route towards the forest, hoping she can slip between the trees without being observed. What really worries her is how, if the rumour is only just beginning to spread, Watchers may already be in place.

When Justica reaches the clearing Paul is exercising. The cloth which covered the top half of his body has been discarded at the foot of a tree. She cannot help but notice how flesh and muscle are beginning to coat his bones. While she watches, a liquid fire stirs in her stomach. No, it's lower than that. Goddess, the heat is intense, it makes her want to... The pulse in her throat flickers as her heart rate increases. She utters a low hoot, filled with such longing and desire, that Paul stops and stares at her. For a moment, Justica feels embarrassed. She has little sexual experience and her feelings are overwhelming. Yet, the look he's giving her... Justica reaches up and begins to unwind her tower of hair. She calls to Paul, hoots her desire softly into the laden air.

"My God," Paul whispers as her golden plait coils snake-like onto the grass beside her. Justica walks towards him, her hair slithering across the clearing. Most of it remains in the spot where she first stood and inadvertently voiced her longing. She undoes her dress, sliding it off her body to pool at her feet, deftly revealing her naked form. Paul looks at her. His hand trembles as he reaches out to touch the pale fur which completely covers her tawny skin. Uttering soft hoots of pleasure, Justica crouches. Removing what's left of his clothing,

Paul falls to his knees; his hands stroke her fur, and his lips press softly into her flesh, arousing her further. Before Justica can turn around, Paul pushes her backwards onto the ground. She squirms uneasily. Paul's fingers stroke down her belly, soothing Justica's instinctive fear, yet she nips his shoulder in warning when he tries to enter her. A sharp intake of breath, a lifting of pressure and Justica swiftly turns over. Raising her haunches, she presses herself against Paul's erection, shuddering when his hardness slides into her.

*

It is late. Justica slips in through the city gates just before they're locked for the night. Street lamps flicker and windows are shuttered. She hurries home before anyone notices her hair isn't as neat as normal.

"Where have you been?" Mamin asks angrily, grabbing Justica's face with hard fingers. Her mother's eyes pierce Justica to the bone.

"I… I fell asleep in the park. Sorry Mamin, I was so tired after work."

"Then why did you not come straight home?"

"Because I always walk in the park."

Mamin nods in acknowledgement, releasing Justica's face.

"That's true." She steps back. "What is that smell?" Justica watches in horror as her mother's eyes narrow. Then Mamin is sniffing and growling, a deep guttural sound from the back of her throat. She surges forward, gripping Justica around the neck snarling, "Understand this, if you have dishonoured me, you will pay for it. Don't think I've not noticed what you've been taking from our home recently."

Justica is thrust backwards into the wall. She sinks to the floor as Mamin storms out of the house.

"Oh holy Goddess help me," Justica whimpers. She's certain Mamin is on her way to the Guard's Tower.

*

Bruised and battered, Justica curls protectively around that which is in her womb. The cloth beneath her is harsh against her face. It looked newly woven when she was thrown in here, but now her blood stains the once pristine blanket. The rising sun is warm and behind her eyelids redness glows, for there are no shutters on the solitary window. Her cell is in the Watcher's Tower and seeing the night sky for the first time was wonderful. Now, it's become ordinary.

A creaking door rouses her fully. One eye is swollen shut. She opens the other as Mamin enters and locks the door. Justica sits up, feeling the life within stirring as she does so. Her belly is so large, Justica is certain she will bear more than one cub. She rises and begins moving towards her mother, who she hasn't seen since the Guards brought her to this circular prison.

"Mamin!" Her voice cracks.

Mamin's movements are a blur, her slap a force which sends Justica back to the floor. She lands awkwardly and her unborn cubs kick in protest.

"I am not your mother. I took you in when your parents were executed."

"No. That cannot be. Please Mamin, I am your daughter!"

Mamin purses her mouth. Her distaste for Justica is written upon her face as she continues spewing the harsh truth of Justica's existence. "Your parents were thieves; they held themselves in greater esteem than the rules of our civilisation. You were named after the justice which was served, but like them, you're an aberration, a deviant and you will answer my questions. By the Goddess, if you refuse, I will cut you." She pulls a curved blade from her skirt, one used for cutting herbs. The blade gleams brightly in the morning sunshine. Justica has no doubt it is sharp.

Mamin strides across the floor towards the interrogator's chair. Once seated, she waves an expectant hand at the chair intended for Justica. Both are bolted to the stone beneath them, as is the table. From the floor, Justica can see how Mamin's serge uniform sits just above her tightly laced boots. Uniform. Mamin is wearing a uniform. Justica looks just below her mother's left shoulder and sees an insignia stitched into the material.

Carefully getting up, she asks, "Since when have you been a Watcher?"

The sneer which greets this question is as hard as Mamin's eyes. "Since before you were born. You and the poultices provided great cover until recently."

Justica sits down, hiding her quivering hands beneath the swell of her belly. The knowledge that Mamin has been watching her all of her life, has never loved her, pains Justica more than the beatings she has endured.

"It has been found," Mamin announces. "Despite your silence, the Guards have found the creature you've created the abomination inside you with." A snarl of disgust escapes before she controls it. "You will tell me how you communicated with it."

"Only if you tell me where Paul is and what is going to happen to him." Justica braces herself for the flurry of blows that must surely follow. Instead, hooting laughter fills the cell. Mamin's head is thrown back upon her long, graceful neck. Abruptly, the hooting stops, but Mamin's black eyes glitter with acid amusement.

"With pleasure. It's in a lab. It will be treated well until we're able to get the information we require, after which it will still be taken care of, but in a different way." Mamin's eyes flicker to Justica's belly. "And once that *thing* you're carrying is born, I'll take it to join its father."

Bile rises in Justica's throat at the loathing in Mamin's eyes, the knowing twitch of her mouth.

*

71

Not knowing what to do, Justica sits looking out of the window. Giving birth had been easy compared to this. Her two cubs had been wrapped in cloth and taken from the room by Mamin before Justica saw them. She heard hungry cries, so knows they were alive. Her teats are producing milk, but this is beginning to dry up and her belly is returning to normal. Days are passing and, although food and water is being shoved through the slot in Justica's door and waste is being collected, no-one has visited to cut her hair in recognition of the birthing. She shakes her head, feeling her towering hair sway with the motion. How can she expect tradition to be followed when she has broken the most sacred of rules?

Each day, she sits, wondering how Paul and her cubs are faring in the laboratory assigned to them. She has no doubt they are suffering, but what can she do? Her cell is so high that from her window, citizens look like insects. Yet, the external structure of the tower is not smooth; balconies protrude lower down the building. Presumably there are doors or windows adjacent to these balconies, but Justica feels too inert to do more than wonder. Then the day comes when there is no knock on the door for her waste and neither food nor water are provided. When the same thing happens the following day, Justica realises she has been left to die. She picks up the meat knife on her empty plate, running a finger along its blunt blade. Taking it over to the windowsill, Justica starts to sharpen it. She will not die in a stinking cell. The blade rests momentarily as an even stronger resolve surfaces. She will find her cubs and Paul.

*

Evening falls and Justica is using the knots Paul taught her to bind strips of her rough blanket together into a rope. She'd had to resharpen the knife twice so it would cut cleanly through the densely woven cloth. Next, Justica unwinds the coil of her golden hair, unravelling its length onto the stone floor. Then she unplaits it and, pulling the hair into one thick strand, begins tying her hair into sections with smaller strips of cloth. The first is tied where it reaches her shoulders, the second is bound near her waist. Justica plaits the final section very tightly and ensures the final strip of cloth binding the plaits' end will hold firm. Taking the cloth rope, Justica ties half-hitches to secure it to a leg of the bolted chair closest to the window. She then uses a double sheet bend to secure the cloth rope through the plaited section of her hair. Finally, she re-hones the knife.

Night falls and Justica slowly lowers her cloth and hair rope out of the window, down the side of the tower. She hopes it is long enough to reach the balcony she can see when leaning over the sill. The point where she has to start climbing in order to give herself more hair to use, arrives quickly. Taking a deep breath, Justica pulls the cloth rope taut against the chair leg and lowers herself over the sill, pressing her feet against the stone tower. She steadily lowers herself downwards. The rising moon is just a sliver glimmering faintly in the night sky. Even so, Justica offers a silent prayer to the Goddess that she is not seen.

The moon's journey across the sky tracks her progress as she works her way down to the balcony. The rope is just too short. Placing her toes on the balcony rail and bracing the other foot against the wall, Justica balances. She takes the knife from her pocket and cuts through her hair, as smoothly as she can, just above the first cloth tie. The remaining length should signify an adolescent cub. The sudden lack of tension, of taut support, almost sends Justica plunging below. She topples sideways, landing on the solid stone floor of the balcony.

No sound comes through the open balcony door. Crawling forward, Justica sniffs. The adjacent room is laden with many scents, but is empty. Inside she finds blue uniforms and every-day clothing, hanging from named hooks which line two of the walls. She searches for an outfit with an apprentice insignia that will fit her. One for a male will serve her well. Someone has left food near their clothing. Justica eats, then drinks deeply from the half-full water jug placed on a washstand. A hairbrush pokes from a dress pocket. Taking it to a mirror hung near the door, she brushes her now shoulder-length hair. The cut looks a little ragged, but it will do. Taking the knife from her discarded dress, Justica sharpens it once more, places it in a trouser pocket, then steps out of the room into a corridor with just enough light to walk by. With no idea if she's on the right floor, or where the laboratories are, Justica sniffs to her right. The air is nondescript. That coming from her left carries a faint chemical smell, reminding her of Mamin's workshop. Justica heads towards it.

*

It appears only a small number of personnel work during the night. Doors have a light close by and those she opens lead into offices. The chemical smell grows stronger, and it is with some relief that she notices a sign indicating she's nearing the laboratories. Justica realises she's found them when the corridors are illuminated by light spilling from behind large sheets of glass. Justica looks into each laboratory she passes, seeing nothing but silver and black equipment which glints and gleams under the strong white light issuing from circular mounds on the ceiling. What it does, or why it is there is beyond Justica. At home – what used to be her home – they had candles, cooked food over an open fire. A burner, test-tubes and vials, resided in Mamin's workshop, but what can be seen here makes her equipment archaic. Each laboratory Justica passes has a worker or two, but these individuals are too involved with the machinery to notice her. There's no sign of Paul or her cubs.

The dimness of the grey stone corridors seems darker after the bright light. She almost misses the recessed doorway on her right – it is unlit. She peers at the metal panel just above her head. Justica's insides turn to water when she reads the words, but she senses that this is where she will find Paul and their cubs. Her fear is so great it is as if someone else, not her, pushes the handle down, opens the door, steps through, and enters the Eugenics Laboratory.

The floor slopes downwards. After curving in on itself, the dimly lit corridor levels out. There are three doors ahead, all on the left. Light pools on the floor outside the first, and Justica can hear voices. She slips by in the shadow of the right-hand wall. Just as she reaches the second door, the third opens. Easing herself into the unlit room, Justica watches through a crack as a female walks by carrying a tray of containers filled with fluids. Her uniform is a different colour to those in the changing room. Leaving the room once the female is out of sight, Justica heads for the third door.

This room is lit by light issuing from the machines surrounding Paul and their cubs. Each of them lays on a metal slab with tubes inserted into every orifice. Tubes also run from veins in their arms and from their spines. Leather straps hold their wrists and ankles tightly in place. Paul even has one across his throat. Metal probes have been inserted into their shaved scalps. Each probe has a thin thread which leads to machines sounding like droning bees.

Unable to understand what she is seeing, Justica draws closer to the slabs on which her cubs lay. They are beautiful; both have Paul's five digits instead of her four. Their faces reflect her mouth and nose, but their eyes are shaped like his. Each of them is slightly different; the female cub perhaps takes after her, whereas the male reminds her of Paul. Their backs show none of the spinal curvature that is normal in new-born cubs. They will not need to go through the painful straightening process she had to; will walk, upright with ease. Justica longs to hold them in her arms. She wants to watch them grow, see them develop. Gently, she runs a hand down each of their small bodies. Her fingers register the scars where they have been opened, the flesh folded back, and their glistening insides laid wetly bare in the name of eugenics. They do not respond to her touch; their eyes remain closed. Her cubs are breathing, but they do not live.

A cry begins to build inside her, one unlike anything she's ever felt. Deeper than one of rage, it boils up from the depths of a despair, scouring the core of her being. Her chest heaves. It's as if she's choking on air. She looks at Paul. His eyes are open and she sees that he is in terrible pain. With a strangled cry, she goes to him, trying in vain to wipe the tears from his beloved face. He cannot talk, due to the tube down his throat, but he communicates by moving his head, lifting a finger, with his eyes. And Justica knows what she must do.

She undoes the strap around Paul's throat. His scent fills her nostrils, and she kisses the soft skin, feeling where his life force pulsates. Taking the knife from her pocket, Justica stands above his head, pressing the knife against the pulse. Paul nods. There is no fear, only acceptance of what must be. He closes his eyes when the knife pierces his flesh. His body shakes as it pumps a crimson spray across the grey stone floor. When it stops, she kisses him goodbye.

Knife in hand, Justica goes to her cubs. They look so peaceful despite the tubes, despite the suffering already inscribed upon their innocent forms. Looking at the scars running down their bodies, she cannot bring herself to inflict another cut upon them. The knife clatters to the floor. Justica kisses the forehead of her female cub saying, "Go with peace little one." and calmly places firm hands over the tiny nose and mouth. It doesn't take long for her cub to stop breathing. As she approaches her male cub, Justica recalls the word Paul would have used to describe him. Her kiss is as loving as those which went before it, her hands just as firm.

"Goddess take care of you, my boy, on this journey," she whispers in his ear.

*

Silent and wraith-like in the shadows, Justica makes her way back to the changing room. Once there, she strips off, using what remains of the water to wash away the blood. Fortunately, the male clothing she'd noticed earlier still hangs from its hook. After putting it on, Justica leans over the balcony to establish how far down the tower she still has to go. She can see the streetlights, the guards walking in long established patterns through the city. She takes a moment to wonder why the streetlights are lit by hand when the lights in this tower function without flame and briefly considers the machines she's seen in the laboratories, but there's no sense in trying to understand that which bewilders her.

Back in the grey stone corridor, Justica takes the opposite direction to earlier. She walks at an even pace as the corridor slopes down and around. Before long she is joined by others also dressed in day clothes. Some trot past her eager to be home, others chat in pairs or groups. Like Mamin, these citizens must hold their secrets silently. Justica keeps to herself. A flight of stairs leads to a room with a reception area. There are two desks, one for signing out. Using the name on the hook above the clothing she's wearing, Justica signs *Habain R* then leaves the building with a cluster of other citizens.

Early morning sun lights the road through the city centre. It leads past the building Justica once thought of as home, takes her past a time when she believed Mamin was her mother. Her steps falter. The emotions which ravaged her as she realised what had been done to her cubs threaten to re-emerge. Justica battles for control. She wants to kill Mamin, make the bitch suffer, but she must remain hidden. The knowledge of her escape will be Mamin's undoing. All Justica needs to do to achieve this, is to go for a walk in the park with the multitude who take a morning stroll. From there, she can sneak into the forest, cut through to where it runs alongside the road and make her way to another city. One which has a forest where she can live, harvest herbs, make poultices and potions; build a name for herself as a healer, create a new identity.

Justica passes the guards in the midst of the morning crowd. All they see is an adolescent of no note.

HANDFULS OF NOTHING

The sound of feet running up carpeted stairs alerts Jem to the fact her sister's new friend, Liam, has arrived.

"My sister's room is down here," Sophie says. "She won't mind if I show you."

Despite having her curtains closed to ease the summer heat, Jem's bedroom is stifling. She is wearing just her underwear. If Sophie were alone, there'd be no problem, but she's with a boy Jem has never met. Getting off her bed, Jem reaches the door just as Sophie turns the handle, begins to push it open.

"Wait 'til you see the posters and the books she's got."

Jem speaks through the narrow gap, "Hang on, I'm not dressed."

Sophie doesn't seem to hear, is pushing the door.

"I'll get some clothes on, then you can come in. Okay?"

Jem can't be certain Sophie has heard, but Liam has. He just looks at her, says nothing.

"Sophie? I'm closing the door."

Liam stares through the narrowing crack as she gently pushes it to.

A high-pitched scream pierces Jem's ears. She promptly reopens the door enough to peer through. Sees her little sister holding injured fingers to her narrow chest, as more screams issue forth. Hears their mother racing up the stairs.

"I'm sorry, I thought you'd heard me," Jem says.

Mum glares at her, protectively cradles Sophie in her arms, carries her youngest daughter downstairs. Liam gives Jem one last look, then follows.

Feeling sick, Jem closes her bedroom door, leans against it. Why was there no warning? She often sees things before they happen, knows things she has no way of knowing, but on this occasion, there had been nothing. Nothing to suggest her sister would get hurt when she closed the door.

Jem crosses the room, parts the curtains and looks through the nets at the sun-struck garden. She's wishing she had been forewarned when her bedroom door is slammed into the wall so hard, its handle dents the plaster.

"You bitch."

Slaps land wherever skin is bare, gaining in strength and conviction.

"It was an accident!"

"You did it on purpose, bitch."

Mum's voice is quiet despite the outpouring of rage from her hands.

Jem tries to defend herself from the onslaught. Her mother switches to pinching and twisting the skin on her arms.

"You're hurting me!"

The look on Mum's face is one of absolute fury. Jem feels the force of her rage in every blow. Never before has her mother attacked her in this way. All Jem has ever known are taps to her hand as a child and the occasional smack.

"I'm sorry! I didn't mean to hurt her!"

The pinched line of Mum's mouth, her flushed skin, narrowed nostrils and the hard, hard look in her eyes say otherwise. Angry hands continue their assault. Jem tries to step away as a fist pulls back.

"You knew she was there, hurt her on purpose."

Jem cries out as the fist impacts. Doubles over cradling her belly.

"I'm sorry! I told Sophie I was closing the door. Told her three times. I didn't know her fingers were there."

Liam had heard, Jem is certain, but he said nothing when she closed the door. She can still hear Sophie's scream as it shut on her small fingers.

"Liar."

Mum pulls Jem's shoulder-length hair with such force she yelps, then slaps her across the face.

"Bitch."

"I didn't know she hadn't heard me!"

Jem feels the agonising force of Mum's hard shoe against her shin. She cries out, not knowing where the next blow will land. Mother's hands are everywhere. How can this be happening when she is telling the truth?

"I'll teach you."

The slaps, punches and pinches are controlled, deliberate, relentlessly targeting Jem's arms, head, torso and thighs. Time stretches out, becoming progressively slower as each blow falls. Every pinch twists the skin to what feels like breaking point.

Something in Jem gives way. She falls silent, despite the pain. Stands still, arms wrapped around her waist, as the blows continue. Ragged breathing and harsh words fill her ears. A deep internal emptiness opens up, invites her to step in. She falls to the floor, curls into a ball, sobbing. Her anguished cries are distanced and she doesn't see her mother leave, or hear her bedroom door shut.

*

"Good morning, Jemma," Mum says, as though nothing has happened. Jem hesitates before entering the kitchen. Mum's bright and cheery face falls slightly, but she recovers quickly, saying, "Come and get your breakfast, I'll pour you a mug of tea."

Sophie sits at the table eating Rice Krispies, fingers wrapped around the handle of her spoon. They look a little red, as if more blood than normal was deposited in their tips, but there is no sign of bruising. Her other hand holds the bowl in place. There is no bruising on those fingers either. Jem's breath hitches in her throat. She glances at her mother, who is leaning against the work-surface eating a slice of toast. The promised mug of tea has been placed on the table in front of a chair.

"I'm taking Sophie swimming then doing food shopping," Mum says. "Dinner's at six. Your dad's gone to play golf. Be nice if he ate with us, he's away next week."

"Pigs might fly." Sophie parrots a phrase their mother often uses.

"That's right, sweetheart." Mum ruffles Sophie's hair.

Jem can't speak, has no words for the everyday normality on display. She crosses the kitchen, only lifting her head so she can see to get a bowl out of the wall cabinet. After filling it with cereal and milk, Jem returns to her room, leaving the mug of tea on the table. She'll get her own later. Her stomach knots as she eats. Nausea hits after a few spoonfuls. Putting the bowl to one side, she goes to the square mirror placed at head-height on her wall, brushes her hair. The bristles irritate her scalp, making it sting. No marks show on her face but when she lifts the brush, mottled purple, black and blue bruising contrasts starkly with her cream pyjama sleeve as it drops down. When she removes her pyjamas, the light tan on her skin seems to deepen the shading of those massed on her torso and thighs. Her shin bone hurts, as if the kick she received has done more than bruise it. Jem closes the pain down, boxes it up tight along with everything else.

Net curtains ripple in the slight breeze. They spin sun into sugar-like strands which filter softly through the mesh. The mid-August day promises to be another hot one. Jem is due to meet with her boyfriend Dan and his friends. Ellie and Jack, she knows from drama club. Hannah and Fin, she's met through the Saturday drives they go on. Drama club is held at the church hall, except during the summer holidays. It remains a good place to meet up, though, a short walk and a bus ride from Jem's home. She needs to get a move on. Opening a drawer,

Jem's fingers linger on shorts and t-shirts, but settle on pale blue jeans and a long-sleeved white top with printed poppies growing upwards from the hem to just above her waist. The sleeves are a little looser than she would like, but the poppies go well with a pair of red trainers she loves. Once out of the front door, Jem ignores the pain in her shin and runs towards the bus stop. The sudden exercise is a release until her breathing begins to hiccup and she starts crying. Her heart is hammering. Jem slows to a walk and reaches the bus stop, limping. By the time the bus comes she is calm.

*

Jem kisses Dan briefly on the mouth once she is in the car.

"Get a room," says Hannah from the back seat. Her head rests on Fin's shoulder, one of her arms across his hips. Static lifts her long and fine mid-brown hair to stick against the fabric of the seat.

"You can talk," Jem says.

"Yeah, you don't leave me alone! Not that I'm complaining," Fin laughs.

Their delight in each other and their easy acceptance of her eases the hard knot of emptiness slightly. Jem smiles as she sits back in her seat, reaching for the seatbelt, Hannah's comment to the forefront of her mind. Dan is affectionate towards her, but no more. They've never slept together. Jem suspects this is due to their age difference. She'd been fourteen when eighteen-year-old Dan asked her out, turned fifteen just two months ago. He never treats her as a child, none of the group do. And they believe her when she speaks. Tears form. Jem blinks them away while fastening the seatbelt. Dan's phone pings.

"Jack and Ellie on their way?" asks Jem as he quickly checks it.

"Yep. And we're off!"

Tyres squeal around the corner of the road in front

of the church hall. Jack speeds past while Ellie waves out of an open window as if she were the Queen. Dan slides out from the kerb to follow, not bothering to match Jack's short-lived burst of speed. Dan's calm and measured driving is why his car is always full. Unlike Jack's.

Journey's end is a woodland park with a burger van. Jem, Hannah and Ellie pile onto scorching bench seats with an integrated tabletop, while the lads sort food and drinks. Heat seeps through Jem's jeans. How hot it must feel against Ellie and Hannah's bare legs. Out in the fresh air with friends, Jem finds she is starving. She eats the hot juicy burger, relishing every mouthful, licking grease and juices from her fingers. Finds it hard to eat without the sleeves of her top falling back, but manages. The coffee is slightly bitter, so she adds sugar.

"We'll go to the loo while you get the drinks and snacks," announces Hannah, swinging her legs out from under the table. "Come on girls."

"I thought I was Queenie today," Ellie says while Jem wriggles herself out from her end spot. She follows the other two, listening to their chatter; Hannah is teasing Ellie about going braless and trying to get her to spill the beans on whether she has slept with Jack.

The copse they find is lovely. Just far enough off the beaten track for civilisation to be silent, although Spotify playing on Hannah's phone reminds Jem it is ever-present. She and Dan sit under an old oak tree, their backs against its wide trunk. Above them, branches dwindle in size as they reach out and up. Various shades of green leaves filter the sun's strength and a light breeze rustles through, giving an illusion of coolness.

"That chilled container has kept the J2Os cold," Dan says. His Adam's apple moves as he swallows and contentment seeps from him. Ellie sits with Jack. She drinks orange liquid from a glass bottle as he kisses her neck. Hannah and Fin lie side-by-side, singing along to a

Spotify mix.

"It's lovely here."

"Jack and I found this park soon after we passed our driving tests. The burgers are great, you can walk for miles if you want and there's areas like this," says Dan.

Jem lifts her bottle, sips the chilled liquid then places it back on the grass. She doesn't notice the concerned look on Dan's face until she feels his fingers lifting her hand. He gently pushes her sleeve up, exposing her arm.

"You've been quiet today and I wondered why you were covered up." He runs a finger across the livid marks, from just above her wrist to her elbow. "What happened?"

Images of her mother's hard face make her flinch from Dan's touch. She tugs her sleeve down, pulls her knees into her chest, curls herself up tight. Tender flesh on her belly complains as the metal button of her jeans digs in. It's all Jem can do to not rock on her haunches. A warm hand strokes her back.

"I noticed you were limping on the way here. Just how badly are you hurt?"

A wail begins to build. Jem clamps it down. She doesn't know how to tell him; what happened yesterday makes no sense to her, so how can she explain it? Panic rises in her chest.

"Jesus, Jem, you're shaking. I'm sorry, I had to ask."

Dan gathers her to him, kissing the top of her head the same way Mum used to whenever she hurt herself as a child. Dan's caring nature, the sense of belonging she has with these friends, helps. Slowly she reels herself back in until the trembling stops, the panic subsides. Moving out of Dan's arms, Jem drinks some of the now not-so-cool J2O, sees Dan's eyes drift to Jack. Jem watches as Jack runs a finger along the top of Ellie's right breast where it rises above her camisole. He slides his finger over the material, circles Ellie's nipple. She presses herself towards him and they kiss. Electricity jolts in Jem's groin as if a switch has been flipped. Dan has never kissed her the way Jack is kissing Ellie. Dan licks his lips as if they are dry, swallows hard. His eyes remain on Jack.

Jack… Jem sits bolt upright. *She sees cars bumper-to-bumper on one of the main roads they travelled here on. A silver car, driving too fast. It looks like Jack's. She hears the squeal of brakes, sees it swerve and clip the rear of the last car in the queue. The speeding car lifts and rolls on its roof, metal screeching as it careens into oncoming traffic...*

"Jem? Jem! What is it?"

"Can we drive home a different way? Avoid the roadworks?"

"Yes we can. Why?"

Jem nods at Jack. "He drives too fast, has an accident."

"What? Did you see something? Are you sure it's today?"

Jem traces one of the poppies on her top. Its redness reminds her of blood. "Yes, I saw it and no, I don't know if it will happen today."

"Was it a vision?"

"Yeah. And I feel it here." Jem presses her abdomen, catching the bruise there.

"Are you always right?"

"Not always. I guess things can change what I see."

"You were right about Hannah and Fin. I never thought they'd get back together, but look at them."

Jem smiles at the couple lying contentedly on the grass. Hannah's legs are turning red in the sun.

"And I'll never forget that time you suddenly sat up and yelled at me to slow down and brake. Remember?"

Jem does remember. Each vision is imprinted on her mind.

"If I'd not done as you said, I'd've hit that stag." Dan

checks his watch. "I know a different route. It will take longer so I'll drop you home." He gets up, begins rousing the others. "You follow me this time, Jack," he says. "I followed you all the way here, so it's my turn in front."

*

Jem sinks into her seat when Dan stops outside her home. Despite his questions, the horrible vision, it's been a relief to get away.

Dan leans over, presses his lips quickly against hers, then says, "Shall we go and see a film this week? I can pick you up Wednesday, say six."

"Sure," Jem says. "See you then."

As she waves him off, Jem cannot help but think the date is a reward for saving Jack. Yet, somehow, when Dan texts her on Tuesday saying Jack has written his car off and he needs to be there for his friend, she's not surprised. There had been an inevitability about the vision featuring Jack's car. Jem wants to text: *Follow your heart. Tell Jack how you feel.* But she doesn't need foresight to know this wouldn't end well. Instead, she sends: *I understand. Take care of Jack and I'll c u at drama in Sept.* Neither the message from Dan nor her response says, "Goodbye," yet Jem is certain their six-month relationship has ended.

*

Several days later, most of Jem's bruises are fading to a greenish-yellow colour reminding her of vomit. She can walk without limping, although the bruise on her shin remains purple. Even though her body is healing, there's a deadness as though a part of her has ceased to exist. It makes speaking to or looking at her mother impossible. Words fail to form in her mouth. When Mum talks to her, all Jem can do is nod or shake her head. She finds it best to keep her eyes down, focus on the floor, looking up only when necessary. Jem's feelings towards Sophie haven't changed – she loves her sister dearly – but how she feels

87

towards her mother? The deadness inside holds her emotions in check.

The still morning air is thick with heat as Jem goes into the kitchen. Having been awake since six, she is already dressed. It's too hot for jeans so she's wearing shorts with a thin gypsy top covering her arms. Mum looks at her shin, putting half-eaten toast down on her plate as Jem reaches into the cupboard to get a bowl. Her sleeve slides down, revealing a fading tan and faint bruises.

"Come and join us at the table, Jemma."

Jem's sleeve drops to cover her arm as she places her bowl on the worktop, pulls a spoon out of the drawer. She fills the bowl with cereal, pours milk over, then makes to leave.

"Sit down."

It's a command. Jem hooks out a chair with her foot and sits, putting her bowl and spoon on the placemat.

"We need to get you a new coat for school. You've lost weight, your old one's too big. I'm off work this Friday, thought we could go to London, have a day out. Find you something nice."

There's no hesitancy in Mum's voice, no mention about the lack of tan when it's such a sunny summer, or the greenish bruises. It all sounds so normal – go to London, buy a school coat. It's not though. Before, if Jem had a bad bruise, Mum would have comforted her, put arnica cream on it, made sure she was okay. It has been ten days since Jem was beaten, cast adrift, to become flotsam in the flow of family life, yet this morning it's full-blown normalcy with no apparent room for manoeuvre: sit at the table and have breakfast with me, chat as if nothing ever happened and, oh, let's go shopping.

Jem pushes her chair back. Running upstairs she grabs her bag from her room and races down, jumping the last two steps. Needing fresh air and space, she opens the front door and heads for the local park.

*

On Friday, Mum drives them to the train station where she buys tickets for the forty-minute journey to Victoria.

"Have you had a look online?" Mum asks once they're on the train. "What shops do you want to look in?"

Jem stares out of the smeared window, squints at the grey clouds in the sky. It looks like it might rain. She shakes her head.

"We'll start with Oxford Street. I'm sure we'll find something there."

When they reach Victoria, Jem steps onto the platform unable to take the hand Mum is holding out.

"We need to go up the escalator and find the exit. We can walk to Oxford Street; takes about half an hour. Okay?"

There's a crowd of people in the area before the bank of escalators running up on the left and down on the right. Jem follows her mother through the crush. The moving staircase with its metal steps sliding up out of the floor is just a short distance ahead. Wondering where it ends, Jem looks up. She sees a grey-haired man in a beige raincoat.

A grey-haired man... He's almost at the top when the black handrail reverses. Instead of following the upward trend of the escalator, it pulls his hand down towards the floor. People around him are exclaiming, struggling with the sensation, as is he. He lets go, grasps the rail further along, but the motion of his hand sliding in the opposite direction to his body for a second time, causes him to lose his balance.

He falls back onto the woman behind.

She topples onto the woman and child behind her. They also fall backwards.

Person after person is knocked off their feet. They lie on the hard metal treads screaming at the high-vaulted ceiling above...

Jem stops in her tracks. She looks again at the grey-haired man. He's two-thirds of the way up.

"Come on, Jemma."

Jem tries to speak, but words stick in her throat. Mum takes her arm, puts Jem before her, placing a hand between her shoulders. So fierce is the urge to get out of line, Jem barely registers it. The mass of people behind and alongside them pushes Jem and her mother onto the escalator. They begin to rise.

Jem twists to look at Mum, opens her mouth. The only sound she makes is a whispered croak.

"Turn and face the front, Jemma. Hold the handrail."

Jem does as she's told. The black handrail reverses.

Jem lets go, balances and braces herself. She ignores the comments made by those around her. From high above comes a scream.

Bodies topple like a set of dominoes. Torsos immobilise legs. Panic permeates the escalator; its stairs continue going upwards while the handrail steadily runs downwards. People lie at an angle on the metal steps. The continuous loop of the aluminium track runs under their bodies and nothing is stopping the flow.

One step up from Jem, a plump woman in a brown coat cries out and flaps her arms on seeing bodies falling towards her. Jem bends at the knees, puts her arms out and catches the woman, when the domino effect pushes her over. Jem holds her, but has no voice to tell the woman to stop moving her arms, to stop screaming, that someone will turn the escalator off soon.

"I'm being crushed! My legs, my legs! Get off me!"

Her frantic hands fly back, catching Jem in the face, knocking her over.

"I've got you." Mum is grasping the back of Jem's coat under her shoulders, keeping her head off the metal stairs moving beneath her. "You're okay, Jemma. I've got you."

As the escalator continues its ceaseless progression upwards, the metal rim of each step hits Jem's lower back. The woman on top of her continues waving her arms and screaming. She presses heavily against Jem's legs, yet Jem is calm. She wonders why Mum is panting with the effort of holding her. Jem is nothing; ceased to be anything on the day she accidentally shut her sister's fingers in the bedroom door. Then, Mum's hands had been full of rage. Now, Mum holds handfuls of nothing.

Behind Mum, people are waving their arms in the air, calling for the escalator to be turned off. Those above continue screaming for help. It's a relief when the staircase finally stops. At the top, people begin helping each other up. The stillness of the handrail helps, gives them something to grip as they rise and climb what remains of the steep steps.

"Not long now, Jemma," Mum says, "they're almost halfway down, those who fell."

The woman lying on Jem groans. "My legs, my legs!" She starts crying when assisted to her feet. Jem feels hands lifting her. A man is helping Mum to get her up.

"Your daughter did well," he says. "We saw her let go of the handrail as soon as it went backwards, so did the same."

"And she caught that stupid woman. Are you okay, hon?" The woman with him reaches forward, pats Jem's arm.

Jem nods, smiles as best she can then makes her way up the stopped escalator. A couple of staff are on hand at the top to check people are alright.

Mum steers her around a group of people asking questions. "Bugger that," she says, "let's get a drink." She takes Jem to a Costa with a seating area, gets them a coffee.

"I've put sugar in it," she says, placing the cardboard cup on the table.

Jem prises the lid off, blows on the steaming foam, sips. The sweetness is lovely. Mum probably thinks she's in shock.

"I knew it was going to happen," Jem says. "I saw an old guy in a beige raincoat lose his balance when the handrail went backwards. Saw him fall, saw them all fall just before you put me in front of you. I wanted to say we shouldn't get on and couldn't. I wanted to tell you."

Mother sits motionless, staring at Jem. She takes a sip of her coffee then says, "It's over, Jemma. You couldn't have stopped it no matter what you said or did. Drink your coffee and let's get going."

The latte has cooled enough for Jem to swallow it rather than sip. She drinks, wondering if Mum's comment was about the escalator, or if it's as close to an apology as she will ever get.

LIGHTNING JIM BOWIE

Although Jane sits on a park bench under a tree, she can still feel the scorching summer sun. Her bike is propped against the trunk with a selection of library books stacked in its basket. She's hoping they won't be needed. All it would take is for one of the girls from school to phone, and ask her to go to the cinema, or to come over and experiment with the new range of Rimmel eye shadow. Perhaps they will listen to some music and chat. She could pretend to enjoy Abba's latest hit, or the Top Ten, which most of the girls in her class listen to. A sigh escapes her. The longed-for phone call won't happen.

Leaning over the arm of the bench, Jane plucks a buttercup from the grass. She holds it up to the sun, blinking at the golden glow reflecting from tiny yellow petals. A solitary tear slips down her freckled cheek. Wiping the tear away, Jane looks down the path to the playground area. Younger children play on the slide, roundabout or swinging boat. She envies their pack mentality, their groups of compatibility and rivalry. Getting to her feet, Jane steps towards her bike.

A cold damp nose presses against her leg. It belongs to a small dog. He's tan with white socks and a white blaze on his forehead, which zigzags the gap between his eyes. The dog whimpers, is visibly shaking.

Speaking softly, Jane sits back on the bench, holds out her hand.

"C'mon boy, it's alright."

The dog sniffs her outstretched fingers. Then, with a tail which begins to lift but has yet to wag, he clambers on her lap and presses against her body. Jane can feel him trembling, so she soothes the dog with gentle words and hands. He gazes at her and, for the first time, Jane falls in love.

That summer, although Mother isn't happy to have a dog in the house, fourteen year old Jane has a buddy, a soulmate. She blossoms and grows like a sapling in the hothouse of '76. Her companion is named after her previous idol – David Bowie.

Bowie is a lively dog who senses her moods perfectly. He has a basket, but at night sneaks onto her bed. Jane often wakes with his body curled against hers. She keeps his licence in her secret keepsake box. Puts a black leather collar around his neck where his terrier coat is smooth and soft. It has a name tag detailing his owner as Simmons, the street name and their home phone number. By September, Mother has agreed to keep an eye on Bowie when Jane returns to school. For the first time, she is looking forward to seeing her classmates.

"I'm going to miss you, Bowie," she says on their brisk early morning walk the day term begins, "but I have a photo of you in my bag and I'll tell everyone about you."

The chill winds of October bring Jane crashing back down to harsh reality. Both Bowie and her tan have gone; they disappeared in the sycamore spin of Autumn. She searches for him, knocks on every door down roads they walked to reach the park, asking, "Have you seen my dog?", while holding up the photocopies of the poster she made. Desperation hones her voice as head after head shakes and doors are closed.

Jane sellotapes posters to lampposts, persuades shopkeepers to place one in their windows. Father pays for a notice in the local rag. But there is no sign, no phone call, to say Bowie has been found.

December arrives. What had been budding friendships freeze in Winter's chill grace and Jane retreats back into her library books.

*

Jane stops to catch her breath on the park bench. It might not have been such a good idea to take a walk in the

Spring sunshine, but she feels better for getting out of the house. She has a few months to go, before her baby arrives, and isn't ready to put her feet up just yet. Closing her eyes, Jane immerses herself in the scents of tree blossom and freshly-cut grass. A breeze stirs the air as a cold damp nose presses against the arm draped over the side of the bench. It jolts Jane out of her brief reverie. She looks down. The dog before her is the spitting image of Bowie.

This dog she calls Lightning due to the blaze of white on his forehead. He can't be Bowie as twelve years have passed and this is a young dog, yet they bond as if they know each other of old. Jane buys a red leather collar and an owner's tag. She has the tag inscribed with his name, along with her address and phone number.

"I don't mind you having a dog," says Jon, "but I do object to him sleeping on our bed."

"I find it sweet. I love how he curls against me and have you seen how he sniffs my belly?"

Jon looks up from the fried breakfast she likes to cook him every Sunday, even though the smell of it has nauseated Jane throughout her pregnancy. His eyes linger on her baby bump, then look at her swollen breasts. He licks his lips.

"I don't want him getting between us in bed and do you have to walk him so much over the weekend? I miss your company, would like to do more together, go to the cinema, or out for a meal."

A bundle of fur presses against her leg. Jane reaches down, fondles the dog's ears. She doesn't know what to say. At times like these, she feels suffocated as if her time and body isn't her own.

"Or I could come with you when you take him out."

Taking Lightning for a walk, away from it all, is such a relief. If Jon came, she'd have to think of what to say, make conversation.

Jon shovels food in his mouth, chews, swallows and says, "The neighbours keep telling me you're blooming and I have to agree. You look lovely, but it might be an idea to get some bigger clothes," he points at her chest with a fork covered in congealing yolk. "I can see your clothes are getting tight, especially that dress. We should check out the maternity wear in Mothercare. Could go today. What do you say?"

He goes back to his fried bread, bacon and eggs.

Lightning whimpers as Jane plunges her hands into hot soapy water, scrubs the greasy frying pan. Taking the dog out brings colour to her cheeks, makes her bloom. The fresh air alleviates her constant nausea.

"No thanks," she says, "Lightning needs his walk."

*

As Spring becomes Summer, Jane isn't able to walk far with Lightning and he appears content to play ball in the park or garden. Two weeks before she's due to give birth, Lightning disappears. He chased a ball into the cluster of bushes near the bench Jane favours and was gone. She places posters on nearby lampposts, puts a notice in the local newspaper, all to no avail.

"It's for the best." Jon smiles placatingly. "Our baby is due any day."

Jane is inconsolable.

The last straw comes shortly after their daughter is born. She's only two months old when Jon uses the mobile, recently installed in his company car, to tell her he's leaving.

"I feel ignored," he says. "You never really talked to me. Didn't want to do anything or go anywhere, and now you give all your attention to the baby."

"You don't exactly help," is out of her mouth before Jane realises she's saying it.

"This is your fault, not mine. I should've recognised the signs when that damn dog was around. You always

96

favoured the dog, put it first. I was way down the bloody list."

Jane puts the phone down, walks away. Katie is crying, does so until Jane feeds her.

Later, the TV is on and Katie is sleeping. While Bush is elected president of America, Jane lies on the sofa, sobbing into a cushion. She wants to be strong, to continue. Argues she must for the baby's sake. Finds she is longing, not for her husband's arms around her, but for the comforting warmth of Lightning's body pressed against hers. Jane sits up, wipes her face and acknowledges there is truth in Jon's words; she smothers her baby with love and affection to bury the grieving turmoil from the loss of her second, beloved dog.

*

It's the new millennium. All the London codes have been changed to 020, which is annoying. Jane's had to update her address book, but not to keep track of her own busy social life. No, it is Katie who is always on the go. How easily her daughter makes friends! Jane's own personal life, once the divorce was through, has been solitary. They now live in Jane's childhood home. It was left to Jane by her parents and is nearer to work than their previous abode. She takes comfort from the memories bound within its walls.

Shivering as damp and desiccated leaves swirl upwards in the October wind, Jane wonders what her daughter is up to when movement catches her eye. The lithe body of a young dog with a smooth tan coat races towards her. He has the familiar lightning blaze and white socks. His tail is wagging fiercely as he gives a happy bark. Jane stands, begins backing away, but reason is arguing how these markings are common. There is nothing special about the dog, he is just a friendly soul. Reason wins out. She finds herself bending down to greet the wriggling pooch, who certainly acts as if he knows her.

This time, instead of immediately buying a collar and tag, she takes the dog to a local vet to see if he's microchipped.

Katie thinks the dog is cute. However, as her daughter is a busy, popular girl, Jane finds herself the proud and loving owner of Jim. Her adoration of this lively creature is plain. Mind you, Jane feels embarrassed when a woman she works with asks if there's a new man in her life. To reply that a dog makes her this happy feels a bit odd. Blushing, Jane lies.

In a household where teenage hormones are running riot, Jim's companionship keeps her mellow. She becomes a calmer, more rational parent. People ask if she's joined a gym, not realising many a brisk Winter walk is responsible for a fitter, healthier Jane.

January of 2001 is refreshingly dry after the December rains which preceded it. A light flurry of snow fails to put Jane off taking Jim out for an early afternoon walk. She can give him a run in the park, then return home before daylight fades. They race through streets named after castles with Jim knowing his destination. He leads her without hesitation, pulling Jane through the park gates just as snow starts to settle. Jane is warm, can feel her cheeks glowing, as she unclips Jim's lead from his blue collar. They are playing ball when, just as the day darkens, he doesn't retrieve. Jane finds the ball under a bush. Jim is nowhere to be seen.

The vet assures her Jim's microchip means he can be identified if he's been stolen, or found injured. This does nothing to assuage the tidal waves of grief that slam into Jane as if she were a sea wall. Both home and mobile numbers are on Jim's tag, but she feels no hope,

"This is the third time," she wails while sitting on the sofa. "My third dog – why me?"

"For God's sake, Mum, Jim is just a dog. You only had him for three months. Get over it."

Lightning Jim Bowie

Despite the central heating's warmth, Jane goes cold. In a moment of clarity, a pattern begins to emerge.

*

Today is Jane's fiftieth birthday. She's taken herself to the park with a small picnic and a book. As usual, she is celebrating alone. Katie left home some years ago. Communication is sparse as, apparently, Jane's motherly love has an obsessive, toxic quality. Katie felt smothered, confined and left. After receiving counselling, her daughter decided to keep her distance. Jane misses the bustling energy Katie's presence bought into their home.

There will be no birthday call from her child, yet she hopes this will be a special birthday. One where she doesn't sit on the park bench under the tree for nothing. Hopefully, this will be the day her dog comes home. So Jane sits in the early summer sun patiently waiting, as she has done every day since the year began. Today, her patience is rewarded.

White-socked paws race out from under the nearby bushes. She stands, holding out her arms as a small tan dog leaps into them. This time, Jane has a plan for, twelve years ago, she had an identical dog microchipped. She takes the dog to a different vet and asks him to check if the microchip has moved. It hasn't but the vet recommends she check on her registration as the reference number is old, not quite what he expected in such a young dog. Jane doesn't bother. She buys a green woven collar and orders a tag. This time his name is etched as Lightning Jim Bowie.

Knowing her time with him is short, Jane tries to keep her emotional distance. Lightning Jim Bowie is having none of it. He knows Jane's weaknesses, showers her with affection. He plays and races about, bringing life and joy into a house which was devoid. By the end of two weeks, Jane is back to where she was when she met Bowie. Her rational brain argues this cannot be the same dog, despite the physical evidence, but emotion wins. Although it is no surprise when Lightning Jim Bowie disappears three months later, the devastation is as before. Worse, perhaps, as there is nothing in Jane's life to propel her onward. No parents, no baby, no challenging teenager. Jane feels unbearably alone and her books no longer provide an escape.

*

Jane sits on her bed in the nursing home. Earlier this year, she celebrated her hundredth birthday. The nurses organised a cake, other residents gathered to wish her Many Happy Returns, but the effort exhausted Jane. Her mind remains sharp while her body is failing. Modern technology keeps her alive.

A nurse places a call button on the straightened top sheet, removes the untouched dinner and switches the large wall screen on. She knows Jane enjoys the news, especially on a Friday when there is a slot which investigates all manner of oddities. The program provides a little interest and levity in Jane's otherwise dull routine. She perks up as the presenter appears. He's a quirky looking individual wearing the latest in fashion glasses. To Jane, he looks goofy.

"Do you believe in time travel?" he asks as an age old Time Lord's Tardis warps in the background. "Well, today I'm meeting a man who claims he can prove it exists. His name is Marty Goodwin. The time traveller is his dog, Blaze."

The cameras switch to a nondescript man who looks to be in his early thirties. He's holding a small dog which has a white zigzag and socks. As Marty describes creating a wormhole, using an electromagnetic field and an antigravity device, Jane leans forward. Her hand stretches towards the broadcast image of the dog. Her dog.

"So you set the year on your machine then sent

Blaze back in time. Do you think he always arrived at the same place?"

"I believe so. I timed it so each visit was twelve years apart. It might have varied a bit as to which month Blaze arrived in."

"How did this work? And how on earth did you get him back? You couldn't expect him to be in a certain place at a specific time."

"I chose an established park which existed right up until the housing crisis of 2058. A stable wormhole has a fixed entrance and exit. It was just a matter of setting the coordinates and the year. For a dog to travel, the wormhole didn't need to be big. I picked an area of the park where it wouldn't be obvious."

"Right..."

The interviewer looks knowingly at the camera, raises an eyebrow.

Jane thinks about the discarded ball beneath the bushes near the seat under the tree.

"...so how did you persuade Blaze to re-enter the wormhole?"

"Well, both light and sound travel through space. With sound, the higher the pitch the greater the distance, and radio waves can travel through a vacuum. I built a device which emits a radio wave of a dog whistle and used it to train Blaze in recall. He returns to me when he hears it."

"So it was like a homing device?"

"Kind of. After Blaze travelled through the first time, I re-opened the wormhole three months later, set the device to repeat the signal on a regular basis and waited."

Jane's eyes haven't left the dog. He sits in Marty's arms gazing at the camera as if he senses her.

"Weren't you worried you'd never see your dog again?"

"I was worried, but I reasoned if he was found in a

park, the chances were he'd be walked in that park," Marty shrugs. "It was risky, but I'm certain it worked."

When Marty finishes his sentence, he looks fondly down and kisses the top of Blaze's head. The dog, her dog, responds in a manner Jane recognises and knows. The bond between Marty and Blaze is there, on the screen, obvious to all those watching. Jane's heart breaks anew.

"Do you have any physical evidence demonstrating the dog time-travelled?"

"Yes I do. Blaze went back in time on four occasions."

"Well, that would be faaan-tastic, if it's true." Winking at his audience, the presenter says, "Let's see the evidence."

The camera pans to a table where four collars sit. Jane knows the black one is eighty-six years old. There is a close-up of its tarnished circular tag detailing "Simmons" and a phone number. The camera pans to a faded red collar whose tag states "Lightning" and a different phone number. Next is the blue one with a tag reading "Jim". Under this is a street name and postcode, then two numbers. One begins 020 the other 07932. Finally, a green woven collar comes into view with Lightning Jim Bowie etched into its tag, along with the same residential phone number as the black one.

"You could have got these made yourself!" says the presenter.

"Well I didn't. Look at the age of them, the different details on each tag. Also, when I sent Blaze back to 2000 he returned with a microchip."

The presenter grins. "Microchips are compulsory! Admit it, you've had Blaze microchipped with a name and phone number you researched. This is a scam."

Marty's face turns red. "The microchip number isn't a recent one."

He looks directly at the camera.

"I don't know if you're still alive, but if you are, please contact me. I work at Leeds university. I'm certain your surname is Simmons. I believe you took care of Blaze each time he travelled, and the last tag shows all the names you called him."

He strokes Blaze. Turns him towards the camera so the lightning strike of white on his nose stands out.

"This is Lightning Jim Bowie. You and he can make scientific history. Please, get in touch."

Jane looks at the image of a man desperate for confirmation he is right. She cannot help but see how Lightning Jim Bowie gazes up at him from the secure comfort of his arms. Her keepsake box, a different one from when she was fourteen, is in the cabinet beside her bed. It contains Bowie's dog licence, the Polaroid she took to school and other photos taken over the years. It also holds Jim's microchip certification. Jane reaches for the call button then stops.

Memories of how she felt each time her dog disappeared pour into her mind. The overwhelming sense of loss has never left her. It remains a constant ache, despite how many years have passed. She would love to hold Lightning Jim Bowie in her arms before her life ends, but he isn't hers, never has been, and her love for this man's dog affected her relationship with both Jon and Katie. After over sixty years of wondering, "Why me?", Jane's grief and loneliness consolidate.

Twilight sweeps across the sterile room. The blue-white glare from the screen illuminates a single tear in crystal clarity. It trickles down her lined cheek as Jane's hand falls silently on the white sheet

HAPPY BIRTHDAY

Around nine the fresh scent of schoolgirl flesh passes him by on course for the living room. Coats are removed and he smells the slightly acrid odour of deodorant. He indicates the cabinet in response to their request for a drink. Glass clinks and red mouths are wetted with rum, then with brandy. His father had readied the fire before leaving for work and it has been lit. The red-orange warmth of the flames combines with each girl's internal glow, causing jumpers to be raised over upright breasts, resulting in glimpses of bare flesh as shirts come adrift.

One of the girls in particular attracts him. In his mind he feels the sensation of her soft, yet taut skin under his fingers. He refills her glass. She swallows rapidly and the action of her upturned throat reminds him of the thrust of intercourse. She laughs, wipes her mouth with the back of her hand, holding her glass out for still more, then raises it to toast him, for today he turns sixteen.

"Happy birthday," she says, downing the drink in one.

The other two girls gather round, the birthday greeting is repeated, but the first to toast him holds his attention.

A smile flirts with her liqueured mouth and her body loosens. As the others cluster around the drinks cabinet, she cascades down onto the sofa. Her skirt rises to reveal smooth thighs. Her long brown hair flows backwards from her flushed face. She giggles uncontrollably. His penis engorges and his balls tighten. He turns to see if the other girls have noticed. The shorter of the two is caressing the bottles, stroking the blown glass, sipping from the slim necks, comparing and contrasting flavours. The one with shoulder-length blond hair is pouring port into her glass. Uncertain what to do, he decides to have a smoke.

Leaving the house as instructed, he stands in the raw February air and lights up, draws the smoke into his lungs, feeling it tingle from the nerves in his mouth through to his extremities. This rough warmth exaggerates the outer chill as the wind stirs the t-shirt covering his upper body. He feels very alert, and this increases the sexual ache brought about by the girls collapsing onto the sofa. His desire to just walk back in and take her threatens to overwhelm him. Instead, he focuses on the physical sensation of standing in the bitter cold, observing the clear winter sky with its pale low sun. Once calm, he returns inside.

The girl he left on the sofa rises to greet him. A tumbler of port slops its contents over her fingers and down her hand, staining the white cuff of her blouse. He considers licking and sucking the liquid from her skin and trembles. She puts a warm arm around his cold neck and presses against him. He feels her nipples tighten in response to how cold his body is from standing outside. Kissing her, he probes the moist crevices of her mouth with his tongue while looking at the others. They shrug nonchalantly and make to leave. While they're gathering their belongings, the back gate clunks. It's the cleaner. He'd forgotten she was due today. Quickly, he herds the girls through the kitchen and upstairs into his bedroom. A stale male odour, which even he can smell, greets them as a woman calls from below.

"Hello?"

Adrenaline courses through his body as he rapidly descends the stairs.

The cleaner is in the living room. He watches from the doorway as she looks at the discarded glasses, the open bottles. One lays on its side dripping into a purple port stain on the light-blue carpet. Discarded sofa cushions lay nearby. When she turns towards him, he sees her face harden further as something hits the floor in his bedroom.

"Get whoever's up there down here. Now," she says, heading towards the kitchen.

Inserting himself between her and the bottom of the stairs, he calls up. Two of the girls appear, coats on, school bags slung over shoulders. Apprehension fashions their features, causing mouths to open as if forced by their tongues, which he can see darting out to lick dry lips. Their fear is arousing. He sternly asks them why they have left the other girl in his room. The confused glance they give each other empowers him further.

"Go and get her," he commands.

They retreat, reappearing with the third girl suspended around their shoulders. Her face flops forward as she tries to negotiate the stairs which elude her. Also, the staircase is narrow, too narrow for three. They stumble from step to step and it's obvious the drunk girl is a dead weight. He notices how her stained cuff is pulled back and winter sunlight through the kitchen window shines off the golden down which covers her fair skin. He imagines the sensation of those soft fine hairs against his lips. She misses her footing and falls.

Viewing her curved and twisted body, he collects himself to portray concern, probing the warm bruised flesh with hard fingers, causing her to arch her pelvis and cry out.

"Careful!" three voices chorus, but these are only dimly heard as his brutal enjoyment continues; threatens to overwhelm him.

"Get off her!" the cleaner almost shouts. She grabs then pushes him away. Crouching over the fallen girl, the cleaner tries to sit her upright against the bottom stair. "How much has she had to drink?"

He shrugs, the other two girls do the same.

"I think she needs a doctor." Straightening up, the cleaner goes towards her bag on the kitchen work-surface.

"We'll take her to school and get someone to look after her," the shorter girl says. "Don't worry." The two of them lift their friend off the floor. They guide her towards the door, carrying all three bags and the unworn coat. He has it open before they get there, closes it firmly behind them.

"What the hell's been going on?"

Leaning his forehead against the painted wood of the door he smiles. Despite her adult stance, this woman's role is that of cleaner, not parent. All he has to do is plead with boyish irresponsibility.

"It's not my fault; they came in to wish me Happy Birthday then helped themselves to drink."

"Why aren't you in school?"

"I'm off sick. I couldn't stop them, I'm sorry."

And so on. Eventually, she relents.

While he bathes and indulges his sexual longings in masturbatory remembrance, she cleans the house beyond the closed door then departs.

*

Later, he lays wrapped up on the sofa watching a Blu-ray, curtains drawn against the encroaching dark whilst the fire burns bright. The sound of a hard fist knocking against even harder wood rouses him. Who might it be? He is partially dressed, vulnerable. He hasn't heard the gate above the noise of the film, feels unprepared. The next knock is harder still. It's only when he hears footsteps through the kitchen that he recalls leaving the door unlocked after the cleaner left.

A man, similar in age to his father, enters the living room as he gets up, pulling the fleecy cover he's been laying under around his frame. It's the father of the girl who fell down the stairs. The man marches across the room and pulls the cover off, leaving him naked apart from his boxers. Fear rises from his gut as the man's eyes travel down and then back up his body.

Defensively wrapping his arms around his thin frame, he asks, "Why are you here?" while noting every bone under the thin sheath of blood, tissue and skin that covers his ribcage. All the time, the man's mouth works around words that don't arrive as unspoken rage emanates from his sweeping glare.

Abruptly, the girl's father headbutts his stomach. Pain acknowledges this paternal rage which radiates out like the fire's warmth to fill the room. He gasps for breath while the father stands before him, fists clenched, tears running from his eyes. "You bastard, you bastard, you bastard," he repeats brokenly. This becomes a litany synchronised with punches.

He feels righteous blows on his face and chest. "I didn't do anything. Stop hitting me!"

A fist makes contact with his nose, and he hears the bone snap. The noise in his head is so vast it overwhelms the man's response to his protestation of innocence. Suddenly the balled hands cease their relentless pounding.

"Sara's dead. My girl is dead," says her father. He leaves.

In the bathroom, he wipes the blood from his face and carefully touches his nose, examining it in the mirror. He imagines what happened, sees Sara leaving the house, suspended over the shoulders of the other two girls. They cannot carry her far, so deposit her in the park at the end of the street and make their way to school, hoping they haven't been missed. He pictures Sara's skirt riding high in the cold wind. From the warm security of its waistband, her blouse once again comes adrift. Chill air caresses the strip of naked flesh and pierces the thin material of her school blouse, causing her to shiver. His mind toys with her taut raised nipples and his breathing becomes rapid, causing his bruised stomach and chest to protest. He feels the sour puke rise, feels its solidity pressing upwards to fill

Sara's throat, her nostrils, sees it trickle from her pale soft lips to lay on winter's scorched grass. He vomits. Muscles contract sharply as the liquid spurts through his mouth.

He winces at the pain, but is strangely satisfied.

GAIA'S BREATH

Climbing the steep and narrow spiral staircase while trying to keep a mug of nettle tea steady isn't the easiest task, but it's one I'm well accustomed to. Cliff turns away from the crenulations of the Observation Tower as I reach the top.

"Thanks, Bee," he says, taking the mug in both hands as if they were cold despite the humidity. Across the water towards the Wolds, Gaia's breath is whipping grey clouds, scudding them across the sky. I lick my finger and hold it up. Today She is blowing from the North. Sipping his tea, Cliff grunts in appreciation.

"The latest farmer brought honey."

"Did he say which farm?" he asks.

I shrug. "One of the orchards. Those with him brought fruit."

Cliff keeps his eyes on the land between here and the hills. The castle our tribe lives in has been surrounded by water since before I was born. Nothing remains of the once thriving city below the steep roads that rise out of the lake, or the farmland and towns my mother told me used to exist before the Great Flood. Many years passed before the land between here and the salt marshes, bordering the sea, was reclaimed to grow crops, nurture bees and support wildlife. Now, those who work on the farms are coming here.

"There's no room for any more people. We need all the garden area the castle's got to feed those of us already here."

"Despite what they bring?" I ask.

"Yes. There's only so much you can carry on foot and not many have cars." He points across the water to a lone vehicle on the far shore. "They're useless once they run out of power. The nearest charging bays are on the farms and, if what we're hearing is true, it's not safe to go there." He pauses, then says, "We can't raid those farms anymore, so need to be self-sufficient." I can only agree. Sleeping and feeding extra bodies is difficult in the confined space of our walls. The prison cells we live in number under a hundred and they're stacked over two floors. The ground floor of the building is used for storage and holds various workshops, plus there is a kitchen and an area we gather in to eat. I place my arm around his waist. Cliff leans his hard body against mine and we stand together for a moment.

"Who's taking care of Holly?" Cliff asks.

"Fern."

Taking his eyes off the far shore, Cliff looks at me. His bushy eyebrows rise high in his craggy forehead. "Fern? Well I never." He once again looks towards the Wolds.

"She sees a future for Holly. Others don't."

A brief nod is all the acknowledgement I get as Cliff shades his eyes with his right hand. After focusing intently on the distance he says, "Tell Heather to send two boats. Our hunters return and they've got four others with them."

I head down the steep stairs until I reach the castle walkway. Heather is in the grounds praying to Gaia. The altar of our Goddess stands near the gardens we till and plant from seeds stolen, in the past, from the now stricken farms. It is fitting that where we worship our deity is close to the soil amidst all this stone, for Gaia is a living entity.

Disrupting someone at prayer is never a thankful task, but Heather merely sighs.

"What meat were the hunters carrying?" she asks.

"Cliff didn't say."

The direct stare I get tells me I should know. Heather folds her arms below her breasts saying, "Let's hope they've got more than a few rabbits and hares. There's plenty of wildlife now, but it won't be long before it's as scarce as before, scarcer maybe." She abruptly walks away, heading towards the castle gate to pass the message on and arrange a greeting party. Heather's back is straight and her long plait swings with the sway of her hips. Despite this suggestion of femininity, she is physically commanding, tall and muscular.

Heather is right. Although the land to the East is full of game, like the farmers, it is fleeing and dying. Around the fire, our hunters tell of dead animals, blistered bodies and makeshift graves as they draw near the road leading to the coast. Cliff is on the Observatory Tower not just to watch for strangers and returning hunters, he's there to alert us when the threat draws near. Problem is, we have no idea what the threat is.

*

Fern smiles as I enter the square cell which is my home. It is one of a few corner rooms which are big enough in the prison complex to house a family. Once, the rooms and corridors were painted cream. They would have reflected the sun when it streamed in through the tall arched windows at each end of the building, through the smaller windows in each cell. The black wrought iron staircases between the floors, would have gleamed. Once, the prison would have been full of light. Now, most of the paint has flaked off revealing dull grey stone beneath; curved iron staircases are tinged with orange rust. When the sun does shine through what remains of the windows, the building hums with an oppressive dullness.

Placing a finger against her lips, Fern rises from Holly's bed and joins me by the door. "Holly's just fallen asleep. She loves learning the old tales, but it tires her." Fern glances at my daughter and smiles affectionately. Her face crinkles into deep lines. Fern longed for a child of her own, but that time is gone and she has chosen Holly as her successor.

"Cliff and I are grateful you're teaching her."

Fern grips my arms with firm hands and pulls me into the narrow corridor.

"She must live. Without a Storyteller the old tales will die. Bring Holly to the fireside tonight. Let her hear me tell the tale I'm teaching her so I can see how much of it she knows."

Although the words are quietly spoken, Fern's passion for her trade is undeniable, the fervour in her eyes plain. When her grip relaxes, I hug her.

"I pray to Gaia every day that she'll get well. I know you do the same. Gaia's blessings on you, Fern."

The older woman pulls away, patting my shoulder. We understand each other, Fern and I.

I cross to Holly's bed. My daughter is one of the few children born in the past decade. She has pushed the coarse woollen cover down to her waist. Her fingers are bone thin, her body skeletal and much of her skin is so pale it appears translucent. Her lungs rattle and wheeze as she breathes, they're terribly congested. But, Holly's spirit is strong. Gently moving her brown hair aside, I check her forehead with the back of my hand. She is cooler than this morning. Perhaps her fever has broken. Pressing my lips against the flush of her cheek, I offer a silent prayer to Gaia. Cliff and I have hidden our fear and worry. Nonetheless it is there. It eats away at us.

*

Despite the warmth of the evening, I've wrapped Holly in a thick blanket. Hope and pleasure ran through me in equal measures as Holly woke from her afternoon sleep with an appetite. I helped her to wash, to change her clothes and I've brushed her hair. She is weak and, occasionally, a hacking cough rises from deep within her chest making her body spasm. Sometimes she brings up thick, green matter. Cliff's smile as he crouches before Holly erases the shadow of worry from his weather-worn face.

"Are you ready?"

"Yes, Da."

Holly grins as he swoops her upwards, nestles her against his shoulder and carries her down the rusting iron staircase.

Turning left out of the prison entrance, we make our way up the steep slope to Lucy's Tower. An arch has been cut into the stone that encircles a small grass area. A fire has been lit to ward off encroaching darkness and torches are placed at intervals along the high castle walls. Fern waves us over, patting the ground beside her. We sit. Cliff places Holly between us.

A hum of conversation buzzes in the air. Most of our hunters are present, as are those who work in the garden, kitchen, or workshops. Other children also sit with their parents. Then there are the four brought across the water by our hunters earlier today. What strikes me most about them, is how well fed they look. I doubt they've ever known true hunger. Their clothing is made from bamboo, contrasting sharply with the leathers and furs we wear. They all look subdued and I think this is because once we, the people their government labelled "Outcasts", were the ones asking for help. Or taking it.

Heather stands to speak and the voices cease. "Welcome all, including those who arrived today seeking safe harbour. To them I say that what we discuss at the fireside is aimed at keeping everyone informed of matters which may impact upon the tribe. This is not the place for disputes. Those you bring to me at the appointed time. Does anyone wish to speak?"

Our head hunter, Hawk, nods. Heather extends her hand, then sits near the fire as Hawk gets to his feet.

"Myself and other hunters know these newcomers are running from something, but we don't know what it is, or how to deal with it. I'm a pious man. I worship Gaia. As

115

a hunter I never take more than She can sustain, whether it's roots, berries or game." Hawk pauses, takes a deep breath, then says, "One of those we brought back with us today is a scientist."

An angry murmur runs through the crowd. I see looks of disgust cast, not just at those new to our tribe, but also at Hawk.

"Sit down, man, before you make a complete fool of yourself," someone shouts from behind me.

Hawk's features harden, making his beak of a nose more prominent. His voice rings out. "We would be fools if we didn't get the facts. All I'm saying is that science might help us understand what's going on."

One of the newcomers looks at Hawk and nods. He extends his hand. I cannot take my eyes off the woman as she stands. She's even taller than Heather and, like our leader, has strength in her bearing. Full lips part and the woman speaks.

"My name is Elena and yes, I'm a scientist, but those with me are not. They are farmers and a hunter. My speciality is synthetic biology. If it weren't for the work of my predecessors, you wouldn't have crops in the garden you've cultivated. Like your hunter, I want to survive. We all want to survive, so I'll tell you what I think is happening.

"The history books say that scientists tried to find a way to prevent further acidification of the oceans, but couldn't. A few days ago, a gas formed over the North Sea. It looks as if a mist sits on the water but, on dry land, it has no colour. You cannot see it, but you can smell it and from the way it blisters skin, I'd say the gas contains sulphur dioxide. If I'm right, you don't want to breathe it in. When the wind blows it inland, this gas kills everything in its path. That's why we're here. To survive, we need to stay away from the gas."

Silence greets her words then falls into noisy disarray. Stunned by what I've heard, I pull Holly close, feel Cliff's arms surround us both. His eyes, when the shouting stops and we draw apart, are bleak.

From her place by the fire, Heather says, "Are you suggesting we should be ready to leave?"

Elena nods. "Yes. I'd get ready. We weren't prepared. You can tell if the gas is nearby not just by its smell, but from how it makes your skin and eyes sting. Also, you must take cover when it rains. I was on my father's farm testing crops because, over the past few weeks, the rain has steadily become more acidic."

Heather stands. "Well, that would mean leaving the safety of these walls. Still, we have enough boats if we need to." She pauses for a moment then says, "We follow Gaia here. As leader of this tribe, I will pray to her for guidance. This is our home and I wonder if Gaia's breath would carry this gas over enough land to breach its walls."

Cries of agreement rebound off stone.

"But I will tell those of you who have arrived in the past few days this. If you cannot follow my lead, my orders, you can take what belongs to you and go."

Cliff tugs me and Holly to our feet. Most of the tribe are already on theirs. Illuminated by torches and firelight, fists are punching the air, accompanied by a tribal roar. Looking satisfied, Heather says, "We are done talking. It's time for a tale."

I and others sit back down as Fern walks towards the fire. Holding her hands above her head for silence, Fern says, "Now is a fitting time for this tale." I struggle to read her face in the flickering flames, but her eyes are glinting like sparks from a forge. My insides clench. She's up to something. Fern circles the burning wood, arms level with her shoulders, fingers clicking. I, and the rest of my tribe, clap in time. "For this is the tale of Gaia and the Maiden."

A cry of approval meets her announcement.

"Is this the tale Fern's been teaching you?" I quietly

ask Holly. She shakes her head. My stomach sinks. The fresh faced scientist may find herself outside the castle gates once Fern is done. As more logs are thrown on the fire I glance at Elena. She looks unperturbed, but the slim woman beside her is reaching for Elena's hand as if she knows what's to come. Fern begins.

"Long, long ago the world came into being and she was called Gaia. Life flourished and intelligent creatures developed. Aeons passed and one creature began to purvey all around him with a sense of ownership. However, Man was a selfish beast, taking from Gaia without thought; her coal, her trees, her stone. Many creatures lived in Gaia's forests, thrived in her oceans and rivers. Man saw fit to organise and treat these creatures as his own. Hunting, killing and eating the flesh of another animal is part of the natural order, but Man ignored how Gaia, both within and without, held things in balance. A balance which kept the wheels of life turning.

"Instead of working with Gaia, Man explored every inch and every crevice of her being; learning and applying what he found to create a world which drained Gaia's resources so badly, she began to cry out. But, Gaia's voice was swallowed by industrial noise."

Fern's voice rises and falls. Her expressive hands and body sweep in and out of gestures and postures, creating a rhythmic, lyrical form captivating her audience.

"For years Gaia's voice went unheeded. There were those who thought something was amiss, but they also struggled to be heard. After all, Man was flourishing as a species. His numbers grew and his inventions harnessed power into a matrix which surrounded Gaia, encompassed her.

"With her polar ice caps melting and species important to the balance of her entity becoming extinct, Gaia began to scream. She screamed gales and tornadoes, brought floods and droughts, warning Man of what was to come if he didn't change. Some heard and they began harnessing power from Gaia's breath, from the sun above her, but it was not enough. Gaia realised she needed someone to speak in her name. Someone who would make all of mankind listen. She began calling for such a person."

Fern pauses. She looks around at her audience and softly asks, "And who heard Gaia's call?"

"A child," several voices speak in unison. Holly is leaning forward, mirroring the body language of others, responding to the question.

"And what did this child do?"

"She spoke on Gaia's behalf."

"And what did this child become?"

"A warrior! Gaia's Maiden!" Holly shouts. Her cheeks glow, her eyes are sparkling.

"Holly speaks truly, for this is what the child became. She fought long and hard to try and bring the world to a better place where Gaia could recover, from the damage Man had wrought upon her. She told the mothers and fathers of her time they had betrayed their children. Said they were leaving behind a world unable to support life. Other children, on hearing her words, joined Gaia's Maiden in peaceful protests outside places of learning. Before long, the Maiden had an army by her side.

"Gaia's Maiden showed no fear in the face of her enemies. There were those who decried her prophecies, for after all, how could a child be right?"

Beside me, Holly tenses as Fern falls silent. Everyone in Lucy's Tower seems to be holding their breath. Fern speaks and the intensity of her performance increases as the story reaches its climax.

"The prophecies came true. Gaia's breath ravaged homes, heat-waves burnt the land, scorching new deserts on the surface of Gaia's domain. Sea levels rose, drowning millions of people. Those who said the Maiden was wrong cried out in terror. 'Why did we not listen!' they said, for it appeared all was lost. And, if it were not for those who heard Gaia's plea in the Maiden's voice, all would have been lost. These followers of Gaia persuaded the world to make changes.

"Now we live in a time where we aim to achieve a balance between Gaia's needs and our survival. If along the way we ever feel tempted by how industry and science once served Man, the tale of Gaia's Maiden and her battle to save this world is there to remind us to abide by Gaia's balance."

Fern bows and I join those clapping and cheering. She truly is an artist, but inside I'm horrified at the way she has stigmatised the female scientist. Holly throws off her blanket and gets to her feet. She dances with excitement as this is what she now dreams of doing, of being.

A fresh log is thrown upon the fire. It is damp and the smoke fills the circular space. Holly chokes, doubles over and begins coughing. The harsh, hacking sound causes those near us to move back. It's not long before all that can be heard is Holly wheezing, gasping for breath. She claws at my clothing, then pulls her own down from her throat. Fear and desperation is in her eyes, its scent is on her skin. Quickly, I lower her to the ground, sit her upright as the branch catches fully in the heat of the flames and the smoke begins to clear. Rubbing her back, I say, "Breathe, Holly. Try to stay calm and breathe."

Her face is pale and her eyes bulge as her lips turn blue. She's about to pass out. A large space has formed around us.

"You shouldn't have brought a sick child to the fireside." Heather sounds furious.

"For Gaia's sake!" A voice exclaims, "What the child has isn't catching. It's a reaction to the smoke, that's all."

The woman sitting with Elena comes towards Holly and I. She looks exasperated as she bends over, yet her voice is tranquil. "I'm Lauren. Come, let's get her inside." She scoops the blanket off the ground as I lift Holly. Cliff nods at me and I know he is staying to hear what is said. If it weren't for his sight, we'd have been cast out by now. Straightening up, I carry Holly out of Lucy's Tower. I can feel Heather's disapproval boring a hole in my back.

*

Once Holly recovers, Lauren tips her over the side of the bed onto some pillows.

"This is to drain the matter in her lungs," she explains. "We'll leave her for a while, then I'll show you what to do next."

Lauren looks to be around my own age, twenty-eight summers. Like most women, she ties her long hair back. Her movements are consistent with her frame, small and concise. Lauren's face is oval with a wide mouth. I can tell she smiles frequently from the crinkles at the corners of her eyes. I get us both a mug of water from the jug we keep in our room.

"Did you work on the farm long?" I ask, passing the water to her.

"Thank you. I only arrived this spring. I struggle to stay in one place."

I wait for her to say more, then realise she doesn't know if it's safe to speak. "I'm sorry for what happened earlier, the story Fern told."

"You have a strong leader and an excellent storyteller." A moment passes then Lauren shakes her head saying, "Those of us Heather has taken in know just how right Elena is. The things we've seen." She shudders, drains her cup then places it next to the jug. "How many winters is Holly?"

"Ten this year."

Lauren looks at my daughter. "She may grow out of this. I've seen it happen before. While I'm here, I'll teach her some exercises so she can breathe more deeply.

They'll help."

Tears prickle. "I don't know how to thank you."

Lauren smiles. "There's no need. Come, let's see to Holly."

Holly has fallen asleep, but as Lauren and I gently patter our hands up and down her sides she wakes. This loosens the matter and Holly easily coughs it out. On seeing how much the process has removed from her lungs I feel slightly sick.

Lauren makes to leave. "Do this every morning before she gets out of bed. Will you both be here tomorrow after breakfast? Good, I'll see you then."

After she closes the door I tuck Holly in. She's soon asleep. Lying on the bed Cliff and I share, I cry. For the first time since she became ill, I feel Holly may live beyond childhood. I can't wait to tell Cliff.

I am woken by someone gently shaking me.

"We need to talk," Cliff says, gesturing outside the room. Together we sit on the floor of the corridor, our faces lit by moonlight. What he tells me makes my blood run cold.

*

I'm on my knees before Gaia's statue praying for the strength to face what's to come when Heather says, "Get up, Bee. I need to speak to you."

Inside I'm screaming at her. I want to hurt her for the things she said to Cliff, but I make certain my expression is blank as I stand and face her.

"Are you working today?"

"Yes, in the gardens."

"Before you go, it's come to my attention that Fern is teaching your daughter to be a Storyteller."

"Yes," I say. "Cliff and I are honoured she's chosen Holly."

Heather's face is stern. "I don't consider Holly suitable. I've told Fern she is to train Primrose. Your daughter will not be given any further lessons. Now, leave me. I'm still seeking guidance from Gaia and wish to be alone."

Heather kneels to pray before I can respond. Fuming, I take the pathway to the gardens. I'm only able to work this afternoon because Fern is with Holly. My feet stop and I groan. I may not always like how sneaky Fern is, but teaching Holly when she's been told not to is a dangerous game.

*

Gaia's breath has been calm for several days and the sun fierce. Crops are ripening faster than we can pick them. Holly and I practice her breathing exercises each morning then walk to the gardens and work. She is beginning to recover. Her lungs are clearer, she's not so breathless and the dry heat of the day seems to help. Like the others, I stop work when the sun is high then return to pick crops in the late afternoon. Children of Holly's age aren't expected to work all day, so the lessons with Fern have been continuing while most of us rest.

Tribe members talk excitedly, about the bounty Gaia has blessed us with, as I make my way towards the Observatory Tower. I join Cliff on its uppermost turret where the heat of the day is lessened by Gaia gently blowing a cool breeze. The tops of the bamboo trees near Cobb's Tower are moving slightly.

"This weather won't last much longer," says Cliff.

I scan the sky. There's no sign of a storm.

"How do you know?"

"The breeze." He points past the cathedral ruins towards the coast. "It's coming from the East and is picking up pace. Gaia's gathering breath. She'll be blowing strong by tomorrow morning."

"Oh Mother, the gas." The words croak out as if I'm already struggling to breathe.

Cliff cups my face with his hands. Deep brown eyes

hold mine as he says, "I'll keep an eye on things here. You go tell Heather we've not got much time. She needs to advise the tribe."

*

By next morning Gaia is blowing in earnest and sullen clouds skitter westwards. Heather calls the tribe together. Cliff, Holly and I are waiting near the arch to Lucy's Tower when she arrives. Heather stands on one of the slopes leading out of the tower that are part of the walkway around the castle walls. She looks tired. Strands of loose hair are blowing around her face.

"I have spoken to Gaia at length and prayed for guidance, yet she has not given me a clear answer. There are those among you I have also spoken to."

Heather indicates Elena, the farmers who sought sanctuary and a number of our hunters. But not Hawk. She doesn't include Hawk.

"Days have passed since the last newcomers arrived of which scientist Elena was one. I can only assume others have gone elsewhere or are dead. Yesterday, some of our hunters went towards the East Coast. They told me they could smell the gas on reaching the road over the Wolds to the farmlands, but it was faint. My decision is that we'll wait and see how close Gaia's breath brings the gas by tomorrow. If we cannot smell it at sun up, I will send hunters to find where the gas has reached. This gives us more time to prepare, but we only leave if we must. To those who feel unable to stay within these walls another night, you may take some food from our stores, use our boats. The castle gates will shut at midday."

Heather stands before us looking as impassive as the statue of Gaia she prays to. Then she is gone, leaving her people to decide for themselves.

Cliff and I know what we're doing. We discussed it the night Holly collapsed, the night Heather called him out in front of the tribe. She told him I was not pulling my weight and Holly would never survive another winter. If I wasn't back working a full day by the start of autumn, she would cast us both out. Cliff was to stay. He was a valuable member of her tribe and she would give him a healthy child. Knowing we needed time, Cliff said he would consider her offer and give an answer before the end of summer.

In the moonlit corridor Cliff held me tight, kissed the tears which flowed and told me, "We're leaving, Bee. No matter what Heather says, you and Holly are my life."

We've been waiting for the right time and this is it. I just wish the gas didn't exist.

*

Before we go, Cliff, Holly and I pay one last visit to the Observatory Tower. The three of us stand looking towards the Wolds. The landscape is beautiful despite what lies just beyond the hills. Then we gather our belongings, the food we're allowed to take and begin our walk down Steep Hill, past decaying buildings and crumbling walls, to where the boats are kept.

Lauren is there with Elena by her side, along with Fern who gives Holly a hug. A shout from behind tells me Hawk is on his way.

"We'll take two boats," Hawk tells us, "We won't all fit in one."

"Are any others coming?" asks Elena

"A few might," Hawk says, "but those I spoke to thought what Heather said made sense. Where's the rest of your family?"

"They decided to stay until tomorrow." Elena looks worried. Lauren takes her by the hand and helps her into one of the sturdy bamboo boats tethered by hooks fixed on the side of a building. The boat sways slightly as they settle, then Hawk hands Elena their three packs and his bow. She puts them in the stern. Cliff and I place the remaining packs and Cliff's own bow in the other boat, then we help Holly and Fern get in. Hawk unties the ropes, pushes us off, then sees to the boat he is using.

"We should head west, Hawk," Cliff says.

"Anywhere away from this gas sounds good to me."

Hawk begins to row across the water, telling Cliff which way to turn to navigate the ruins just below the surface. I notice Elena leaning towards Lauren who gathers her in and holds her close. Behind me, Fern and Holly have their heads together, no doubt reciting a tale. Cliff focuses on rowing, in putting as much distance between us and the castle as possible. Gaia begins to blow fiercely. The surface of the water forms rippling waves, rocking the boats. I watch the castle until it is gone from sight.

As the sun lowers, we pull the boats aground and make camp. Hawk goes hunting and soon the smell of rabbit and vegetables, cooking in a pot over the fire, is making my mouth water. The exertion of the day means each of us eats well, but there's little conversation. Gaia's breath has blown long and hard all afternoon. I find myself praying for Her to quieten, to ease the fear each of us holds inside by returning to the calm summer days that lulled us before yesterday's awakening. Lauren takes the first watch. I nestle myself against Cliff, holding Holly in my arms. I fall asleep listening to the quiet wheeze she makes, the rustling of leaves blown on the trees and wildlife moving through the bushes.

*

I've lost track of how long we've been on the move. Every night, we set up camp. I used to hear animals moving in the dark. Not anymore. When day breaks I wake and listen for birdsong, yet the space we occupy is shrouded by silence. Cliff says we must keep going, keep ahead of the wind. Every morning, he checks to see which way we need to go. This is what guides us each day.

The smell of the gas is always present, faint or otherwise. Holly is our early warning system. If the air we're breathing becomes worse, she feels it first. I listen to Holly gasping for breath as her father carries her at the front of our slow procession and wish there was some way I could ease her suffering.

When Cliff speaks to me, the first thing I notice is his red eyes. His voice has changed too. He now rasps his words and I miss the soft tone he used to speak with. Hawk struggles to find game, let alone catch it. Each of us has red skin from the rain, as if we'd been scalded by hot water, but Hawk has blisters from where he's wandered too far into the gas. His eyes now water constantly and he often vomits blood. Before long he'll be too weak to walk. Fern grumbles about how she should have stayed and taught Primrose. She frequently wipes blood away from her nose. It is a slow, but constant, trickle. The love Elena and Lauren have for each other keeps them going, one step at a time.

Sometimes, we come across others like ourselves. They warn us of places to avoid and we do the same for them. I have seen the dead and decaying land lying beneath this invisible enemy that draws ever closer. Other travellers may join us for a short time, but our most frequent companion on this journey has been rain. Holly's cries when it hits her face cut me worse than any knife could. We rush to take cover when it falls, but the once green canopies of the trees we shelter under have turned brown. The grass beneath our feet is dying and the rain is making leaves and berries inedible. We dig roots from the ground, only to find they've rotted in the soil.

At night I hear prayers asking Gaia to spare us, desperate conversations between lovers hoping they will be fortunate enough to survive. Cliff tells me Gaia will recover her sense of balance, allow us to live and flourish in a manner that is acceptable to Her.

127

I no longer pray. I no longer hope. There's no point if what we need to live is being destroyed. Like the animals and birds I am silent. I know Gaia is smothering the life she created, so she can be reborn.

RHAPSODY

Day One

While Greg drives swiftly through the city, Amanda wonders what the emergency call will hold for them. It's rare for a fourteen year old child to suffer with chest pains. When they arrive, the girl's oval face is grey and sweaty, her breathing laboured. Wasting no time, they carry the girl into the ambulance, sitting her upright on the stretcher.

"What's your name?" Amanda asks, placing sticky ECG pads on the teenager's chest.

"Emma Harrison," responds the girl's mother.

She sits holding her daughter's hand as Amanda prepares an IV line. The ambulance swerves slightly when Greg joins the flow of early-morning traffic. Amanda centres herself before piercing unblemished skin. She finds a vein first time.

"Don't let them put me to sleep, Mum."

Mrs Harrison gently smooths tousled hair from a pallid forehead.

"Don't worry. The paramedic knows what she's doing."

"I mustn't fall asleep!"

Imploring eyes turn towards Amanda, who is checking Emma's heart rate. It is rapid. Too rapid for comfort.

"I won't put you to sleep, Emma, but I do need you to relax."

The girl is panicking, her breaths becoming short and shallow. Emma's brown eyes hold nothing but fear, all-consuming fear. They are surrounded by dark shadow. It's possible she's been using caffeine pills to stay awake and study, but Amanda's first priority is to calm Emma before her heart rate climbs even higher. She places gentle hands on Emma's shoulders.

129

"Look at me, Emma. We need to calm your breathing down. Breathe with me."

Amanda begins breathing and counting in a fashion designed to prevent Emma from panicking further. Pursing her lips, the girl joins in, blowing out. Before she has chance to draw a new breath in, her body becomes rigid. Emma's eyes roll back into her skull and a gurgle emits from her suddenly slack mouth.

"Emma? Emma? What's happening?" Mrs Harrison is on her feet.

Amanda checks Emma's heart rate. It's risen to over two hundred. The lower ventricles of her heart are contracting and pumping too fast. Amanda bangs on the plastic separating her and Greg. The siren blasts its wail against city buildings. Mrs Harrison places both hands over her ears. The sudden increase in speed nearly sends her flying.

"I need you to move. Now. Go to the rear of the ambulance and stay there."

Amanda's tone gets the desired result. She works quickly to assess the type of arrhythmia she's dealing with. It seems only seconds have passed since Emma was placed in the ambulance. The girl's bladder releases when Amanda lays her flat. Urine darkens the pale pink bunnies dancing on white pyjama bottoms. A short tube is rapidly slid into Emma's mouth to ensure her airway stays securely open. It will also prevent her from swallowing her tongue. Once the teenager is intubated, Amanda attaches a bag to deliver oxygen. She knows Greg will have phoned ahead.

"Stand clear. Don't touch her."

Amanda reaches for the defibrillation pads and shocks her patient. Emma's body jolts. Locking her elbows, Amanda begins CPR, compressing Emma's sternum in a firm short sharp motion. She feels ribs break and prays it is only one, not two or more. The last thing she wants to feel is broken ribs grating against each other as she continues pressing down on Emma's now-concave chest. Even after all the years she's worked as a paramedic, the sensation of broken ribs grating still turns her stomach. After counting to thirty Amanda switches, squeezing the oxygen bag twice. Next, she reassesses Emma's rhythm. Nothing. Moving fast, she injects Emma with adrenaline using the IV she inserted earlier. Behind her, Mrs Harrison quietly sobs. Amanda resumes CPR. While she counts, her mind screams, *Come on! Start beating! Wake up, Emma!*

The van swings around a familiar bend. Traffic allowing, they've not long to go before reaching the hospital. Emma is flatlining. Refusing to give in, Amanda returns to compressing her chest. This girl is only a year older than her own daughter. She compresses and counts, squeezes the oxygen bag, checks for a pulse then starts again, keeping the routine going until they arrive at Accident and Emergency. Emma is wheeled straight into resuscitation by a waiting team. A soft spoken nurse guides Mrs Harrison to follow. The journey has taken a mere ten minutes, yet Amanda feels depleted. At no point did the girl's heart restart. The resuscitation team will continue to work on Emma for a further thirty minutes. They will give the fourteen year old every chance of recovery.

Amanda sits at the rear of the ambulance. Limp legs dangle feet onto the tarmac beneath.

"You okay?" asks Greg. "That was a tough one."

"Yeah," mutters Amanda.

"Shitty job to get mid-shift."

Amanda says nothing. She doesn't know how to explain the disquieting dread she's feeling.

Greg nudges her. "Let's get the van tidied for the next one. We can grab a coffee afterwards and you can tell me what you really think about this last call."

*

It's a struggle to put one foot in front of the other by the time Amanda walks into the kitchen. Chris greets her. His hug squeezes her aching arms just a little too tightly. She sits down while he dishes up the meal he put in the slow cooker before going to bed. The smell is nauseating. Amanda hasn't the heart to tell him she's sick of casseroled meat. Often all she wants to do after a night shift is go straight to bed. Instead she smiles.

"Thanks, hon."

Normally she manages to eat enough to satisfy her husband, but this morning all she does is push food around her plate. She can't put last night's shift from her mind. Aware Chris's eyes are on her, Amanda puts a forkful in her mouth. Chews and swallows. The fork slips from her hand, clatters on the pine table. Chris takes hold of her hands. His face is wrinkled with concern.

"What happened?"

"We lost three teenagers last night. I did my best to save them, but they didn't respond to CPR. They just died."

"Car crash?"

"No, three separate incidents. Two close to the hospital, one further away."

Amanda pushes her chair back, gets up and walks to the kitchen window. She tears a piece of kitchen roll off, wipes her mouth and looks out at the autumn leaves strewn across the grass. The sun isn't yet strong enough to heighten their rich colours.

"I had to pronounce one boy dead in front of his parents at their home, two died in the ambulance. The resus team worked on them, and those the other paramedics brought in, but none recovered." Amanda falls silent, waiting for her words to sink in. It doesn't take long.

"Hang on. What do you mean, 'those the other paramedics brought in'?"

The hollowness inside Amanda shapes her voice,

"We weren't the only crew to have teenagers die. There were six in total."

"Six kids dead? Shit. Poor parents. Were the others in a fight that got out of hand? A prank? Suicide?"

Amanda shakes her head, aware of the need to rationalise, make sense of how these children died.

"Then what killed them?"

"I don't know, Chris, but there was something about the way they died. I checked with the other crews and we all saw the same symptoms, the same age range."

"Meaning?"

All Amanda wants to do is drop into bed. Her body aches for the comfort and her eyes need to close, but her mind is wound tight. Worried Chris will dismiss what she is about to say, Amanda turns away from their leaf-littered garden to face him.

"They were all exhausted, terrified of going to sleep. Most were fourteen or fifteen, one was thirteen. Penny's age. Their parents made the emergency call. No matter what any of us did, each kid suffered cardiac arrest. One paramedic said the girl who died in his van was hallucinating. She kept saying something was in the ambulance with them." Amanda steps towards Chris. "The kids I treated were so scared. I've never seen such fear."

"It might be a new drug. One that's just hit the streets. I'll keep an ear to the ground in the classroom." He stands and pulls her to him in a brief embrace. "Go to bed. You can eat later. Give Penny's door a knock on your way. It's time she got up for school."

Chris could be right. A new street drug was something she and Greg wondered about as their shift was ending. Despite her exhaustion, Amanda needs to see her daughter before falling asleep. Needs to feel Penny in her arms. She makes her way upstairs.

*

Day Four

Yet again Amanda has a teenager in the van with a rapid heartbeat. The terror in the boy's eyes is heartbreaking. Amanda can't imagine ever becoming accustomed to how these kids are acting. This one is exhausted. His sunken eyes flicker to the back of her van as if something stands by the rear door.

"What is it?" she asks.

But the boy ignores her, turns to his mother saying, "I'm sorry, Mum. I… we didn't mean to do anything wrong."

"Hush, Aaron. It's okay, I'm not angry about the pills."

The courage of these mothers is humbling. Amanda's seen a number of them since Emma died. They comfort their children, then calmly follow Amanda's orders when cardiac arrest hits.

"It's not the pills, Mum. It's the other thing I told you about."

"What other thing?" Amanda wants to know. His heart is beginning to clamour. She sends his mother to the back of the van knowing what is coming next. Aaron's eyes flit once more but not to where his mum is standing. Whatever he sees is near Amanda. His breath begins to rasp.

"No!" he screams. "Leave me alone!"

She lays his legs flat, ready to slide him down the cot the instant his eyes roll back. The teenager's body jerks.

"Step on it!" she yells to Greg.

*

Later that morning, Amanda steps into the room where the boy is lying. His mother is holding her child's cooling hand.

"Thank you for what you did on the way here. You gave my son every chance you could." The woman's voice is dull with grief.

Amanda's not in the habit of speaking to relatives

of the dead. Finds it distressing.

"I'm sorry I couldn't do more." She places what she hopes is a comforting hand on the woman's shoulder. "May I ask a question?"

The woman nods.

"In the ambulance, your son said it wasn't tablets, it was the other thing he told you about. Please tell me what he meant."

"It was nothing," she says. "Just nonsense. You know the kind of things kids dream up."

"Please. It might help other children."

The woman sighs, hangs her head. Expecting to be told to leave, Amanda holds her breath.

"Aaron told me he and a group of friends messed with something they shouldn't have, and it was causing problems. He became scared to go to sleep. The longer he stayed awake, the more disturbed he became." She reaches out, strokes her dead son's arm. "His behaviour changed. He was angry all the time. I found caffeine pills in his drawer and binned them, but he fished them out and..." She bites her lip. Fresh tears run down her face. "I ended up with a black eye. Once he'd calmed down, Aaron said it was because of Rhapsody."

"And Rhapsody isn't a street drug?"

Aaron's mother shrugs. "I thought it was, that he was lying the way kids do when they get caught." An embittered smile contorts her mouth. "I was so relieved when he fell asleep on the sofa. I prayed he wouldn't wake up with those dreams which had been plaguing him over the past couple of weeks. I was upstairs, searching for this Rhapsody, when he started screaming. I ran down. He was clutching his chest, telling me they were here for him." Fresh sobs shake her body.

Amanda gives the woman's shoulder a brief squeeze. "Thank you for telling me," she says, leaving Aaron's mum to grieve. She should report this new information. If a drug is responsible for causing teenagers to die, they now have a name. Despite the brightly lit corridors, clatter from the café in the atrium, the disquieting dread she felt after Emma died is deepening.

*

Day Seven

This is the first day since ending her five-night shifts Amanda has woken feeling rested. She's not due to go in until tomorrow evening, but a phone call from her manager changes things. She's got today to spend with Penny, but their family film night will have to be cancelled. Chris raises an eyebrow as she resumes eating her breakfast.

"What did he want?"

"Me to do the late shift. One paramedic has the shits and another's taking a stress break – feels traumatised."

"So one's drunk too much and the other can't cope with seeing more teenagers die." A frown creases his forehead, "I'm surprised there's been nothing on the news."

"I suppose it's early days, but yeah, it's odd. Doesn't feel right." Crumbs fall on the plate as Amanda bites into lukewarm toast. "Have any of the kids in school said anything? A few days have passed since you began telling them to steer clear of any drug called Rhapsody."

"The usual. Some looked gone out, others exchanged knowing looks and sniggered." Chris shifts in his chair.

"Out with it."

"I told the kids I'd listen if they'd taken this drug and needed to talk. One came to me just as the last lesson ended yesterday, said Rhapsody isn't a drug. When I asked him what it is, he told me he'd be in trouble with his mates if he said anything. How the hell do we find out if they won't talk? It's almost like a secret society. Weird. But kids are weird nowadays. Look at Penny, always chatting on WhatsApp or Messenger instead of meeting up. Or she's on YouTube watching videos."

Amanda's mug stops halfway to her mouth. The fine hairs on her arms are standing up.

"Oh my god, Chris. Where's your laptop?"

*

Forty fruitless minutes have passed since Chris logged on. Amanda has entered every variation of "Rhapsody" she can think of as a search term. She has found a musical site, musical and dictionary definitions and, of course, the band Queen. The closest she comes to finding a society is the Christian Devotional who have published a book, *Rhapsody of Reality*. Chris puts the kettle on.

"Morning." Penny's unruly blonde hair announces she's just got out of bed.

Their daughter hitches her pyjama bottoms up with one hand, opens the fridge with the other. She grabs orange juice, unscrews the top and slugs from the carton. She seems surprised when neither of her parents correct her.

"What's going on?" she asks.

Looking at her daughter, Amanda notices a slight trace of shadow forming under her hazel eyes. "Did you sleep okay?"

"I've been in bed over nine hours. Duh!"

Penny's glance towards her Dad is the one which asks if Mum is stressed out.

"Maybe you can help us," Chris says, taking the carton from Penny's hand.

"Sure." Penny drags a chair across the floor to sit beside Amanda.

"We're trying to find out what Rhapsody is," Amanda says.

Penny's eyes flicker down and right. She knows something. Fearing the worst, Amanda speaks firmly. "It's important, Penny. Tell us what you know."

Penny squirms, pulls her hands free, begins tracing a grain line in the pine table. "I'm not supposed to say."

Amanda goes cold. Across the room, Chris puts the mugs of tea he's just made back down on the work-surface. The tension in his back and shoulders is mirrored by her own body. She hopes the fear on his face when he turns around isn't.

"What have you done?" His voice is quiet, almost a whisper.

"I've not done anything!"

Penny's on her feet. Amanda places a hand on her daughters back.

"Please, honey, we need you to tell us what's going on."

"I'll be a joke at school if I do. Just like you are, Dad. I heard what you did."

Chris is across the kitchen, hands on the table, his face inches from Penny's in a moment. Amanda pulls a shocked Penny back into her chair, but Chris isn't raging, he's crying.

"I don't want to be one of those parents your Mum's been to in the past week whose child dies at home, or in the ambulance. At least one was the same age as you."

Amanda can feel Penny trembling, wills Chris to step back. As if sensing her thought, he does. Uses his jumper sleeve to dry his eyes then gets the tea. Places the mugs on the table and sits down.

"Sorry, Pen."

Penny shifts as if uncomfortable, then says, "You're looking in the wrong place. There's nothing on YouTube."

"Then where do I look?" asks Amanda.

"It's on an app. Messages and videos aren't monitored. There's a word for it."

"Unregulated?" suggests Chris.

"Yeah."

"So is it a group you join?"

Penny sighs at Amanda's question. She looks down at her hands. Her fingers begin twisting her favourite ring back and forth.

"Sort of. You get initiated."

Amanda switches into paramedic mode. It keeps her voice calm.

"What happens when you're initiated?"

"I'll show you."

Penny leaves the room, returning with her phone. She plugs it into her father's laptop.

Shaky video reveals eight teenagers in an ordinary living room lit by candles. Furniture has been pushed back to create a big enough space on the carpet for a tall girl to lie down. She's surrounded by six of her friends who are kneeling. Flickering shadows cast by candlelight dance upon her jeans and tee-shirt. The boy at her head speaks.

"We're ready to start the initiation ritual, which will open a gate between this world and the next and allow Lucy to transcend." The camera leans in. "Put your fingers under her, like this." He demonstrates by sliding just the very tips of his fingers under the girl's head. "You ready, Luce?"

A nervous giggle issues from the girl lying in the centre. The person videoing steps back. Amanda and Chris can see the entire scene.

The boy at Lucy's head says, "Relax your toes. You are feeling relaxed."

Other voices follow, one by one circling the girl's body. They repeat the process, telling Lucy her feet, then her legs feel relaxed, gradually moving up her body until her head is reached. Their words form a mantra which resonates calm and relaxation throughout.

"You are falling asleep."

The girl becomes visibly limp as the chant progresses. Voices remain smooth and fluid throughout, telling Lucy she is becoming weightless. Amanda realises

Chris is holding his breath. When the last voice tells Lucy she weighs nothing, a gasp escapes his mouth. The girl is levitating.

"We will raise you into Rhapsody," The kids chant in unison.

Lucy is raised on their fingertips until she reaches their shoulders. With the litheness of youth, the group stands, continuing to lift her as if she truly does weigh nothing, until she is above their heads.

Beside her, Chris places his elbows on his knees. Rubs his forehead with his hands. Amanda leans forward as the teenagers bring Lucy back down to the carpet, using the same manner of rhythmic mantra to return her to consciousness. While she watches the group celebrate their successful ritual, Penny makes more tea.

*

Amanda finds she has no answers, just more questions. Chris hasn't touched his tea. His hands clasp the mug, while Penny fidgets in the way only a thirteen-year-old can. Amanda has no doubt that showing her parents her own private world is the last thing their daughter wanted to do.

"So what we've just seen is a ritual which leads to someone being levitated," Amanda says.

Penny nods.

"And afterwards, the levitated person is then considered to have experienced Rhapsody?"

"Yes, Mum. That's obvious."

"But what's this gate that's been opened?"

"It's a spiritual one. A good one. You go through it when levitated and touch heaven."

"If it's a good spiritual gate, why are some kids dying?" Amanda leaves out how terrified those she has treated have been.

"I dunno. None of my friends have died and it's a while since we did this. Maybe they were doing drugs and Dad made an idiot of himself 'cos he got the name wrong.

Can I go now?"

Amanda puts her hand on Penny's arm. Her daughter's skin is soft and warm. The impetuousness of youth pulses through her veins.

"Just one more question, hon. When did your friends levitate you?"

And there it is. The pause which tells Amanda her daughter is about to lie.

"I didn't want to be levitated. Are we going shopping or not, 'cos it's past ten."

Without waiting for an answer, Penny goes back upstairs. Amanda hears her bedroom door slam shut.

*

Day Eight

Amanda has introduced a new line of questioning when they answer emergency calls where teenagers are suffering with chest pains. Tonight, she and Greg are on their third. Like those before her, this girl is grey, sweaty, her eyes sunken in shadow. Amanda has already established she's been taking huge quantities of caffeine tablets. Much larger doses than is safe. While she places the ECG pads Greg drives at a pace on the wet city roads.

"Have you recently taken part in a Rhapsody ritual?"

The girl nods than glances towards her mum who looks confused by the question. Her husband is following in their family car. Amanda wonders if her question will be reported back to him.

"How long ago?"

This time, the teenager glances at the back of the van. Fear blossoms. She gasps, "Three weeks."

"Look at me." Amanda commands. The girl's heart is racing faster as terror grips her. "There's nothing there, just look at me."

The girl snaps her eyes back on Amanda's.

"Yes, there is." Her voice is fierce, "We opened a gate and let them through."

The girl's eyes flit as if something stands beside the stretcher. Pupils dilate and her young mouth opens to reveal perfect teeth as she tries to draw breath and scream. Her head slams back. Her body jerks.

Yet again, sirens blast the lamp-lit night while Amanda works on what she knows is just a husk. Recent experience tells her life left the instant cardiac arrest occurred.

*

"We need to talk."

Greg has never used such a stern tone with her during all the years they've worked together. They usually spend their breaks eating and chatting in the manner old friends do. Tonight they've grabbed a burger and coffee from a drive-in, parked up and were eating contentedly. Or so she thought.

"What's up?"

"This new line of questions you've introduced, it needs to stop. I will not tolerate you questioning any more young patients in that way."

"I showed you the video!" Amanda now has the app on her phone and insisted Penny forward the one she and Chris watched. "This ritual is what's behind all of these deaths. I'm sure of it."

"The video is just kids being kids, it's not solid evidence. The autopsy results are evidence. Hard evidence. They all show high caffeine levels. Each kid we've attended showed signs of sleep deprivation. A number of parents told you their child wasn't sleeping well."

"They're too scared to sleep. Don't tell me you've not seen or heard their fear. What they call Rhapsody is the cause of this. Instead of opening a gate to heaven, these kids are opening one to…to…some kind of hell."

"Can you hear yourself?" Greg thumps the steering wheel. "All this video proves to me is that you're too involved to think clearly. You have a teenage daughter who you *think* has been initiated." His fingers form quotation marks around the word "think". "Your questions aren't professional. What Penny took part in is a fad. It'll pass – get replaced by the next one. You've no right to suggest to patients under our care, or their parents, a fad's the root cause of these symptoms. We both know what lots of caffeine and lack of sleep can do to your heart rate."

"But you're ignoring what the last child said."

"You prompted her. Instead of dealing with her symptoms, you asked a question which fed her fear. It stops now."

"And if I don't stop?"

"You take a stress break, or I report you."

Despatch calls. This time it's a fifteen-year-old boy with chest pains. Feeling betrayed, Amanda angrily stuffs her half-eaten burger and their rubbish in a bin. She watches Greg readying the van as she wipes the grease and stench of fried food off her hands with a napkin. Bins that too. Sod him. She'll ask about sleep deprivation and hallucinations. Find the link which, so far, has eluded her. Time is running out. Amanda's certain Penny was levitated, but when? She must save her child. If Greg doesn't like the questions her mind is forming – tough.

*

Day Eleven

After pushing the guest bed under the sash window, Amanda places a desk and pasting table in the room. On the pasting table are trays. Most already have information in them, yet one remains empty. For Amanda, it represents the solution. Hopefully, at some point in the near future, she will have figured this out.

On the wall above the pasting table are copies of autopsy reports Amanda surreptitiously took photos of in the two days before Greg reported her. Statistically, they detail a worrying trend in age and cause of death. Amanda wonders if the situation is the same countrywide and just how many teenagers are dying. As far as she knows, none of Penny's friends have been affected and her daughter hasn't mentioned any bad dreams. At home, Amanda hears hushed conversations taking place behind Penny's door. Conversations which stop if she enters.

Looking at her collection of autopsy reports, Amanda settles on one. Today, instead of making house calls as a paramedic, she is calling as a concerned mother. A scary prospect as she'll be asking questions without the protection of her paramedic uniform. Leaving the room, Amanda heads downstairs to the front door. Her hand trembles as she locks it.

*

Sitting on a plush sofa which is so new it doesn't fit with the tired wallpaper and chipped paint of the living room, Amanda sips the coffee she's been given. Nerves are butterflying her stomach causing the coffee to churn. She quickly places the "Keep Calm And Carry On" mug on a nearby side-table. Aaron's mother clearly follows this advice. Her face is thinner than when Amanda last saw her. Its colour reminds her of wallpaper paste. Only her eyes show any emotion. Dull and red-rimmed, they project grief.

"I had to get a new sofa," she says, sitting down. "Couldn't sit on the last one after what happened." Aaron's mother sips her coffee and grimaces. "Why are you here?"

"I've got a daughter, slightly younger than Aaron. I'm worried about her. I…need to ask you some questions."

"Call me Laura." She places her mug on the table alongside Amanda's. "I would do anything to spare another child or mother from what happened to Aaron. Ask away."

"When we were in the ambulance, your son said he and his friends had messed with something."

"Yes, he called it Rhapsody, but the name changed a few days later. I can't remember what to." Laura shakes

144

her head as if to dislodge the information.

"Do you know what Rhapsody is?"

"I thought it was a drug. Told you so."

"It's something else." Amanda plays the initiation footage, sees realisation dawn in Laura's face.

"Hang on." She leaves the room, runs upstairs. Comes back down holding a phone, passes it over. It's fully charged.

"I kept it because I thought it would be easier to contact Aaron's friends about his funeral. I even answered a couple of calls from one of them, a boy sounding scared. He died a couple of days back. I've not looked at it since. Not wanted to."

Amanda does though. She opens the app and checks the video links. Finds a recording of Aaron's initiation rite. It's almost identical to the one on Penny's phone. By the end, the kids are excited. Joyous. The datestamp on the video is three weeks before she and Greg received the emergency call.

Pausing the video on a shot showing everyone apart from the kid holding the phone, Amanda asks, "How many of these children are still alive?"

Laura looks at the phone. She points at a girl in the background. "This one died a few days before Aaron. Killed herself. He came home from school and cried. That was when he started saying his nightmares were linked to what they'd done, that they'd opened a gate which should've stayed shut." Laura strokes the image of her son with her finger. Tears slide down her cheeks. "I told him not to talk rubbish, that she'd had problems. I don't know about the others, but I recognise the voice of the boy recording this. He's the one who died recently."

Amanda takes a tissue from her bag, passes it to Laura. "Tell me about Aaron's nightmares."

"He saw a figure coming into his room. It wore a top hat and gradually got closer to his bed. Aaron said he couldn't breathe or move, would lie there paralysed, silenced, thinking he was going to die, until something gave, and he would find himself screaming. His screams were so loud, I expected the neighbours to complain. I took him to see a doctor."

"What did the doctor say?"

"That it was night terrors. Unusual in a teenager, but not unheard of. She gave Aaron sleeping pills. He refused to take them, said he needed to stay awake else he'd be taken. Then he started to see the figure even when he was awake."

"He was hallucinating from lack of sleep and saw what he feared most." Amanda gives the rational answer, the one Greg would pat her on the back for.

Laura snorts. "You wouldn't be here if you thought that."

*

On her way home Amanda picks Penny up from school. Apart from a brief greeting, Penny is uncommunicative during the journey. Amanda waits until they are in the kitchen before asking what is wrong. Penny pulls her phone from her blazer pocket.

"I got a message from Sarah after lunch. She hasn't been in school today." Her thumbs swiftly find the text message.

We shouldn't have done it. It's evil. And we shouldn't have laughed at your Dad. At least he saw something was wrong. I can't stay awake anymore and I'm too scared to sleep. I'm gonna do what the site says. Love ya, bye. S xx

"I tried ringing her. Didn't get an answer. I went to the teacher, but he confiscated my phone. Told me to sit down."

"Do you have her parents' number?"

"No."

"What's her address?"

146

Penny starts crying. She stumbles over the words. Amanda hugs her daughter, kisses the top of her head.

"Stay here," she says, then runs to her still-warm car.

Wishing she had a siren, Amanda drives as fast as she dares, pulling up outside Sarah's home. October sun dips towards slated rooftops as the afternoon draws to a close. The moist scent of autumnal decay hangs in the air. Sarah's mother, Mrs Armstrong, is unloading shopping from the boot of her car.

"Your daughter's in trouble," Amanda yells as she sprints up the drive, "Where's her bedroom?"

Shopping spills over the driveway. Mrs Armstrong has the front door unlocked by the time Amanda reaches it. "Upstairs, front right," she says, following Amanda as she races up the stairs, bursts through into Sarah's room.

Sarah is on the bed. Her face softly slack, amongst auburn curls and vomit. Her small, plump body lays supine on a cream and rose quilted bedspread. An almost empty bottle of vodka sits on the bedside cabinet and silver paracetamol foils, scattered like confetti, lay amongst the empty boxes on the carpet. Finding no pulse, Amanda clears vomit from Sarah's airway before beginning CPR. The girl is still, too still. Amanda tries to resuscitate her. A phone near the body flashes almost in time with her compressions. Amanda is certain there are many missed calls, not just the one from Penny.

*

Day Twelve
Amanda blows Chris a kiss when he checks on her and Penny before leaving for work. It's been a difficult night and Penny is now sleeping peacefully. Amanda holds her close. Telling Penny her friend died is one of the hardest things Amanda has ever faced. There's no longer a need to ask Penny if she was initiated. The expression on her daughter's face on hearing about Sarah, her subsequent

breakdown, were confirmation enough. Later, Amanda spoke with the mother of each girl in Sarah's initiation group, telling them what she feared all parents of Rhapsodised children faced. Some had blown her off, others fell silent. Two had thanked her, grateful as their child was suffering with nightmares involving shadowy figures.

Scared Penny will die before she's been able to find a way of halting the process, Amanda considers what she knows. On recalling the text message from Sarah, she gently lays her daughter down, tiptoes into the guest room.

The trays on the pasting table are now full of information about night terrors and shadow people. Much of it is disconcerting. Amanda has information dating back beyond the Victorian era. A common factor throughout the ages is a reoccurring figure who wears a top hat. Top Hat is as much a part of modern night terrors as he was of old.

Amanda sits at the desk, switches the laptop on. Once online she types, *help site for Rhapsody* into the search bar. As she presses return, her phone buzzes against her leg. It's a message.

Hi Amanda, I've just remembered what Aaron changed the name to. It was Rhapsody Noir. I hope this is useful. Laura

The first thought that enters Amanda's mind is how apt the name is for a heavenly experience which becomes so darkly relentless. Could this be the name of the site Sarah mentioned in her text? Intending to change her search term, she turns her attention back to the screen. It takes a moment for her brain to process what she is seeing.

Penny told her and Chris how Rhapsody is secretly passed from teenager to teenager. A digital whisper, an adult exclusion zone via mobile phones and a free, innocuous looking, unregulated app, meaning Rhapsody snuck in under the radar of adult supervision. Now

Rhapsody is global. The initiation ritual can be viewed on YouTube. There are videos from China, America, Spain, Africa, Brazil, the UK, to name but a few. Amanda begins opening links, watching, reading, finding nothing detrimental. Video testimonies from the recently converted radiate euphoria. She types in 'Rhapsody Noir' but the search returns nothing. Resisting the urge to slam the laptop shut, Amanda gets out of her seat, goes to the wall where the autopsy reports are and rips them off. Once the wall is bare, she grabs a permanent marker.

Reaching up, Amanda writes RHAPSODY on the wall. Large black letters break the smooth blue surface. She draws two arrows downwards in opposite directions, placing EUPHORIA at the end of one, NOIR below the point of the other. The smell of pear drops lingers when she steps back. Amanda views the capitalised words and slaps her forehead. Under EUPHORIA she writes MEANS TO AN END? Amanda is certain her deduction is correct, but why? What is the purpose of the euphoria teenagers experience? Under NOIR, she details all the terrible effects she and other paramedics have witnessed, draws a short arrow beneath, and pens NOIR WEBSITE. She needs to find this website and a way of stopping Rhapsody rituals. Another thought flits through her brain. Amanda doesn't understand quite how this fits, but she's certain it has a significant role to play. Drawing a line directly down from RHAPSODY, she places the words, SPIRITUAL GATES on the wall. Under this she instinctively puts, SHADOW PEOPLE. Glancing at the laptop, at the list of sites and YouTube videos now available, Amanda knows the cases she and other paramedics have dealt with are the tip of the iceberg. Society is about to be confronted with a huge problem. She looks at her flowchart. Asks, *Am I being rational?* Self-doubt threatens to overwhelm her.

Penny enters the room. She looks so vulnerable. Amanda wraps her arms around the slim form of her daughter. Kisses the top of her blond hair. Penny's slender arms entwine Amanda's waist. This brief comfort ends when Penny looks at the black blemishes upon the once perfect wall.

"Cool," she says. Then, pointing to NOIR WEBSITE, "You'll find it, Mum."

*

Day Sixteen

Amanda takes a break from writing her blog. The increasing number of Rhapsody videos are damning evidence the trend is growing. Chris is speaking about it in school assembly. Enough pupils have died for the headmaster to be concerned. Hopefully the kids will listen, unlike the counsellor her NHS Manager has appointed. Like Greg, he thinks she is irrational. Mentally unstable. Amanda doesn't care what either of them thinks. The response to her blog has been mixed, but encouraging. Despite the haters spewing bile, insisting she's got it wrong. Shrugging off their comments, Amanda finishes her latest entry. She's been writing about her daughter, telling other parents what to look out for if a Rhapsody ritual has already taken place.

Penny is suffering from the effects of Rhapsody Noir. She's not sleeping well, beginning to look oh so tired. Each night, her daughter has gone to bed in her own room without question, yet in the early hours of this morning, a frightened Penny had climbed into bed with them.

It's gone two o'clock by the time Amanda stops for a break. She goes downstairs to make a cup of coffee, collecting post off the floor. Whilst the kettle boils, she opens it. Amongst the bills is a letter from her manager asking her to attend a formal review in two weeks' time. Amanda notes the date on the calendar, feeling strangely unconcerned about the fact she is likely to be suspended. She spoons coffee into the mug, grabs a cereal bar. Chris phones as she's making her way back upstairs.

"Are you at your desk? I've got a lead for you."

"Almost," she replies, "How'd assembly go?"

"I was approached by so many kids afterwards, the headmaster's put me in his office to speak to them individually."

"How many are we talking about?"

"Enough for me to be working late. The kid I've just spoken to told me Rhapsody Noir is a community site. For teenagers who experience bad dreams and see shadow people. He said it's hard to find as it's often a link in a comment on teenage advice sites. Like Teenline. You'll find it somewhere in the discussion forums. The problem is, it's unofficial, so..."

"Moderators close the thread with the link in, or remove it."

"Yeah. Plus the IP address of the site keeps changing, so it stays hidden."

"They're trying to avoid being traced? What kind of help site does that? I'll get on to it."

"Okay. Because of the response I got in assembly, the Head is calling a parents' meeting. I'll put it on the calendar when I get home."

Something stirs in Amanda that has been sleeping. It is hope. Maybe, just maybe, this will be the start of an army of voices that will shut Rhapsody down.

*

After dinner, while Chris tidies up downstairs, Amanda searches the teen help and community sites. Penny lies on the guest bed re-reading texts from her friends for clues on where to look next. Using Rhapsody as a keyword, Amanda is soon finding relevant discussions, but it's past Penny's bedtime before they find what they're looking for.

A recent comment in a thread reads; *Need help with Rhapsody Noir?*

Amanda clicks on the link.

The landing page contains a single message.

Has your Rhapsody experience taken a dark turn? Do you need help? Create an account or login HERE.

"Use the same pretend name and date of birth," Penny says, stifling a yawn. She looks exhausted and the shadows under her eyes are deepening.

"Time you went to bed."

"But Mum..."

"I don't want you seeing this. Give your Dad a shout, will you."

"Can I stay in here, Mum? I'll sleep on the guest bed. Please. At first it was just one." Penny glances at the trays. "They're like moving shadows with red eyes. There's one with a top hat. I think it's in charge." She plays with the ring on her left hand.

"I understand the dreams are scary, but if you deprive yourself of sleep, it causes physical problems. Go to bed, hon. You're worn out. I'll check on you in an hour."

Penny makes as if to speak then closes her mouth, moves towards the door.

"Would you feel safer if you slept in our bed?"

She smiles. "Thanks, Mum."

*

Chris enters the room carrying a glass of wine in each hand. He passes one to her.

"Got much more to do?"

"Not tonight." The dry smoothness of the wine is mouth-watering after an hour reading testimonies and advice. It helps to soothe the rising anger she feels. "I've been looking at the site Penny and I found, the one which is supposed to offer help. It's full of messages from teenagers around the world. Since being Rhapsodised, all of them are seeing groups of shadow people. There's four moderators. They all say the same thing."

"Which is?"

"Kill yourself before they take you."

Chris splutters, almost drops his wine.

"Then they ask about the kid's personal circumstances and give advice on the best way to commit suicide."

"Bloody hell."

"I've reported it, but by the time my complaint is looked into, the link to the site will have been moved to another forum."

"I'm already talking to teachers and headmasters from other schools. I'll ask for student and parents meetings to be set up. Get the word out there. Sorry, Amanda, that's all I can think of to do."

Amanda sips her wine. It's plain from her blog many people are in denial. Part of her wishes she was still on the vans, she'd have a better idea how many teenagers Rhapsody is currently killing. She has no idea how many may have died since Greg reported her.

"I feel as if we're just two people against a global teenage movement, Chris. What happens in a couple of weeks when the impact of recent and ongoing Rhapsody rituals hits? If the amount of new videos uploaded to YouTube today is anything to go by, there will be thousands." The wine is turning to acid in her stomach. Amanda puts her glass on the desk, pushes it away. "How do we protect Penny, the children you spoke with today? You said there's over two hundred names on your list and that's just one school."

Chris, who stood tall and strong as she walked down the aisle, crumples miserably.

"I don't know how we protect her," he says. "Maybe we can't. I think all we can do is warn people. Try to stop other kids taking part in rituals. I don't think we can do anything for those already Rhapsodised."

As the finality of his words sink in, Amanda hears Penny screaming.

*

Day Twenty-One

Amanda wakes for the third time that night, places her arms around Penny, soothes her until the screams soften to sobs. The night terrors have increased in the past five days. Shadow people are drawing closer, surrounding the bed. Amanda doesn't comment on how she can't see them. They're real to Penny and that is what counts. Instead, she gently cuddles her daughter's increasingly thin frame. Penny feels brittle in her arms. If Amanda were to squeeze her too tight, she might break.

"Shall I make us a hot drink?"

Penny nods.

"Chocolate?"

The hint of a smile.

Penny presses herself against her father's back as Amanda gets out of bed, pulls on her dressing gown. Making hot chocolate to lull Penny and herself back into sleep is becoming a nightly ritual. Chris is so tired from dealing with the number of Rhapsodised children coming forward, Amanda expects he'll sleep through.

Mugs are ready, the kettle just boiled, when Penny clatters down the stairs and runs into the partially-lit kitchen.

"Mum! Mum!"

Amanda barely has time to return the empty milk pan to the hob before Penny flings herself against her.

"They're here, Mum, they're here!" Penny's voice is shrill. She's shaking from head to toe. Fully expanded pupils turn her eyes black. She pivots away from Amanda, screaming, "Go away!" at the open door.

"Sit down, Penny." Amanda pulls a chair out from the kitchen table, nudges her daughter towards it. Then she crosses the kitchen, shuts the door. The work-surface lights are on, but Amanda flicks a nearby switch. The light above the table is bright. Penny sits, but her eyes are darting feverishly around the kitchen.

154

Keeping her tone firm, Amanda says, "You're safe, Penny. You're awake. The dream has gone."

Greg would be proud. Turncoat. She ignores her internal critique. The words are intended to calm Penny. Amanda doesn't have to believe them.

She places the steaming mugs on the table, sits beside her daughter. Penny turns to look at the door as she picks her mug up, spilling some of the milky liquid.

"It's shut. there's no-one there, hon. Drink your chocolate whilst it's warm."

Penny sips. Her breathing is calmer despite her obvious fear.

"Don't let them take me, Mum."

"I won't." Amanda squeezes Penny's knee reassuringly through the thin cotton pyjamas, picks her own drink up. Amanda can't help but check the door while the hot sweet liquid caresses her throat.

It's partially ajar. She can't have closed it firmly enough.

Penny shudders as if a sudden chill has swept through the room.

"Are you cold, hon?"

Her daughter appears to be pulling herself visibly inwards.

Amanda checks her forehead, finds it cool. She takes her dressing gown off, drapes it around Penny. The bulb above the table phuts, flares briefly and dies.

"It's nothing to worry about. I'll get a fresh bulb." Amanda begins to rise from the table. Penny grabs her wrist.

"Don't go, Mum."

Amanda checks the kitchen, The atmosphere has undergone a subtle change. Work-surface lights emit a pale imitation of the welcoming glow they first gave. It's as if they are pulling themselves protectively in, just as Penny had seconds ago. Glancing at the door, Amanda thinks she sees something. It's gone before she can bring it fully into focus.

The grip around Amanda's wrist is tightening.

"They're here Mum. I'm not dreaming. Don't leave me."

"I'm not going anywhere. Try to relax, honey."

Penny looks over Amanda's shoulder, then twists to look towards the hallway and gasps.

The door is wide open.

Her face is anguished when she turns back to Amanda. "There's so many! They're coming through the door, can't you see them?"

All Amanda can see are shadows lengthening, encroaching upon the feeble light issuing over the work-surface and pooling on the floor. A peculiar smell pervades the air. She sniffs, finds a bitter taste in her mouth. Is it gas? Penny is already on her feet, pulling Amanda towards the nearest pool of light. The dressing gown slips, drops to the ground, mimicking a fallen body as it dissolves into the murky shadow spreading out from under the table.

They stand in a fading half-moon of light against the cabinets. Amanda pulls her trembling daughter against her.

"Make them go away," pleads Penny.

She's breathing too fast for Amanda's liking. About to panic. Lifting her daughter's face with one hand, Amanda says, "You need to listen to me and do as I say."

Penny is panting, her eyelids flicker.

"Look at me. Nowhere else. I am real. You can touch me, feel me."

The pulse point under the two fingers Amanda placed in the soft groove next to the windpipe on Penny's neck, is horribly fast. Penny's eyes dart sidewards. She wails. Urine runs hot and steady onto the kitchen floor, soaking Amanda's nightshirt where their bodies are close. It splashes over their feet, puddles on the floor in the ever-shrinking pool of light. The stench of urine combined with the earlier smell fills Amanda with dread. She focuses on Penny.

"I'm not letting you go. Breathe like I do. Listen to the count."

Penny tries to do as asked while gasping for air. Tears stream down her cheeks.

Watching her daughter fighting to regain control, Amanda struggles to remain composed. Against her fingers, she feels Penny's heart flutter. It's beat becomes irregular. She channels all her strength and knowledge into encouraging her child to relax.

Darkness rears up behind Penny. Shadows reach across the top of her head, dampening the blond into a dirty light brown. Amanda feels her eyes widen in unison with Penny's as insubstantial fingers grasp her daughter's skull.

"Mum..." croaks Penny.

Her eyes roll back. Her body jerks in Amanda's arms. A solitary scream pierces atmosphere thick with an unearthly presence. The bulb above the kitchen table splutters back on as she collapses onto the now brightly-lit floor, holding her daughter's limp and lifeless body in unresponsive arms. While Penny's pyjamas and her nightshirt absorb the now-cold urine, all Amanda can do is scream.

*

Day Thirty-One

Heavy rain slashes across the windscreen, almost defeating the efforts of the wipers. Amanda knows Greg is looking at her. She pointedly refuses to meet his gaze. He said all the right things about Penny before stating he still doesn't believe in the "Rhapsody Phenomenon", as the newspapers are calling it. Greg is merely expressing what many believe. The number of teenagers dying has escalated dramatically since Penny's death. News reports are full of the dangers involved in partaking in a ritual, emphasising the links between death, excess caffeine consumption, lack of sleep and hallucinations. Medical practitioners and scientists have explained how shadow people can't and don't exist. Except in people's minds.

Amanda knows otherwise.

She also knows other voices are arguing against this perspective. One is her husband. Penny's death lit a fire within him. Amanda hopes it will never be extinguished. Others belong to parents he has spoken with at school meetings, some to people like Laura. In addition, religious factions around the world are preaching about the dangers of entering into communion with spiritual entities.

The battle for the lives of children around the globe is being fought on two fronts. The differing opinions she and Greg hold epitomises this. He continues to regard her as mentally unstable. Doesn't understand how the Review board could reinstate her.

"It's a mad world," she mutters under her breath.

Greg clears his throat. "I need you to confirm you're happy to follow the latest guidelines for Rhapsody sufferers."

"Yes, Greg." Amanda hopes she sounds as pissed off as she feels, "We attempt to resuscitate once using a shield. We intubate them if we manage to restart the patient's heart. Tell me, in all the teenage deaths which occurred while I was off, how many times did you, or any other paramedic, get a heartbeat going?"

Hearing Greg's teeth grate in frustration is strangely satisfying.

"Not once. Look, drop the attitude. We've got to work together. If they die in the van, we take them..."

"...to the mortuary," Amanda finishes. "What happens once the mortuary is full? I ask because it's going to be. It's nineteen days since Rhapsody hit the World Wide Web and we're about to be smothered by an avalanche of death. Shall we take them straight to the crematorium?"

"Shut the fuck up."

Their first call comes in and it's not for a teen. This time they're going to a middle-aged man with chest pains.

Upon arrival, Amanda and Greg are ushered upstairs. The woman who let them in is vaguely familiar. Her husband sits upright in bed clutching his chest. Amanda starts checking him over, Greg asks the questions. The man doesn't appear to see Greg. It's as if his eyes are tracking a non-existent spider on the ceiling until it sits directly above him. Sweat pours down the man's panic-stricken face. Greg repeats the last question as if it demands an answer. No response.

Amanda calls the man's wife over. "Here, sit on the bed and comfort your husband."

"I need to get this done," says Greg.

The woman follows Amanda's instruction. She sits, strokes her husband's face. Tells him she loves him. Amanda moves nearer the door to give the couple some privacy. Greg's face is the colour of pickled beetroot when he joins her.

"Who the hell do you think you are, interfering like that? You said you'd follow protocol!"

Spittle decorates Amanda's cheek. She calmly wipes it away, as the man they were sent to treat jerks then slumps against his wife.

"How did you know?" Greg's words remain peppered with anger.

Amanda shrugs. She's not told anyone, not even Chris, about the strange smell in the kitchen when Penny died. It had been in the room when they entered.

They're about to leave when the newly widowed woman runs out onto the street. Amanda feels fingers grasping her arm.

"There's something I must tell you," the woman says. "Our daughter took part in a Rhapsody ritual. Died in the back of your ambulance. Her father suffered with night terrors as a child. He understood what she was going through. After her funeral, his nightmares returned. At first, I thought it was just a sad coincidence. Not anymore. They visited me last night. These kids, their rituals, opened lots of gates. So many shadow people are coming through. Age, rituals, none of it matters any more..."

Greg pulls Amanda away. Shoves her towards the ambulance door. "Get in."

Amanda does so.

The woman grabs the handle. "I know you believe in them. These demons are stealing our souls! You must put that in your blog. Warn people!" She removes her fingers as Greg slams the door shut.

Amanda uses the side mirror to watch the woman as they drive away. She stands illuminated by a cone of light from a lamppost. Black shadows gather behind her, reach out.

Greg takes their next call. A few minutes into their journey he says, "What the hell was that about a blog?"

"I've been writing one."

"What about?"

"Oh, about flowers and cute fluffy bunnies. C'mon, Greg."

"Do you have a following?"

"Yes." She looks out the window at the houses rushing by.

"How many?"

"Over a thousand." Amanda lies. Best not to tell Greg how many followers she does have. It's closer to three million. Her stomach lurches as Greg swerves into a supermarket car park and slams the brakes on.

"What are you doing? We've a patient to attend to."

"You really don't get it. You're so far up your own arse you can't see what damage you're doing. I remember that woman. Her daughter was one of the ones you questioned about Rhapsody not long before I asked you to stop. Her father was following us in his car."

"You didn't ask me to stop. You told me." Resentment slips out with her words.

"Can't you see what your suggestion has led to? The daughter is dead, Dad has just died and Mum believes shadow people are coming for her. She also thinks they're stealing souls." He turns in his seat, gives Amanda a look of desperation that tugs at her. "I'm fighting an irrational belief system. Something based in the mind, not in reality. You're spreading a spurious and dangerous concept. Don't report what she said on your blog. Please, Amanda, I'm begging you. Shut the blog down."

Greg restarts the engine when she goes to answer. Resumes their journey. Amanda decides to keep quiet. When their shift ends, she will insist on a different partner.

*

Day Forty-One

Amanda makes herself a snack in the kitchen which used to be the hub of their family life. It's dark by four. The clocks have gone back, and Chris should be home from school in a couple of hours. His class is half the size it used to be. So many pupils have died. Worldwide figures are emerging for the number of young children and adults also succumbing to the effects of Rhapsody. It's as if humanity is stumbling ever more rapidly towards a point of no return. Mankind is on the brink of an inexplicable extinction. She wonders just how many people will be alive by the end of this coming winter.

Leaving the lights on, Amanda makes her way upstairs, tea and toast in hand, enters the bedroom. Once it's dark, every light in the house is turned on to banish shadows, keep them at bay. Her last shift was exhausting, and she's done nothing but sleep. Well, on and off. The nightmares which assault her make sleeping soundly difficult. Chris can't get a decent night's sleep either. It won't be long before both of them are too tired to function. Amanda plumps her pillows and gets comfortable. Taps Spotify, selects a Motown mix. Music plays. Amanda eats her toast, sips her tea while song lyrics and rhythms wash over her. It fails to relax her. She barely hears it. Her mind keeps replaying how many have died, how the age range is increasing. Ten days have passed, but for some reason, the woman whose daughter and husband died is foremost in her thoughts. All were victims of Rhapsody, no matter what Greg said, and the concept that shadow people were soul-stealing demons... She removes the earphones, placing them on the duvet. Amanda doesn't believe in God. The notion of a soul is alien to her, but she's witnessed the point where a person departs life so many times. Is the idea too nebulous to contemplate?

Could Greg be right? Can a suggestion carry so much weight it eventually tangles humanity into a web of self-deceit, leading to millions of deaths? Are the Rhapsody rituals responsible for these deaths, or is it down to people like herself, who bring to the illusion a belief that something concrete is happening? She sits, the tinny sound of discarded Motown beside her, wondering how much responsibility she bears. It's not self doubt which gets her out of bed, moves her towards the guest room. It's the niggle in her head saying the woman left standing under the lamppost might have a point.

Although she writes her blog in this room, Amanda stopped seeking answers when Penny died. Her grief remains raw. When staff shortages won out over compassionate leave, she boxed it away. Stored it at the back of her mind. Buried it under work. This was the only way she could cope with seeing other teenagers die. Looking at her flow chart, Amanda considers what pieces of the puzzle remain missing. Her brain is insisting something the woman said is the key to unlocking them.

Black marker in hand, she re-examines the chart,

crossing RHAPSODY NOIR out, as human agency is behind the suicides. This leaves two arrows under RHAPSODY. The first leads to EUPHORIA, the second to SPIRITUAL GATE. Amanda understands how the euphoria, felt by those partaking in Rhapsody, and the manner in which it was kept secret, has led to an increasing number of rituals. It became a cool thing to do. Yet the feeling this is A MEANS TO AN END remains. She underlines the questioning capitals. Then, bracketing SPIRITUAL GATE and SHADOW PEOPLE together, Amanda puts GROWING IN NUMBERS.

Her mind is in overdrive, recalling snatches of conversations, how the number of shadow people seen by those who were Rhapsodised grew from one or two to many. Penny's words, spoken on the night she died, come flooding back. *"There's so many Mum… I'm not dreaming."*

Overcome with emotion, Amanda whispers, "You weren't dreaming."

A piece of the puzzle falls into place: the Rhapsody ritual has led to the conscious opening of spiritual gates. Gates which would normally be incidentally opened in the dreamscape of the human psyche. It's as if the divide between the subconscious and conscious mind has fractured. No longer confined to the world of night terrors, shadow people are accessing the conscious world. Amanda recalls the shadowy fingers gripping Penny's skull, how her eyes rolled upwards, and her body jerked. The final piece clicks into place and the growing numbers of shadow people makes frightening sense. It's not souls she's seen taken.

"Life-force, energy…our bodies are full of electricity. We're a resource, fuel! They're draining people and getting stronger, growing in numbers."

"Can you hear yourself?"

"Fuck you, Greg." Amanda says, scribbling her thoughts on the wall. She is left with one question, which

163

she writes underneath. WAS THIS PLANNED OR DID WE CAUSE IT TO HAPPEN? She can't ignore how Rhapsody rituals might be the instigator of the shadow people's actions.

The lights flicker as Amanda turns the laptop on. She wants to write a blog entry while everything is fresh in her mind. It blinks off when the lights flicker for a second time. Movement from the landing catches her eye. Standing up, she calls, "Is that you, Chris?"

Silence.

The landing light goes out.

Hungry red eyes glint in the dark beyond the doorway. Shadowy fingers curl around the doorframe. They dissipate slightly, as if there's a breeze, then reform until there's a hint of solidity, revealing long fingers tapering to sharp, pointed nails, Amanda backs away. The guest room light flickers for a third time. A split second of complete darkness is all it takes for three figures to enter the room, accompanied by a smell Amanda recognises.

"No," she whispers. "Not now."

Miasma pours from the shadow people before her. This ethereal substance has a noxious reek. Amanda breathes in the sulphurous odour, with its sour, vinegary edge and finds a familiar bitter taste in her mouth. Seeing these presences when awake fills her with dismay. Weakens her limbs. Fear of succumbing makes her move. She clambers across the double bed, reaches the sash window. Looks over her shoulder. Two of the shadow people glide seamlessly towards her. The lightbulb dims as they close the gap. They stop on reaching the bed. Long slender arms stretch, the vaporous stench of them ripples the fabric. It is hard to tear her eyes away, to find the turn-lock in the centre of the window. Amanda fumbles with it as her eyes are drawn back to the entities. Their heads have no discernible features apart from the red eyes. These resemble embers from a dying fire. Their hands are the same as the one which ripped Penny from her life.

The third shadow person is different. It has more substance to its body, appears thicker, looks as if it is wearing a tailcoat. Apart from deep-set crimson eyes, its facial features come and go, as if seen through thick windblown smoke. They suggest a stern visage. On its head is a top hat. Top Hat smells worse than any decaying body she's dealt with. He advances. The light in the room flickers when he passes. Top Hat stands between the other two shadows and doffs his hat to her. This acknowledgement only increases Amanda's fear. Heightens her desperation to escape. He signals for those waiting on the landing to enter the room. Blackness speckled by scarlet embers, surges through the doorway. Amanda's fingers are slippery with sweat. She whimpers as the turn-lock refuses to budge. Rotates it the opposite way, releases the window.

Hordes of shadow people press into the room. The carpet between Amanda and the door is a black pit filled with scorching eyes and menacing claws. Her heart is clamouring, her nightshirt soaked. She cannot breathe. Her fingers slip on the window frame. Precious seconds are lost in the struggle to open the window slightly. She pulls the sash upwards, widening the gap, but it is so stiff she needs more leverage. Amanda puts her shoulder under the sash. As she forces a wider gap, cold air chills the sweat on her body, eases the fetor surrounding her. Top Hat raises his arms, brings them swiftly down in a chopping motion. The shadow people are upon her so fast, Amanda doesn't notice them move. Clawed hands swoop towards her, nails rake into her flesh, pierce the hard bone protecting her brain. The window gives. Opens. Amanda's eyes roll back. Intense pain jolts her body as they drain her. A sad truth occurs to Amanda at the moment her heart gives out. Whatever began this process of assimilation, it's too late to stop it. Even so, she hopes Chris reads what's written on the wall.

TO HAVE AND TO HOLD

I sense a presence behind me and linger near a shop to see who it is. The entrance to the mall frames a slender woman in a shaft of summer sun. The material of her dress is rendered translucent by the glare, revealing supple, athletic limbs. She trembles; perhaps in anticipation of finding him whom I also seek. I too am in physical turmoil at the concept of meeting and touching him. It seems we are united in our desire, but he will be mine. I swiftly walk away lest I am seen. The hunt begins.

While I search this man-made forest of steel girders, glass and concrete, my thoughts are on the man I love. Having glimpsed him once, I cannot wait to have him fully in my sights. The recollection of his finely-chiselled features and the strength of his physique send a shiver through my loins. The intensity of the sensation has me looking around the mall, seeking somewhere to relieve the dominant pressure of sexual longing, but I may miss him if I indulge myself. Once I regain control, I check the mass of humanity that surges through the mall as people continue their absorption in material delights. Wondering what draws them, I examine the displays behind the leaves of glass. There, amongst the people mirrored in the window's facade, I see her and realise from her expression that she has found him.

Her body is alert. She demonstrates a doe-like timidity in her approach which is hesitant, nervous. Despite her timidity, her movements are fluid and I see, reflected in the pane, her hands reaching out and suddenly, he is there. I gaze upon him as he turns his well-formed frame away from her, nonchalantly shrugs off her appeal. His beauty is precise, almost clinical. The longing to touch him causes my heart to flutter. I shake as I reach towards him.

167

Fingertips butterfly against my bare arm; they drink the nectar of my skin. Recoiling from the person's touch. I lose sight of him.

"Who's there?" I ask, swiftly turning.

All I see is a cluster of people crowding the window.

"Who's there?" a voice echoes my query. This is followed by a giggle. It's probably kids mocking me. Something else is said as I leave, but it is lost amongst the foliage of humanity.

The centre of the mall has a fountain beneath a pinnacle of glass piercing the sky. I go there in the hope that the patter of water, raining gently down upon the shallow depths, will calm my thoughts. I glance up as I sit on the low and curved concrete edge of the pool. All I see above are white clouds. Did my rival manage to touch him? Can she win his heart? Her approach was so timid! As was mine. Sighing, I look at the child who has sat beside me. He reaches towards the water and is briefly reflected in its surface before his hand dips, swirling his image into nothingness. Soft footsteps approach from behind and I see an ethereal figure whose dress flutters in the rippling water. I stand to face the woman I noticed at the shopping mall's entrance.

She says, "I... I'm sorry if I startled you earlier, when I touched you. I didn't mean to, it's just that I saw you in town and had to follow."

Her long dark hair hides her face as she stares at her feet. When she looks back up, her eyes meet mine. They're the colour of the sea on a bright summer's day, but I have no desire to drown in them.

She swallows, takes a deep breath, then says, "I don't know if you believe in love at first sight, but it's what I felt from the moment I laid eyes on you."

I say nothing. She's making me uncomfortable. Tentatively, one hand reaches forward, softly taking mine. Her skin feels cool. Holding my gaze, she moves closer, cups the back of my head with her free hand and pulls my mouth down. She fastens plump lips onto mine, flitting her tongue into my mouth. Letting her hand go, I grasp both of her shoulders and push her, none too gently, away. She staggers backwards, red mouth wide, and falls to the floor. I wipe my mouth on the back of my hand before I speak.

"What the hell! I don't care who you are, leave me alone!" Unable to resist, I stick the knife in: "Your beauty is nothing but a pale echo compared to that of the man I seek."

I know the water in the concrete pool isn't the cleanest, but I'm desperate to wash my mouth out. Sunshine streams through parted clouds making the fountain's spray glisten. When I straighten up, there is no sign of the woman. Hopefully she'll leave me be, allowing me to focus on finding the man I desire.

The afternoon is drawing to a close as I leave the mall. Its automatic doors part to reveal quietening streets. The sweat of thrumming humanity has been dispersed by the aroma of fish and chips, the cooling salt breeze from the sea. Seagulls wheel overhead; they call to me with their metallic cries. Many hover near the cafés, awaiting the right time to swoop, but one flies inland. Weaving my way between the remaining locals and tourists, I follow. The bird spirals upwards, then dips down heading towards the trees bordering the common. This piece of land stretches between the town's two major roads. I feel the rhythm of the music before it reaches my ears above the drone of the traffic. I dance between the trees towards its source as the lone gull flies ahead. The fair has arrived. Walking through the unlit multi coloured lights strung between stalls and rides, my excitement mounts. He could be here when night falls. Who can resist a summer fair?

*

I dress carefully. If he is there, I want him to be drawn as a moth to a flame. I choose jeans that fit snugly around my

169

hips and a tight t-shirt. There's no romanticism in my clothes; I have decided upon raw sexuality. Feeling confident I walk to the common where the sounds of carnival lift my spirits. I stride assuredly amongst the attractions, smile benignly at complete strangers, watch the flow of bodies past the stalls and rides looking for him. Music blares, a cacophony of sound mingled with the joyful screams of children and adults, the tumult of excited shouts and comments. Faces, lit by the garish colours of the bulbs, are akin to hybrid blooms. On the Waltzer, blending shades become a myriad blur but, as soon as the ride slows, their beauty withers.

Time passes. The sweet scent of candy floss, the spicy aroma of fried food arouses hunger. It's getting late. The initial bloom of people has thinned into stray blossoms littering the grass avenues throughout the fairground. Although I haven't seen him yet, I'm not concerned. I'm certain he'll be here. Somewhere.

Whilst waiting for my hot dog to be served, I examine the attraction across from the vendor's stand. It looks to be older than the others travelling with the fair, standing higher off the ground than many, with a porch-like area before it. I count the steps leading up to the paybox. There's eleven of them, almost a full flight of stairs. This high off the ground, the ride seems to loom over those who pass by. The sign on it proudly proclaims *The Hall of Mirrors* in large letters formed by flaking red paint. *Will you find your way through the maze?* sits in smaller, blue letters beneath. The wooden boards forming its frontage are splintered, ramshackle, and I can't see any mirrors within the dimly lit entrance. The vendor coughs, passing the hot dog to me once he has my attention. I'm starving. I eagerly bite into the orange-pink flesh, savouring the caramelised onions. I tenderly probe the meat from the white bread roll and find myself imagining him naked and pale, standing before the heat of my desire. Then I smell his scent above that of the fat on the metal fryers. It's carried to me on the cool night breeze, but I cannot see him. Movement on the stairway to *The Hall of Mirrors* catches my eye. The attendant has his back turned on the amusement's dilapidated opening. Has the man I seek just entered? Throwing what's left of my hot-dog away I swiftly mount the steps, slipping past the attendant before anyone notices.

The floor of the maze takes me back to childhood. Duct boards are neatly interlocked forming a passage extending before me. They creak beneath my feet, occasionally bend under my weight and I fear they may split, tumble me beneath. I enter a room filled with brightly lit distorting mirrors set before panelled walls. They look old, very old. None give a clear reflection and he's not here. I run past self-images of fat-thin, tall-short, enlarged head-wavy body until I reach the exit of this section. A smattering of letters proclaims, *Mirror Maze*.

This passageway is narrow – two adults would struggle to pass. It's dimly lit from above by single bulbs that hum and jitter. Flickering pools of darkness form where the lights spasm on and off. Mirrors, cracked and silvered with age, line the walls. As I walk between them, music from the fair dulls to an eerie drone and I can hear no footfall ahead of me. It's as if the decrepit mirrors drain energy, diminish all sound. Faced with a choice of left or right, I choose left. It doubles back into a dead end where an old mirror stretches my head. When I open my mouth and hold my hands either side of my face, I resemble an elongated version of *The Scream* by Edvard Munch. Shuddering, I turn back, retrace my steps, then take the right turn. The further I twist and turn along the next passage, the more choices the poorly-lit reflective corridors reveal. Mirrors with spots and fissures, reveal nothing apart from the shadowy shape of my passage jittering in time with the lights. My body becomes disparate parts separated by cracks in ancient glass. No noise penetrates from outside; I must be in the middle.

The lights go out.

Pressing my hands against the darkened glass on either side, I call, "Hello?"

No answer.

"Can anyone hear me?"

Silence.

I repeatedly thump on the mirrored wall to my right, shouting, "Can you hear me?", but the only sound is of glass splintering under my fists.

"Shit!"

I lash out and slap the unsplintered mirror on the other side. Unless he snuck inside the maze like I did, there's no way I'm not alone in here.

"Help!" I scream.

Nothing.

Chances are the fair-folk are retiring to their beds, congratulating themselves on a successful evening. Damn it. This has been a waste of time, a waste of a day. I begin edging my way forward, feeling for openings in the walls. I know how to get to the centre of a maze so, logically, working the theory in reverse should get me back to the exit. The thing is, despite the age of the damn thing, no light leaks through anywhere. I'm surrounded by pitch black. Fumbling my way into yet another dead end, the only noise I hear is my own panting breath. I'm certain that night and the sea breeze will eventually cool the air, but right now... I wipe sweat from my brow, lift the damp t-shirt away from my sticky back, then press my forehead against the mirror I'm certain is in front of me. There is a brief sensation of coolness, then the mirror clicks open.

I stumble down several steps. The smell of trampled grass and earth is strong but, thankfully, it is cooler here. My hair brushes against the boards above as I carefully move forward. If I can find the front or back of the amusement, I may find a way out. Arms outstretched, I begin navigating my way around. My hands brush against solid wooden supports and my left arm snags on the rough edge of a broken mirror.

Damn it. Blood is running down my arm from a shallow cut. I need to be more careful.

A glimmer of light catches my eye. It's set in the board a little way ahead of me. I'm feeling around the edges of what must be a hatch set into the board above my head, when my knee knocks against a mirror. It slides to the ground. The hatch resists the pressure of being pushed open, but a forceful blow with both fists slams it upward. The cut on my arm reopens and blood splatters my trainers, drips to the ground. Bright moonlight streams in. My eyes adjust and I crouch to lift the mirror on the ground back against the prop it slid away from. Instead, I gasp and find myself kneeling beside the bulrushes carved around the mirrors frame. Blood is running freely down my arm, but the cut no longer bothers me.

He is there, captured by moonlight in a perfect pool of glass, its bulrush rim surrounded by sweet smelling grass sprouting from dark earth. Nearby trees are shaped to hold the duct-board sky steady. Steady enough for hordes of feet to move through its mirrored heavens. I hear shallow breathing as his chest moves in unison with mine. For the first time, I get more than a glimpse of his features. In the moonlight his eyes are green. They reflect passion, longing, yet what I feel is no longer purely lust.

"I love you."

The words are out before I can stop them, but clearly he feels the same. His mouth forms the words the same time as mine, and the smile he gives immediately afterwards mirrors mine.

"I've been looking for you," I say, reaching to trace the line of his jaw with my fingers. His fingertips rise to meet mine. They block the contact. I frown and so does

173

he. I know he wants contact as much as I do – I can see he longs for me to touch him. Sitting back on my heels, I look at him, then reach out again. The fingertips of his left hand meet those of my right, but I cannot feel him. The surface of the pool is a barrier, it separates and divides. Reflected in his eyes is my desperation for us to be together, to be joined as one. But how? Looking at his beautiful face I'm filled with love. And desire. My emotions combust into flames, burning me to the core. I feel them scorching my lungs with each breath I take. Fire spreads through my torso, down my arms until it reaches my fingertips. The glass barrier between us begins to shift as I melt into its surface. I scream in agony as I tip forward and the glass pool begins absorbing my body. The intensity of my passion melds me with the man I love.

As I entwine my fiery limbs around his, from within the mirror, I see pale, cream coloured flowers issuing from ground saturated by my blood. The flowers are blossoming, softly speaking the depths of my insular desire through the golden flame at their heart. I linger for a moment while they whisper my name.

"Narcissus, narcissus, narcissi."

DEATH ON THE *MARY CELESTE*

My wrist phone interrupts breakfast. Damn it, my flakes will go soggy.

"Joe Jansen speaking."

"We've got three dead bodies on the *Mary Celeste*. Come see me as soon as you arrive."

Boss-man taps the call off. This is the first "job" I've had during my six month stint orbiting Sirius. It will be a change from my usual day of pushing paper around a desk, but I doubt it's a change for the better. You see, intergalactic theme parks are not all they're cracked up to be. While the rides are functioning perfectly they're harmonious places, enjoyed by visitors from every known galaxy. Sure, the occasional fight breaks out – they're easy to handle – but when an accident happens whoever gets hurt tends to point fingers at their ancient enemy. You know, the one they were at war with aeons ago before the Council was formed. So when a number of those on a ride die? Oh boy.

Every ride in the Mystery Theme Park has been taken from its original location. Only one mysterious item from each planet is allowed and, to minimise disruption of the space-time-continuum, an identical replacement is installed. This is a popular theme park with those who enjoy unsolved murders, disappearances, supernatural happenings et cetera. Opened just four months ago, it's seen a steady stream of visitors.

The mystery of the *Mary Celeste* is how the Captain, his wife, their child and the crew all disappeared, right? Well, the ship was Time Rescued just before the crew of the Dei Gratia spotted her floating in the mid-Atlantic. Now you can walk her tightly-nailed wooden deck, see the dining table set for the meal which never came, examine her cargo, touch the rough cloth of her tattered sails. The sway of the sea and the force of the wind? These you have to imagine. Here, the ship is docked in space under a dome catering for all the denizens who visit.

*

"Sit down, Jansen," Boss-man says as I enter his office. He indicates the chair across from his desk. "One of those dead is human, the other two are Talinessens."

Crap. Talinessens are humanoid beings with both fins and lungs. They also have four arms. Then there's the way they can change colour, blend into the scenery. They make excellent thieves and assassins. The Council has stipulated Talinessens must stay their natural blue when in any theme park, but this doesn't mean they do and it doesn't make me feel safer around them. And, for some reason, I find their natural skin colour makes me uncomfortable.

"The Council has decided a representative from Earth and Taliness must work together on this case. Apparently, the Talinessen detective currently serving at the park is very experienced. You're to do as they say."

"So there's no room for free thought or action, eh, Boss?"

Boss-man's face reddens. Then he's on his feet, leaning over the desk at me.

"You can think what you like, but this isn't a time for smart-alec comments, Jansen. An incident like this puts the future of the park at risk. Don't overstep the mark – is that clear?"

Shit. I nod. Relief floods my body as he sits back down.

"So, work with this detective and find who or what is killing visitors to the *Mary Celeste*. We need to get the ride reopened asap."

He dismisses me with a curt nod.

For the first time in my life I wish I wasn't a

detective.

It's quite a walk from Earth's department to where the *Mary Celeste* is located on the outermost ring of the park. Meandering streets contain visitors of all shapes and sizes. Many are some approximation of our form – different, but similar. There are those whose tentacles slither along. They leave a glimmering trail, easy to follow in the event of an incident. Others have claws and fur. They tend to meander from ride to ride, twitching noses sniffing the air, rising onto hind legs when near any savoury meats or sweets on offer. It never ceases to amaze me how popular candyfloss is with those from other planets. Animated billboards proclaim information about the rides on offer. They blast their announcements in various languages amidst the hubbub created by the intergalactic hoards thronging amidst the theme park's pathways. Quite the crowd has gathered near the *Mary Celeste*. Many of those present are Talinessens. I push my way into the cordoned area in front of the ship, check my wallet and keys are still where they should be. According to my wrist-phone, it's just before midday.

Due to the ride being one from Earth, it's subject to police procedures from my home planet. I step onto the deck, make my way towards the stern nodding my head approvingly at the officer charged with securing the scene. The bodies lie in close proximity to each other. The human's eyes and mouth are wide open. He lies alongside two Talinessen corpses. All three bodies have their fingers intertwined. Why on earth would they be holding hands as they fell? I notice the blue skin of the Talinessen corpses has faded to a dull grey colour, how each of them linked fingers using their uppermost hand. I briefly wonder what it would be like to have four hands.

Crouching down I look for gunshot and knife wounds; find no obvious injury on any of the bodies. The man and Talinessen female are dead in that blank life-has-exited way I'm used to seeing. The Talinessen male is different. Something of what he experienced lingers. Hovers expectantly in the body as if seeking an outlet. It's odd. Weirds me out somewhat.

I examine the deck around the dead hoping to find something. According to witnesses, all three dropped at the same time. Died on the spot. Right now, the only physical evidence is the three bodies. Perhaps the autopsies will reveal more.

The officer who secured the scene interrupts my thoughts. "Sir, the Talinessen detective is waiting for you outside."

"Tell him to get on board." I chuckle at my own joke.

"She says she can't, Sir. She's waiting on the walkway."

"Well, that's just great." I press on my knees as I stand, "I'd better go see her then."

"Yes, Sir."

Stepping off the *Mary Celeste* I find Talinessen officers are working alongside mine to clear the crowd. In time, only a few curious onlookers will remain to press up against the boundary. Right now, news of the incident is still spreading, drawing individuals to cluster. A billboard flashes a headline:

An accident has occurred on the Mary Celeste. *This ride is closed until further notice. There is no cause for concern.*

This is closely followed by:

NEW RIDE! The Intergalactic Mystery Theme Park is proud to announce the opening of the, ALPHON POWER PLANT RIDE. Experience the tension of an imminent explosion with no apparent cause!

And there it is, a distraction. The Alphon ride wasn't due to open for another week.

The Talinessen detective stands as far back from the ship as the cleared space allows without becoming one with the crowd. Like most of her species she's tall, but the planes of her face are angled and she's slender. Most of the female Talinessens I see around the park are fuller of face and body. They remind me of Kali – a goddess representing sexuality, violence and death. Talinessen females usually dress in thin material which hides little, wear it low on their hips and barely cover their breasts. Part of me admires their boldness, yet it makes me uncomfortable.

From what I understand of Talinessen culture, the detective doesn't have the roundness of features perceived as beautiful. Nor does her clothing push the boundaries, of what I would consider decent, until they break. Her knee length dress is modest. Perhaps it's the job. When she greets me, her brown eyes are level with mine. She offers a hand. Before I can stop myself, I'm pushing my own deep in my trouser pockets. The smile on her face falters. She dips her head. Shoulder-length brown hair falls forward.

"Yeah, I'm not the handshaking type." I'm trying to cover my own discomfort as well as hers. "Why won't you come onboard? I'd value your perspective on the position of the bodies."

She glances at the ship. An involuntary shudder runs through her. "I cannot, the emanations are too strong."

"Emanations?"

"Yes, psychic vibes. I felt nothing from the *Mary Celeste* when she arrived, but in the two weeks this ride has been open, they've grown. If I were to examine the bodies in situ, I… I might struggle." She looks troubled. "It is why I've sent none of my men to join the search for physical evidence. Have yours taken photos? Made notes?"

"That's all in hand. I'll arrange for the bodies to be taken to the mortuary. You know where that is?"

179

She nods and visibly relaxes. "Yes. I will read them there."

"I'll get the photos and copies of our notes sent over to your department."

"Thank you," she says.

I'm already moving away, striding back onto the ship so I can tell my men, they're on their own. Bloody Talinessen. They're too sensitive for their own good. I don't remove my hands from my pockets until I'm near to where the bodies fell.

*

I'm finishing my second coffee of the day when the voice call comes.

"Detective Jansen?"

"Yeah, who's this?"

"Detective Serinal. We met yesterday. The *Mary Celeste* incident."

"You took your time. The photos and notes were sent with the autopsies first thing this morning. You looked at 'em yet?"

"Yes, Detective..."

"And?"

"What do you mean, and?"

I can't resist. "Any psychic vibes?"

Silence.

I turn to grin at the officer next to me, notice the frown on his face, follow the grin through with a wink. He gets up and pointedly walks away. He was working with the Talinessen to control the crowd yesterday. Clearly they got to him. Removed his sense of humour.

"It's a joke, Detective Serinal, I'm pulling your leg."

"I doubt you would pull my leg, Detective Jansen. Yesterday you could not shake my hand."

Ouch.

"Okay, what can I do for you?"

"You can join me in the mortuary."

*

Twenty floors of Council offices are situated at the centre of the dome covering the theme park. It's as if the building holds this cover in place. The dome flows seamlessly, from the entry points on the rooftop docking bay, down beyond the outermost rides. Each planet has its own department situated over the first and second floors. A corridor separates the circular walkway around them into two halves. In the corridor's centre are a number of lifts. I enter one, press B for basement.

Amidst the bright lights, the Talinessen detective's blue skin has an iridescent sheen. She is reading the names on the storage drawers, turns at the sound of my footsteps and notes how my hands are already in my pockets. Is that disappointment I register in her face?

"What do you need me for?"

"I wish to examine and discuss the bodies with you, Detective Jansen."

She pulls open one of the drawers, her manner brisk yet tense. My jibe has got to her. I bite back regret as she walks across to a nearby table and begins shuffling papers with those four hands of hers. Upon the metal, with his head towards the centre of the room, lays the body of the man whose fingers were linked with those of the Talinessen woman. Rough stitching with thick thread forms a Y on the sliced torso, but the skull has been left intact for what this Talinessen needs to do.

I clear my throat, "We both know from the reports that there's nothing suggesting anything other than natural causes for each of these individuals."

"So why did they all die of heart failure at the same time?" She's rooting through the photos. "Background checks have shown no medical conditions that may have caused this."

"True. So where do we go from here?"

She holds a photo forward. It's the one showing the

position of all three bodies. "Would you agree it looks as if the three of them were linking fingers? Holding hands?"

"Yes, I noticed this yesterday, on the ship."

"I wish you had told me when we first met. It would have been useful."

"Why?"

"Because the pattern of the bodies tells me I needed to start my investigation yesterday."

"Okay." I perch on the desk, "What does the photo tell you? I'm all ears."

"My people do this when they're facing a psychic emanation which is too strong for them. Pretty much all of us have some psychic ability. We are taught as children how to use this method to ground ourselves and someone who is in danger." Detective Serinal places the photo on the table. Her fingers trace from body to body.

"So this was a rescue attempt?"

"In a way. It is a survival technique. Someone suffering from psychic...vibes..." – her voice sounds slightly bitter – "...will link with someone who cannot sense the emanations. These then pass through the link and are grounded, absorbed even, by the lack of sensitivity."

I get it, understand what she is saying, but it raises other questions. I gesture towards the cadaver. "So why did this man take hold of the Talinessen's hand?"

"I can only surmise it was an attempt to help her."

"Perhaps he had no choice," I say. "She grabbed him."

Detective Serinal lifts her chin. "Perhaps he linked his fingers with her to try and save them."

"You can't know that."

She gives a thin smile then says, "Detective Jansen, why these three deaths occurred is far more important than who took hold of whose hands."

My face reddens. I turn and walk over to the prone body with its scream of a Y, look at the waxy skin. "So why did they die?"

"That is where my expertise comes in. Can you record what I say?"

"Sure." A few taps pulls up the voice recorder on my wrist-phone.

Detective Serinal positions herself behind the man's body, flexes her fingers, then leans over, placing one left and one right hand on either side of the corpse's head. She presses her fingertips against its forehead, closes her eyes. I lean against the wall of drawers, tap my phone to start recording.

Her eyeballs move rapidly in their sockets.

"The images are fogged, not as obvious as they would have been yesterday. In the memories I can access he is exiting through a door onto the deck. He looks around, walks towards where a couple stand. The Talinessen man is collapsing, grabbing a hook embedded in the wood of the ship. The woman reaches for him. Their fingers entwine, she writhes, stretches out her free arms.

"'Help me!'

"He runs over, takes each of her hands in his own. Copies how she is holding her partner's hands. Locks his fingers with hers." Detective Serinal gasps. "Images – so many. He is afraid, terrified at what he sees, yet does not see. There is a smell." Her head turns to one side. "What is it? Oh, it is gone, whipped away by the wind..."

She falls quiet, then says, "There's just blackness now."

I watch as she opens her eyes, gently removes her fingers from the dead man's skull.

"This victim gave us little additional information." Detective Serinal says as she pushes the cadaver drawer back in place. "Shame the images were so rapid. I don't think he had time to make sense of them. Might be why he felt such fear. That's what caused his heart to give out. Let's try the woman next."

"Hang on, he died from fear?"

"Yes."

"How in hell do I know what you're telling me is true?"

"You think I am making it up as I go along? Twisting the facts to avoid admitting you are right? That in fact the woman grabbed his hands, forced him to hold hers?"

Oh crap. I hold my hands up. "Okay, I'm sorry, the joke about vibes was a bad one. I apologise."

She sighs. "If you think it was your joke that upset me, Detective, think again. It merely confirmed what I already suspected."

Double crap. And I'm under orders to work with this...female. Something holds me back from thinking of her as a woman. I try to ease the tension between us.

"Look, I'm sorry I upset you. We need to work together, so lets start again. No need to call me Detective Jansen, it's just...my name is Joe. Okay?"

Her eyes are pensive. I can tell she doesn't believe me, but protocol kicks in.

"Very well, Joe, but please accept my methods are different to yours. I access what people experienced using a psychic ability you do not possess. I merely report what I see through the eyes of the dead." She opens the drawer containing the Talinessen woman. "Call me Serinal."

"Isn't that your surname?"

"We have just one name in our society, carefully chosen by our birth mother. Serinal means I am a 'Sentinel of life'. Do you know what Joe means?"

"I have no idea."

Serinal laughs as if I've cracked the best joke ever. The sound is infectious, I find myself grinning as she places her fingers on the forehead of the woman.

"Give me a moment, I am pushing through fog to reach the memories of what this woman saw... Ah, she is entering a cabin at the rear of the deck. There is a bed where the captain and his wife slept, a cot which held their daughter captive at night. Her husband, Hanoni, gasps. His eyes are vacant. He appears to be listening to something she does not hear; moves swiftly ahead, disappears. She follows, finds a ladder leading below the first level.

"'Hanoni?' she calls.

"He is climbing up the ladder, but his eyes do not see her. Hanoni lurches across the deck. Stops. Stands still. He sways then weaves his way to the main deck.

"'Hanoni!'

"He does not respond. When he turns and staggers to the stern, his face is full of fear. She realises what is happening, tries to ground him. Images assault her. She sees… fear, anger, panic and out at sea… a turbulent vastness moving towards them. Horror, fear, overwhelming fear… She cannot save him. The wave is too strong. Some part of her calls for help, but she feels...distant, is submerged by the current. A human rushes to help her, their fingers lock and she is…a conduit."

Beads of sweat run down Serinal's face. She struggles to remove her hands from the dead Talinessen's forehead. Uses her free hands to assist with pulling them off. Staggers backwards, almost lands on her arse. I would laugh, but her skin looks dull. It's lost its sheen.

"Time for a break?"

She nods.

"You like coffee?"

"Never had it."

"Then it's time you tried some."

I lead the way out of the Council offices to a nearby coffee shop. Its customers are mainly human, but there are other species who've discovered it a useful boost. No heads turn as we enter. Why should they? Meeting up with intergalactic friends at theme parks is now the norm.

Serinal sits on a seat next to the window. Looks out onto the busy walkway. I keep a surreptitious eye on her while I queue, notice how her exhaustion shows in the tremor of her hands. She places her head in two of them. Dark hair curtains her face.

"Two Americanos with milk on the side. And two pieces of the chocolate cake." Some carbs might do her good.

"Thank you," she says as I set it all down, park myself in the opposite chair. She devours the cake before trying the coffee. Screws her face up, adds all the milk and three of the sugar cubes from the pot on the table. Stirs, sips, nods. "It is good."

"You've just ruined it as far as I'm concerned."

Mine is as it comes, unadulterated black.

"Well, as you Earthlings say, it takes all sorts."

"Mind telling me what happened?" I indicate the Council Offices which tower into view no matter where you are under the theme park's dome.

"The psychic power emanating from what her husband was experiencing is strong. The strongest I have ever come across." She drinks. Puts the mug down.

"I guess the husband was psychic; was she?"

"From how he was seen to be acting, I believe Hanoni had a strong ability. His partner though? Hard to tell. The psychic phenomena he encountered caused her to become a conduit. For that to happen, either it used pathways in her brain which existed, or it created them."

This time it's me pausing to drink coffee. I go to take a bite of my cake, find I've no appetite. Push it across to her. She's looking much better. Takes her time eating this slice. Between mouthfuls she asks, "Did you notice anything when you examined the bodies? Feel anything?"

"I've been checked and know I've no psychic ability, but the Talinessen man. Something lingered. Just felt like it was seeking an outlet. Somewhere to go."

186

Serinal freezes, cake halfway to her mouth. "Shit," she says, "I might need your help."

*

Back in the basement, Serinal opens the final cadaver drawer. It's clear she can feel the effect from the body as soon as its head is in view. After a few moments she crosses the room and sits on the table. Looks at me. I've already assumed a position against the closed drawers, hands in pockets.

"I take it you're right and need my help."

"I believe so, but let me check with my department if anyone else is available. Wait here."

She gets off the table, walks away. I hear the hiss of elevator doors as they open and shut, go to the male Talinessen body. The sense I had on board the ship of something 'hovering' has gone, but how powerful must it have been for me to feel it when I examined him? Clearly, for Serinal, the emanation remains strong, despite the passing of time. A surge of fear rises in my throat. I'm choking it back when Serinal returns. Her shoulders are slumped, face unhappy.

"No help from upstairs?"

She shakes her head. "Someone with no psychic ability is rare amongst our people. No one in the office fits that category, nor does any Talinessen visiting the theme park."

Recalling what Boss-man said earlier, I say, "You're the more experienced detective in this case. You could order me to do it."

"No, the person has to be willing. There are risks involved."

"Like what?"

"You saw how I struggled to break free from the woman? I might need you to help me break free of this victim during the examination. I might not be able to do it alone."

187

"Go on."

"I will be walking in his shoes but, if the vision becomes strong enough, fearful enough, it may begin to absorb me. If his point of view becomes mine, I need you to interlock your fingers with those on the two hands which are free. Instead of standing there grounding me, I need you to think about me, gather me in, pull me back before he dies."

"And if I don't?"

"I die."

I may be getting on with her better, but I'm uncertain I can hold her hand? However, I don't fancy her dying on me, that's for sure. Boss-man would kill me.

"In fairness, I may die anyway, but my only chance of surviving a psychic power-storm of this nature is to have a non-psychic individual pull me out. Your records confirm you are a human with no ability, who happens to be my partner for this investigation." She shrugs. "You have what we need to solve the case."

I swallow before asking, "Could I die? The man who tried to help the female Talinessen did."

"No. I'm trained in what I do, but there is one situation which may occur."

"Which is?"

"You might come out of this with new neurological pathways. There is no guarantee my mind will be intact, either."

Fuck. This just gets better and better.

"Can we do this tomorrow?" Damn it, my voice is cracking. "Give me a chance to get used to the idea?"

"If we want to understand why these people died it has to be today, Joe. Even in people with good ability, psychic memories get fogged up if left. Those of the woman were not easy to reach."

What can I say? She's risking her life, her state of mind whereas all I might get is new neurological pathways. Considering she does this as a job, I kinda admire her.

"Hell, let's do it."

*

This time, Serinal's entire body jolts when her fingertips touch the dead Talinessen's forehead. Me? I'm anxious as hell about what she's doing as I tap the recording button. I don't fancy her chances of coming out of this unscathed. Nor mine, for that matter. I breath in, remind myself of how I need to pay close attention to what she says in case her perspective becomes that of the man whose memories she is accessing.

"Ah, at last. The fog is breaking and Hanoni's images are clearer than those from his partner and the Earth man. He is walking the boards of the ship, watching ghostly figures move around the deck. Is amused; his ability is weak."

The dread I feel throughout my body isn't from being in the mortuary. Serinal's gone into this believing Hanoni's ability to be strong. What does the fact it's weak mean?

"Pull out, Serinal, we need to talk."

She doesn't respond, continues relating what she sees while linked to his memory. Chances are, I'm worrying about nothing. Serinal is trained in dealing with these situations. I leave her to it. For now.

"Ahead of his partner, he enters the Captain's cabin, sees the cross above the bed, the bible on the desk. A young child is resting in the cot. This image has depth. It is tinged with pale colour. Reminds me of old photos I've seen in the History of Earth museum. Faded brown hair against a slightly grubby pillow. She looks ill."

Serinal's head turns. "He hears a voice.

"'I won't have it. Drinking alcohol is banned, ungodly, and what we're hauling is denatured! You know as well as I do it's what made him blind and he denies it!

189

All but one of the redwood barrels are empty. Evaporated! That's what he told me. The man is taking me for a fool, I tell you! And the crew – they're acting like halfwits. The dizziness and nausea, I've told them it will pass. We've all been suffering from it. Eaten something rotten, that's all. We need to check our food stocks, throw overboard anything else which might cause us to suffer.'

"There's that smell again, the one the human experienced. Hanoni goes to the first deck trapdoor. It is stronger at the top of the ladder leading down into the hold... the scene is becoming more defined... as if he is there.

"Four men are drinking in a space cleared amongst hundreds of barrels. One of them is the blind man the Captain spoke of. Another sailor fills his flask, presses it into his hands. The blind man is speaking.

"'...cursed I tell you. Look at 'er history; three captains dead, one on 'er first voyage and I've 'eard tale of all manner of mishaps. It's why I can't see, why we're all sick. I've not had the shits, so it's not the bloody food. Hey, I'll drink to that. Unless we've drunk the barrel dry!'"

Serinal coughs. Twists to one side, retches.

"The stench of the fumes thickens the air down here. Hanoni cannot help but feel as if he is inhaling them." She tilts her head. "People are shouting. The sailors put their flasks in their pockets, help the blind one up the ladder. Hanoni is dizzy, feels sick, as if he's become hungover on the fumes... The hold extends beneath the galley where meals are cooked, the cabins those on-board sleep in. Fumes are rising into those areas.

"Now he's moving towards where two sailors and the Captain are standing. They are looking out to sea. The sky is stormy, wind is picking up, sails pull taut. A sailor rushes to assist another secure a loose rope. Hanoni staggers across a deck rising and falling with the swell of the sea. Looks up. An enormous funnel-shaped cloud is descending from a black and purple sky. Fierce wind drives it towards the ship until it fills the horizon. Orders given by the Captain are whipped away, but there is fear in his voice. The Captain and one of the seamen run towards the main deck house. Hanoni follows the other to where the lifeboat sits. This sailor shouts for someone to get a coil of rope, for others to come and help him. They free the lifeboat. Carry it to the stern. Use the coil of rope to lash it to a hook.

"Wind pushes the men, who lean into it. Tears at the sails, threatens to shred them. The lifeboat is pushed over. Rain lashes clothes and skin, makes the deck slick. The Captain's wife cradles their daughter into her bent-over body. The Captain and the sailor who went with him carry instruments. Using the rope they go, one by one, through riled-up waves into the tiny boat lifting and dropping with the ocean. The massive cone-shaped cloud draws close. The Captain is the last to leave. I watch the rope move against the wood of the ship as he swings himself towards the lifeboat. It is fraying."

Hang on. Did she just say, 'I'? Has she become one with Hanoni? I step towards her. "Serinal?"

"It is breaking! The rope is breaking!" Serinal rocks on her feet as if hit by something. Her free arms rise to shield her face. "The cone is hitting the ship! Encompassing it! The deck is swamped with knee-high water, there is so much water! The Captain's gone and the lifeboat is being dragged into the cone's vortex. The screams! I can hear them screa..."

I grab her hands. Push my fingers into the spaces between hers and grip tightly. Brace myself and think of our time in the coffee shop, of her eating cake, of her brown eyes, so full of life, her laughter, her smile, all the time gathering her to me, pulling her away from the water drenched boat, the wind, the sea, out of Hanoni's mind and off the *Mary Celeste*. Along with these thoughts, my mind is saying, *I've got you, I've got you, I've got you, and she's here. She's with me and I can see her form, feel her fear easing, her gratefulness. I become aware of how much she gives of herself so others can be safe, her love of life in all its forms. And I feel the horror and pain embedded in the thick, jagged knife scar, which runs from just below her left breast to her right hip. The distress the memory and mark on her body causes her. And she sees me. Experiences the shame I felt aged twelve after finding those images of Kali on my father's computer. Knows how my body pulsed and came. The horror I felt at what had happened. She feels my disgust at the mess soaking through my pants, penetrating the material of my trousers. How I thought my immediate ejaculation was unnatural; Kali was unnatural. Serinal sees how smothered my desire has become by self-perpetuated loathing, my avoidance of intimacy. I try to pull back, but she holds me, lifts a hand, strokes my face. Stop punishing yourself, she says.*

Then Serinal is gone and I'm holding her grey lifeless body in my arms.

*

The lift doesn't come quickly enough for my liking. I also want the corridor and walkway leading to the Taliness department to be empty. They're not, but people scatter before me as I run, shouting for them to get out of the way, until I'm through the door.

"Help her! Somebody help her!"

A Talinessen officer takes her from my arms.

"I think she's dying!"

"We will do our best to save her," he says. "It will take time. Come back in two days."

I think he's speaking to Serinal as he walks away, but his mouth is still.

Relief, hope, tiredness and aching muscles all hit in one go. I slump into a visitors chair. Sit for a bit. Think on what to do next. Guess I should go put Hanoni away. Take the recordings to the Council; they demonstrate what danger the *Mary Celeste* holds to anyone with the slightest psychic ability. By the time I return Hanoni to cold isolation, I've an idea. The replacement *Mary Celeste* should be Time Rescued for use in the Mystery Theme Park, and the original returned. Let the actual ship end up wrecked on some Haitian coast so the powerful emanations held within its wooden body dissipate in the sea. A handful of visitors might suspect the replacement isn't the real thing, but none would truly know. More importantly, nobody else would die. It's a marginally better idea than setting fire to it although, right now, part of me thinks flames are the best solution.

*

I couldn't help but be outside the Taliness department before the doors opened. The receptionist smiled as I entered.

"You're expected. Go down the stairs, someone will meet you at the bottom." She nods towards a staircase in the centre of the back wall.

A Talinessen wearing a tunic and trousers is waiting. We walk a little way down the corridor, stop in front of two huge doors. A scanner reads his eyes and we're entering a space which reminds me of a hospital ward. Equipment and beds, also a desk, are on one side of the room. Along the opposite wall is a water tank, filled with a variety of plants and fish.

"Serinal is in the recovery chamber," he says.

Life within the tank is vibrant, colourful. I notice Serinal gliding through the water, twisting her form around rock formations and through arches. As she comes to rest upon a large rock, I can see her skin has returned to its natural glistening blue. The gills on her neck open and close as her hair lifts upwards in the water. She looks so at ease in the water I find myself wishing I had gills. When she pushes off the rock to swim towards the surface, the scar on her torso serves to enhance the fluidity of her movement. It flexes with the musculature beneath.

I walk up to the glass, unsure of how to make my presence known. Serinal spots me, swims over. We smile at each other. I'm pretty sure my smile is the goofiest grin ever.

Hello Joe.

It's good to see you looking so well.

I am about ready for coffee. Want to join me?

Are you paying this time?

You did such a good job of choosing cake, you can treat me again.

She somersaults then holds still. Her four hands, her feet gently stir the water. I both see and sense her beauty, her quiet, unassuming beauty. She reminds me of what it's like to be a teenage boy, but in a good way.

I… I'd like that.

A blue palm is pressed against the glass, I mirror her action.

Guess you are buying me coffee then.

REMEMBRANCE DAY

The early summer sun is warm as Hannah walks across the lawn to the small walled herb garden her grandfather often weeds. Her favourite t-shirt and black calf length trousers absorb the heat while Hannah strides towards her destination. The t-shirt details the cover of a favourite album – *Phantasmagoria* by The Damned. Her gelled and spiked hair reflects one of her musical icons: Siouxsie Sioux. Smiling happily, she steps through the arch set in the walls. The pungent smell of thyme, parsley and basil greet her.

Before Granddad arrived, railway sleepers were used to construct raised beds high enough for the old-timers to perch on and tend the plants with ease. Today, Granddad's trowel rests beside him on the wooden bench in the centre of the garden. His shoulders are rounded, and his body appears slack, deflated. His hands sit limply on his thighs. Usually Granddad holds himself upright, shoulders firmly back, despite his frailty, and his hands are busy pulling out weeds or planting seedlings.

"Hi Granddad." The cheerful greeting belying her concern, Hannah sits on the sleeper opposite the bench. His hands are clean; he's done no weeding today then. The face which looks towards her is thin, already browned by the sun and heavily lined, but Granddad's eyes are alertly focused as he smiles.

"Hannah! Good to see you." Granddad falls silent, then looks across at something in the raised bed.

"What is it?"

"It's a poppy." He pats the bench, "Sit here and you'll see it."

Clearly the poppy has just bloomed. Its red petals glow with health. Hannah knows this flower holds a difficult place in her grandfather's life. He's never spoken to

195

anyone, not even Grandma, about his experiences in World War One. A few months before Grandma died, she told Hannah how Granddad would wake screaming in the night. His skin told no story, it bore no scars, but Grandma said he screamed as if he was in terrible physical pain. According to one of the carers in the home, Granddad still suffers with nightmares.

"Would you like me to remove it for you?"

His large hand takes hers and squeezes hard. It's as if her offer has given him strength, for Granddad straightens his back, pushing his shoulders into place. Although not a tall man, once Granddad is sitting upright, his bearing makes him appear so.

"No Hannah. The colour reminds me of blood…of the trenches, but leave it be." He pauses then comments, "It's made me think about a particular day on the Western Front."

His body and breathing remain calm, but tension has entered the walled space they sit in. Despite the sun's warmth, Hannah shivers and goosebumps briefly flare upon her bare arms.

Turning towards her, Granddad says, "What happened on that day beggars belief." His eyes hold an unspoken plea.

"Do you want to talk about it now?"

"I need to." It's almost a whisper, yet the torment in his voice makes her blood feel like ice. Steeling herself, Hannah squeezes Granddad's hand just as hard as he squeezed hers moments ago.

"It's okay Granddad. You can tell me."

The sun continues to warm the stone which surrounds them yet, as Granddad speaks, Hannah finds herself rubbing her arms as if she were cold.

*

19th September 1917

Tom felt the man's eyes on him as he wrote a letter home

whilst sitting in one of the dugouts under the front wall of the trench. He was surrounded by damp mud, but Tom's uniform was relatively dry. The incessant summer rain, which had turned the narrow sandbagged channel into a quagmire of mud, had eased considerably. Six months had passed since Tom signed up. He'd just turned seventeen. Lying to serve in the war felt right at the time, but Tom missed being home. Some men were hardened, others just waited to die, causing Tom to wonder if surviving this war was an option; for if the Germans didn't kill him, foot rot probably would. The soldier's continual staring made Tom feel increasingly uncomfortable. He folded his unfinished letter, stuffing it into one of his pockets. Without making eye contact he quickly made his way further down the trench to where Harry, Ernie and Jim were playing rummy.

"Can I join you?"

"Sure." Jim's cigarette stuck to his bottom lip as he spoke. "You fed up of being eyeballed?"

"Yes." Tom picked up the cards Harry had dealt him.

Ernie leant towards Tom, "'E's a bit of an odd 'un. Not seen him before, nor's 'Arry."

Harry grunted in agreement.

While they played cards, Tom couldn't help but glance at the newcomer. The soldier's uniform didn't fit; it was as if he'd pieced it together himself rather than being kitted out. The trousers were far too short, and the sleeves of the jacket didn't reach his wrists. He was clearly very tall. His eyes were a piercing light blue, with what looked to be arching blonde eyebrows, but his hair was hidden under the large helmet which almost covered his forehead. He was clean, too clean, and very pale. Despite the rain, Tom's skin had browned, unless it was ingrained dirt, but no other soldier in sight was that pale. Despite the narrowness of the trench, those walking by avoided the man.

"Rumour 'as it we're fighting tomorrow," Ernie said, "We're taking the Menin Road Ridge to move us towards Passchendaele."

"Let's get through today shall we." Jim sounded irritated.

His mind on his cards, Tom didn't notice the others abruptly standing. When he looked up, they were saluting an officer. Swiftly joining in, Tom caught a disapproving look and quickly apologised. The officer switched his gaze to Harry.

"You, come with me."

As Harry left, they settled back down to play. Taking a pack of cigarettes out of his pocket, Jim offered one to Tom.

"Take two, and give one to the new soldier. Might as well welcome him, he might be alright when you get to know him. I can tell you're curious." A wink accompanied this remark and Tom felt his face flush. Taking two cigarettes he made his way to where the soldier sat.

"Here." Tom proffered the cigarette.

The gaze which met Tom's made him inwardly recoil. The cold depths of the soldier's pale blue eyes washed over Tom like a wave of despair. All he was certain of was that the man was suffering. When the newcomer smiled, a brief gleam of hope shone bright.

"Thank you." His voice was lilting, almost musical.

"Are you from Wales?" Tom asked.

"No. I'm not." The soldier replied. He didn't take his eyes from Tom's as silence grew between them. Unsure of what to do, Tom looked at Jim, but he and Ernie were smoking, having a quiet laugh.

"Well, I'd best get back to the game."

The soldier gave a knowing smile and nodded. "Thank you for your kindness."

Tom felt the man's eyes boring a hole in him as he walked towards Jim. The short distance stretched out before him, his friends never growing closer. Jim laughing at something Ernie said. An eerie silence was all that reached Tom's ears, as if he was in a vacuum. Fear welled, stirring his gut, his limbs turned to jelly and suddenly he couldn't move, became an observer in a bubble of exclusion. The soldier peering over the trench wall with a periscope turned and Tom lip-read,

"Minnie coming in!"

A shell exploded in the centre of the trench. The shock wave ricocheted off the sandbagged walls; thick mud and body parts landed in dug-outs. The ground shuddered as the impact rippled outwards. Tom lost his balance. Skin, blood and bone evaporated into a red pulp which sprayed over the ground, sandbags and survivors. Jim and Ernie climbed out of the trench onto No Man's Land, rifles in their hands and grim looks on their faces. Tom's ears were ringing. Realising he was unarmed, he dizzily stumbled to a nearby dug-out looking for a rifle. His hands were painted red from the blast, his uniform splattered with matter – it was in his nostrils and mouth. Tom retched. A hand on his shoulder roughly pulled him around.

The man looked calm despite the bloodbath as he shouted in Tom's ear, "Stay with me if you want to live."

Tom realised it was the blue-eyed soldier leading him rapidly in the opposite direction to the one Jim and Ernie had taken. Seconds later, another blast thudded into the sandbags. Glancing back, Tom saw it had landed where he'd been standing. Suppressing a shudder, he continued following. A wave of soldiers made movement through the narrow, slippery trench difficult. Some looked at Tom as if wondering what he was doing, but his coating of gore meant no comment was made. They probably assumed he was injured, unable to fight. That or a coward. Tom didn't fancy getting shot for cowardice, so he grabbed the arm of his rescuer.

"We can't run away. We need to fight."

The man's icy eyes were tinged with guilt. "You will fight, but from a position where you can win and live."

"What the hell do you mean?"

Pointing further down the trench, the soldier said, "We climb out there."

"I need a rifle."

"There will be one on the ground. Keep low as we reach the top."

Tom's mouth went dry. Why did this man expect a rifle to be ready and waiting on the ground? Something was off. After a few more yards, they climbed out onto an empty section of No Man's Land. A discarded Enfield P1914 lay a few feet away. Grasping the gun, Tom asked, "How did you know?"

"Later. First we need to go that way." A slender hand pointed towards the infighting, "Then we go deeper into No Man's Land. We skirt the battle, but you will get to fight."

"Why the hell didn't we follow my mates and go straight there?"

"The ones you were playing cards with? Because you die."

Keeping in a crouched position, the soldier hurried towards the gunfire and earth-shattering explosions a short distance ahead. Tom knew they were getting close when the screams of men and horses became a howl amongst the rapid Maxim and Vickers machine guns, the deafening bombardment. Sunshine tinged the hazy battlefield smoke yellow. It was hard to tell who was German or British. Ahead someone swung around, shooting a soldier Tom could barely see.

"To your left." The instruction was quiet.

Tom swiftly dispatched not one, but two Germans before they had a chance to register his presence. A hand signal to go right sent Tom scurrying behind some sandbags where a dead war horse lay. It had a fresh bayonet injury to one of its hind legs, indicating that not long had passed since it had been shot. The soldier placed his hand against the bullet hole in its forehead and sighed.

"I'm always too late. If you didn't talk before leaving the trench, I might have reached this magnificent animal before they kill him. His leg has an injury I can heal, but you always talk."

"What are you on about?" Tom kept his eyes peeled for enemy movement, but the noise of war seemed to be moving further away from them.

"Not now. German soldiers are beginning to sweep across behind those who are fighting. They aim to find and kill enemies who are injured. We need to move."

"You can at least tell me your name."

"Call me Glenhalidral."

"Sod that. I'll call you Glen."

Not knowing what else to do, Tom followed Glen out from behind the sandbags. Yet again they skirted around the fighting. Hearing men dying didn't appear to affect Glen, but every time a horse screamed, his hands formed fists. As they crept into a blast hole littered with the remains of bodies, Tom remarked, "I've had enough of this. You've got me creeping around, hiding amongst dead bodies, while my mates are fighting. I'm a soldier, Glen. I need to get out there. That's what I joined up for."

"Fine." Glen waved him out of the crater.

Tom didn't stop to think why the change of heart. He scrambled out only to be hit by a stray shot. Clutching his shoulder, Tom slithered back into the crater. Blood streamed from the wound. The bullet hole had exploded through, fragmenting bone.

"Shit!"

"Indeed," commented Glen, "but I've learnt that no matter what I say, you leave. If I try to persuade you to stay, that shot never happens and instead you die. This injury I can heal."

Glaring at his companion, Tom removed his hand to find it coated in fresh blood.

"Try not to scream this time," Glen said taking Tom's arm and immediately inserting one of his thin fingers into the wound. Tom bit back a yell just as Glen's free hand covered his mouth. But Glen's warning glare did nothing to prepare Tom for what happened next.

*

He is in the trench after the first blast. His ears are ringing so badly, he doesn't hear the second shell. It hits him and in the brief second before his body disintegrates, into a scattered mess of unidentifiable body parts and splinters of bone, every nerve in the body Glen is healing alights with searing pain. Then Tom is following Jim and Ernie, having been handed a rifle by Glen. He is immediately in the fray of battle. A bullet shatters his knee, causing Tom to collapse in the damply churned mud of No Man's Land. At first, he is grateful the mud is firmer now, at least he isn't sinking into the stinking gloop which swallowed so many soldiers during the summer. Then a German soldier kicks Tom flat and a hot, savage pain erupts from his stomach as he is sliced open by a bayonet. Leaving him for dead, the German soldier moves on. Tom stares at his gaping flesh, tries in vain to push the sides together. Blood is pooling around his body when Glen appears. He pulls a small package from the top pocket of his uniform. It unfolds into a fine, gossamer cloak which glistens briefly before assuming the colours around it. He covers them both. Glen's hands plunge into Tom's guts. He screams in agony, shocking Glen into pulling his hands out. As he does so, Tom's intestines spill over the slippery soil. He can no longer feel his body; his life is ebbing away and darkness claws inwards until there is no existence. Next, Tom is climbing out of the trench and a rifle is before him. He picks it up and, following Glen, he moves across the ground towards the infighting. After Tom notices the soldier killing an enemy, Glen motions him to wait. The shock of the bullet entering his skull from behind stuns Tom who falls forward. Something is oozing down his neck onto the boot churned mud. The last thing Tom hears is a man crying in despair, but it isn't him.

Tom sustains a number of injuries before Glen gets the timing right to secure him safely behind the sandbags. Then comes the trek across uneven mud to a shell crater. Each time Tom is injured, Glen heals him. Every time he does this, Tom relives the deaths and injuries prior to getting this far in the day. Then comes the moment Tom first leaves the crater. Angry after arguing with Glen, he scrambles out running towards the fighting. But his anger blinds him and instead of watching where he's going, Tom runs straight into the pathway of a war horse. It rears, throwing its rider who lands awkwardly. Tom hears the man's neck snap, sees a British arm patch as a limp body bumps across the mud. A hoof clips his forehead and Tom falls. The weight of the horse lands on his thighs, snapping the bones. Then it charges across him, forcing his body into the partially dried mud which resists the pressure. Finally, it's hooves smash his ribcage puncturing his heart, which pumps out until his veins run dry. This is an agonising death enhanced by Tom's guilt over the British soldier. As Glen continues healing his current gunshot wound, Tom's body registers, yet again, every crushing step the war horse made.

*

Tom sobbed. Tears cleared streaks of dirt-ingrained skin through the blood on his face. Time passed, but Glen seemed in no hurry. When Tom could catch his breath he said, "What the hell did you do to me?"

"I healed you. It's a simple task for me, but clearly a hard one for you to endure."

Wiping snot from his nose with his sleeve, Tom

drew a ragged breath. He could taste the stench of death surrounding them. "Just tell me what's going on."

Glen shifted uncomfortably before speaking. "You recall I told you I wasn't from Wales." Tom nodded. "I'm not from this time or place and I'm not human. I'm an elf."

"Sod off, you're pulling my leg!"

Glen shook his head, his expression remaining serious.

Tom gave a bark of laughter. "God help me, you're insane."

"Then how do you explain the healing you've just received?"

Pulling his uniform away from where the bullet had entered, Tom could see his skin was perfect. No blemish, no bullet wound. Yet the hole left by the path of the bullet through the stained fabric was as clear as day. He gasped as memories of dying began to swamp his mind. "Bloody hell," he whispered, quickly shrugging his shoulder back inside the rough cloth, trying to ignore the dizzying terror which filled him.

"Elves are peaceful," Glen remarked. "We do not seek war, but where I'm from, a great evil is growing. Usually our bows provide food, but now they are being used in combat. Many of us have been trained to fight with swords forged from the finest metals available to our smiths. There is honour in fighting evil, but we rely on tactics and skill. Your warriors use machines, which blast a body to pieces no matter where they're aimed." Glen nodded towards the rifle resting beside Tom. "Then there's the way you abuse your mounts. I have a horse and together we're skilled hunters. Whiteflame and I are in accord, or at least, we were. Since war began, hunters have been sent out with warriors and used for scouting missions. I found although I relish hunting, I don't enjoy battles."

Glen fell silent, then drew a strange pattern in the

thinly crusted mud. Wiping his finger on his uniform, he explained, "That is the rune of my city. The camp I scouted for was ambushed; became over-run. I deserted, fled full of fear and returned, the bearer of bad news. Or so I thought. On nearing home, I gave myself an injury, but our healers are skilled; they knew the wound was too recent. Also my beloved horse refused to meet my eyes when I groomed him in the stables. Whiteflame has a warrior's heart and I'd forced a coward's retreat upon him. When those I'd left behind won the battle and sent news, my people discovered the truth. A Council was called to pass judgement on my actions. They asked a wizard to throw me into an abyss of time and place until I redeem myself."

"How will you do that?"

The impact of a shell blasting a fresh hole nearby shook the damp ground.

"We're out of time."

Glen pulled Tom to his feet and together they left the crater.

The fighting had moved nearer. Glen signalled for Tom to stay close. A quick look established they were roughly in the centre of No Man's Land. Glen began sneaking forward, using every sandbag or dead body pile and crater to avoid being seen. He moved in a manner Tom now saw was that of an experienced hunter. Knowing he was clumsy by comparison, Tom did his best to keep his movements smooth. After a while, Glen stopped near some sandbags, placing a hand on Tom's arm as he drew level.

"We stop here, but need to hide. Stay still and be quiet."

Glen sat down against the sandbags, motioning for Tom to join him. Covering them with his cloak Glen said, "You speak, you get shot and I have to heal you."

Tom swallowed his words; boots were moving towards them. It wasn't the thought of a shot to the head or bayonet to the belly, that kept Tom silent as the German soldiers searched, it was the fear of another healing. More than once, Tom heard a man scream. When the German soldiers were out of earshot, Glen shifted slightly so he could look at Tom, but kept the cloak over them. Sweat ran down Tom's back. The air under the cloak was becoming humid and dampness was seeping into his underwear.

"Now I will answer your question. To redeem myself, I must save a warrior from death in battle. I am saving you by taking steps to keep you alive; learning what happens to you, when and how you get injured. As soon as this battle ends, we'll return to your trench."

"But that may be hours away." Tom protested. "Do we sneak around like this all day?"

"Yes."

"And how many times will I get injured?"

"I don't know. Not yet."

"And I go along with this?"

"Yes, because you want to live."

Tom couldn't deny he wanted to live; to survive the war, to return home and feel his mother's arms around him. Glen whipped the cloak off, creating a brief breeze in the still air.

"Follow me."

They inched forward. Due to their slow pace, Tom's thoughts began intruding; how Glen knew things, the way Glen had made him act and what had been done to him in the name of redemption. Tom realised he would rather die than suffer another healing. He began to tremble at the thought.

Glen said, "Up ahead."

Shakily lifting his rifle, Tom shot at the soldier who'd turned to look behind. He missed. Luckily, his next shot hit the German in the chest, but the second soldier was in the process of firing. The bullet went through Tom's side. Clenching his teeth, Tom aimed. The second German fell.

Glen's face was white. "Before today you've not missed, and we've gone forward. I don't know what this changes. I cannot be certain the soldier you shot in the chest is dead. Still, there is no time for debate, we must go."

He scurried forward keeping his body low. Tom followed as quickly as he could, hand pressed against his side, ignoring the pain. Blood was soaking through his uniform. Glen used a pistol tucked into one of his boots to swiftly dispatch the soldier wounded by Tom's shot. Clearly Glen was an accomplished killer, swift, silent and deadly – when he chose to be. It was also obvious, from the way he threw the gun aside, that using the pistol was abhorrent to him. He stopped when they reached a mired Mark IV tank. The barrel of its side gun-turret just cleared the mud, and the front end was tilted further skyward than design intended. Glen scooted beneath the upraised Mark IV. When Tom hesitated, a hand shot out and pulled him under.

"It won't topple," Glen declared, as Tom slumped down. "Now I'll heal you."

"No. I don't want you to."

Glen frowned, shrugged his shoulders, then swiftly jabbed two fingers into Tom's throat. Tom gasped for air as Glen pulled him flat on the ground and calmly undid his jacket. Feebly Tom tried to push him away, but Glen folded Tom's arms across his chest, then rolled Tom on his front. After lifting the jacket and shirt so the exit wound was revealed, Glen sat on Tom's body and calmly pushed a finger into the shredded flesh, while pressing Tom's face against the ground with his free hand. Disabled by the blow to his throat Tom felt he was in danger of suffocating as, once more, he was slammed into memories of death and agonising pain. This time, there were more instances to recall.

He struggled to stop screaming after the healing.

Although his face was no longer pressed into the dirt, Glen's hand remained firm against Tom's mouth. His blue eyes were cold, uncompromising. They passed judgement on when to let Tom go, when to allow him to sob without restraint. They looked away when Tom vomited bile onto mud which had seen countless deaths, sucked living bodies and machines filled with men, under to suffocate and drown as fodder for the hungry earth. Mud for which those deaths suffered by Tom were as nothing. Once he'd mastered himself, Tom said, "Remove your helmet."

"Why?"

"Because in children's tales elves have pointed ears. Plus, you're too bloody tall to work for Santa."

Glen undid the strap and pulled his helmet off. Tom prayed his ears were normal, the same as his own. They were pointed. The tips stuck through roughly-shorn blond hair. Glen tucked it behind his ears, revealing not just how large they were, but also how angled his face was. His high forehead had been hidden, the true shape and slant of his eyes had been shadowed and the arc of his eyebrows disguised. Helmet removed, it was clear Glen was not human. He was also breathtakingly beautiful.

Awestruck, Tom spluttered, "Just how many times has this...happened?"

Amusement flickered across Glen's face. "I've lost count."

"And if I die today?"

"We start again. Only next time I have to allow for the fact you may miss a shot you've managed several times before. Listen, we need to hide. They've not spotted us under here so far. Just remember, stay still and be quiet." Glen began unfolding his cloak.

"Did your Council give you that to help you redeem yourself?"

"You've not asked me this before. Why are you asking now?"

208

"I'm curious."

"No," Glen replied. "I just happened to have it with me on the day judgement was passed. It was woven for me by my mother. She began it the day our Council declared we were joining the war."

Tom instinctively knew Glen had taken the cloak with him in the hope he could evade whatever judgement the Elven Council passed. He didn't say that though. Instead he asked, "If the Council had known you had the cloak, would they have taken it from you?"

Glen shook the cloak out vigorously. The face he turned to Tom was devoid of expression. However, under the chilling blue veneer of his eyes was guilt.

"They'd have taken it off you."

"Be quiet." Glen draped his cloak over them.

Tom pulled it off. "Why me?"

"The answer is simple. You showed me kindness. I felt you deserved saving."

Horror swept over Tom as he realised the simple act of offering Glen a cigarette was what had caused him to be chosen.

Choking back his immediate response, Tom said, "Look Glen, you may be an excellent hunter and an efficient fighter when you have to be, but you're not brave. I think that to save someone from death in battle, you need to be brave. Perhaps you need to sacrifice your life for mine. When the soldiers you wish to hide from get here, I'm going to fight. You should join me."

"That is madness! Get under the cloak and they will pass us by."

Tom peered out and saw a group of Germans emerging from a bank of sandbags they'd passed a short time before reaching their hiding place. He shook his head then stepped out from under the tank saying, "I hope I don't see you again."

*

19th September 1917

The soldier's continual staring made Tom feel increasingly uncomfortable. He folded his unfinished letter, stuffing it into one of his pockets. Without making eye contact he quickly made his way further down the trench to where Harry, Ernie and Jim were playing Rummy.

"Can I join you?"

"Sure." Jim's cigarette stuck to his bottom lip as he spoke. "You fed up of being eyeballed?"

"Yes," he said picking up the cards Harry had dealt him.

Ernie leant towards Tom, "'Es a bit of an odd 'un. Not seen him before, nor's 'Arry."

Harry grunted in agreement.

While they played, Tom kept looking at the new soldier. At one point the man's cold blue stare met his. Turning back to his companions, Tom said, "There's something not right about him. I'm steering clear." In truth the sensation which filled Tom wasn't to steer clear, but to run. Belgian soldiers were stationed roughly a mile further along the line and Tom had an overwhelming urge to join them.

"Pick your cards up Tom," Ernie said. "Rumour 'as it we're fighting tomorrow. We're taking the Menin Road Ridge to move us towards Passchendaele. Be nice to get a few games in before we go."

Instead, Tom got to his feet, saluting the officer who'd just entered their section. The officer nodded at Tom, then frowned at Ernie who'd been immersed in his cards.

"You, come with me," the officer said, motioning for Tom to follow. Overwhelming relief flooded Tom's body.

"Yes, sir."

Tom couldn't help but glance back as he followed the officer. The soldier who'd been staring at him was on his feet, anguish then anger curdling his face as he

210

realised Tom was leaving. Time slowed and Tom felt as if he was being sucked down into wet mud. Fear welled, stirring his gut, as he struggled to move forward. The blue-eyed soldier walked towards Tom with ease. His mouth began forming words and one of his hands clasped, as if holding a ball, then drew back and threw *something*. Tom instinctively tried to run as it hit him in the back. He bit back a yell as *something* spread out, soaking through his uniform as if it were water. It rippled across his skin like a swarm of insects. Tom's hands clawed at his uniform, desperate to get beneath the material, to brush away whatever was now crawling across the flesh of his back. Too late. *Something* wormed inside, mingling with his cells, with the very fibre of his being. Tom's mouth opened to eject the scream his lungs had formed. Suddenly the day jolted into motion and the scream died in his throat as Tom almost crashed into the officer, who was heading towards the Belgian section of the trenches.

The officer began briefing Tom. "There was infighting further along the line yesterday. You'll be checking those bodies you can find for identification and personal belongings. There will be a truck to remove those you've dealt with for burial."

"Will the bodies be going home, sir?"

"No, Private. A mass grave is being dug. You may find there are German soldiers doing the same as us. Let them be. They've as much right to deal with their dead as we have. This is a peaceful operation, but I warn you now, not a pleasant one. However, it is of the utmost importance to the dead and their families that we do this."

An explosion sounded behind them causing the ground to shake. Turning to see where the shell had landed Tom gave a gasp. An image flashed into his mind of a body exploding into bloody pulp. The officer pulled Tom back as he automatically went towards the sounds of warfare.

"Leave it, Private. You'll get the chance to fight tomorrow." The officer looked stern, so Tom fell back into step behind him. Some of the nearby soldiers began climbing out of the trench.

*

Tom turned yet another mangled body over to the sound of distant warfare. This soldier had been sliced from chest to groin. Intestines slid out onto the churned and bloody ground. They stank. The whole area reeked of death, shit and rotting bodies. Trying not to retch, Tom glanced at the man's face and saw his own. Suddenly he was there, on the battlefield feeling the pain this soldier had suffered. Knew how he'd clutched his sides together in an effort to keep his guts inside his body. Saw a soldier with ice-blue eyes appear beside him. This soldier threw a strange cloak over them both and plunged his hands inside Tom's ruined body. The pain was overwhelming. Tom pushed the corpse away. He sat on the gore-strewn ground panting, wanting to vomit. Another soldier on the same duty as Tom, looked sympathetically at him. Tom got back to work, methodically checking the pockets of the dead, loading those he'd finished with onto a nearby open backed farm truck. The day progressed and the fighting near the British trench continued. Tom found many of the bodies he touched were triggering visions. He was unwilling to call these occurrences memories as he'd suffered no injury since arriving on the Western Front. Yet Tom recalled the circumstances which surrounded each wound or death, felt agonising pain. Almost every remembrance featured the blue-eyed soldier. When one of the visions revealed what this soldier did to him, something in Tom began to give.

He curled into a ball on the ground sobbing. Felt arms picking him up, knew he was being carried. The nurses in the Field Hospital were tender – Tom could tell from their eyes they'd seen soldiers like him before – and the doctor, who briefly checked him over, complained bitterly about sending a boy to do a seasoned soldier's job. Tom didn't trust himself to speak. He knew the injuries and deaths he experienced in his visions happened. Also, if he told anyone that one of the soldiers in the British contingent was an elf, they would label him insane, lock him up. He felt a coward for leaving the blue-eyed elf before the first shell hit. His desertion meant another British soldier would be chosen in his place, and that soldier might be one of his friends. He'd condemned someone else to suffer an unbearable fate at the hands of the cast-out elf.

During the night, Tom woke screaming from memories of the deaths he'd evaded.

*

Hannah puts her arms around Granddad when he stops talking. She holds him tight against her as he quietly sobs. Tears trickle down her cheeks, but in truth she's uncertain how to respond to the tale she's heard – found it unnerving. Then, there was the jolting pressure and weird crawling sensation she felt in the centre of her back on hearing the elf threw *something* at him. After a short time, he untangles himself, pulling a crisp white handkerchief from his pocket, while Hannah grabs a tissue from her bag. Wiping her face, she gives a rueful laugh.

"That's one heck of a tale, Granddad."

"Yes, but I feel better for telling you." He smiles, then frowns saying, "It's a horrible tale and I know it's hard to believe."

"The First World War was horrific. You should have been at home, not fighting in the trenches."

"I couldn't sit back, nor could a lot of others my age. After six months I was coping well. What's always bothered me most is how, by leaving with the officer, I put one of my friends through hell."

"You don't know that Granddad. It's possible

213

the…soldier realised he needed to do as you suggested." Hannah can see he doesn't look convinced. "What happened once you were in the hospital?"

Granddad leans forward, placing his forearms on his thighs. "I was diagnosed with shell shock and sent to a treatment centre. Never did go back into the trenches. The treatments were questionable, but some good came out of being there; I met your Gran. She was one of a group of women who volunteered to visit and spend time with injured soldiers. Some were physically injured. Others, like me, suffered with mental trauma. Your poor Gran had to put up with my nightmares our entire marriage."

"She didn't put up with them, Granddad. She loved you and knew they came with the territory."

Granddad wipes his eyes once more, checks his watch, then gets to his feet. Hannah wonders how long they've been sitting; her bottom is numb.

"It's teatime. Will you walk with me to the dining room?"

Hannah takes the proffered arm and assists her grandfather across the lawn. He whistles jauntily, chirruping with the birds as they cluster amongst the cherry trees. Hannah feels out of sorts, strangely weighed down by the tale Granddad told her. It's almost as if a mantle of despair has settled around her shoulders. The day seems dull, compared to when she arrived, and there's a chill in the late afternoon air. She wishes she'd brought a jacket.

*

Hannah runs across uneven, dense mud. The air is cloying, thick with smoke coloured ochre by the sun. It's hard to see and breath. She hears a wailing noise to her right, the sound almost sings to her. Then the earth shakes, causing her to stumble. Picking herself up, Hannah carries on and doesn't notice the horse. It rears and Hannah sees a British arm patch as the man's body bounces across the mud and she is kicked to the ground. The pain when her thighs snap screams up her body and out of her throat. She screams again as her body is trampled into the damp earth, its thinly dried crust cracking under the pressure. Her heart punctures, begins to pump blood out and death approaches...

Hannah wakes screaming.

SURVIVAL

Garth draws a deep breath. Despite the fact that he's tied the loan shark's arms and legs to a chair, the man still tries to control him.

"Well boy? Are you gonna get on with it and slit my throat or what?" Baron's eyes narrow. "I never had you down for a pussy."

An image shoots across Garth's brain: his Mum, held down by a henchman while the bastard before him rapes her. Clenching his teeth, Garth slaps Baron's face hard, splitting the man's lip.

"Shut up."

He returns to sharpening his knife on the whetstone he found in the kitchen. Blood oozes from the wound, causing Baron's sneer to become almost clown-like.

"You'd have been nothing without me." Baron spits bloodily on the expensive hardwood floor.

The sharpened blade glints as Garth lifts it to the hall light. Its surface reflects the staircase behind him where a bodyguard's legs swing gently, but all Garth can see is his Mother's dangling body. He recalls her purple face, her limp hands, how her mules had slipped off in her death throes to lie upon the stairs.

"Oh, I'm something alright." Garth looks the shark in the eye. "I'm a trained killer. That's what you turned a simple schoolboy into."

"Ah!" Baron nods. "So that's what this is all about then, eh?" He gives Garth a knowing look. "I get revenge, boy, I really do. So come on, untie me and let's talk. I'm sure we can reach an understanding."

Looking at Baron, Garth sees his father: throat slit, life blood soaking into the carpet. He tests the sharpened blade by slowly drawing its edge down the loan shark's forearm. The man's face goes white. Blood beads, then begins to drip. Garth smiles.

"When your henchmen killed my Dad, you offered me a choice. Join him, or work for you."

Garth draws the blade down Baron's other forearm, enjoying the tenderness of parting flesh as his knife slides in. It always excites him. This time the loan shark winces as blood flows.

"I was terrified, but wanted to live. I still do, just not in your house." Garth steps back to survey his handiwork. "But this isn't merely revenge. It's about putting the past behind me and finding redemption."

Baron throws his head back laughing uproariously.

"Redemption! Oh god, that's priceless. You fucking halfwit. Look at you! Torture and killing, you love it. They're what you are."

Swallowing the bitterness arising from his gullet, Garth uses his knife to cut into the fabric of his prisoner's shirt. Ripping off a strip of material he gags Baron and gets to work.

*

The pub is dead during Nate's shift. In fact, since the curfew has been instigated, trade is almost non-existent. As he holds a glass up to the light, checking for smears, Nate prays he won't lose his job as a result. His student loan is almost gone. That debt is far more than Nate hoped it would become, but at least he's in his final year and on target to do well. It's a relief when his only customer approaches the bar. The TV has been his main companion during this evening, but repeated news of multiple murders is depressing. The tally of violated bodies grows each night and, a few minutes ago, a reporter stated that there were still no leads on who was responsible.

"Jameson's on ice, mate – make it a double."

Nate nods, grabs a tumbler and turns to the bottle behind him. Just as he finishes serving, Richard, the landlord, returns from replacing a barrel. Nate watches him scan the bar then check the pub's clock. Richard shakes his head.

"This curfew's killing trade. The sooner they catch these cultist bastards the better. You might as well make a move, Nate. Go on, get home, it's almost closing time. I can manage here."

"Sure. I'll see you tomorrow?" Nate hates himself for the question, knowing he should have said nothing, just turned up for work as if everything was normal and people didn't have to be home, safely behind locked doors, by ten pm.

Richard shakes his head. "Nah. Give it a miss tomorrow." Then he quietly adds, "You free for a lock-in on Friday? We'll go through the night 'til curfew lifts and make your hours up that way."

The look Richard gives Nate says it all. A lock-in is illegal. However, it's a profitable move if they dare. Nate nods. His natural instinct is to be law abiding, but with the loan decreasing fast he is barely managing.

"Okay, let's put the word out," says Richard.

Lifting the flap separating bartender from customer, Nate crosses the floor, grabbing his jacket off the coat stand.

"Get home safe, Nate," Richard calls as the pub door swings shut.

Outside, the October air is unseasonably warm. Usually there is just enough time to get home once curfew sounds and Nate now hates this lamp-lit walk home. He begins down the long avenue which will lead him towards student bedsit land. Setting a brisk pace, he can't help but think about the murders taking place all over the country. Fear has infected the internet, the papers, radio stations and most individuals. Various rumours are circulating, but many agree with his boss that a cult is responsible. Nate looks nervously around, hoping to see someone he can walk with. The police are stretched to breaking point and tonight's news reported the army is being drafted in to assist. Nate can't wait for this to happen; an army presence in the city during the night would be comforting. When the sun goes down a terrible disquiet settles in his bones which remains until a glimmer of dawn breaks the black.

To his dismay, there is a small group hovering towards the end of the avenue. He can hear them chanting, which means they are amongst the few protesting that the curfew affects their civil liberties. Quickly Nate ducks into a front garden before he is spotted. One of their tactics is to delay then attempt to persuade people to stay and join in. Nate's skin prickles; he feels increasingly uneasy as he hides in the garden's darkness. Is he more at risk here than if he tried to walk past the protestors? Slightly further down, on the left, is an alley which cuts across into his street. It runs behind an old factory unit. During the day, Nate uses it all the time – it cuts a huge chunk off his journey to lectures and work. However, using it in the dark is an altogether different matter. Apart from one lamp-post roughly halfway along, the alley is unlit. Glancing down the street Nate can see the protesters are already haranguing a couple, surrounding them to cut off any exit. This is his chance. Nate slips into the alley unseen just as curfew sounds.

*

While I crouch atop the deserted building I've been teleported to, this world's sun is setting. Clouds slowly move across the darkening sky pushed along by a light wind. There will be a wait before I can serve my people. My role gives me great pleasure. If, when I was younger, I'd been told I'd become a Harvester, I would have laughed in the face of the cretin who dared say so, all the while plotting revenge for the insult. Then, I thought being a Harvester was nothing – a role for those subjects who wish to be mere servants to our scientists. Later, I realised that for a female of our race to be good at Harvesting was rare. Now I'm revered as being the best amongst our kind. After this mission, I'll be in a position to claim a good strong mate.

I try to recall the last time I saw a Desurite I desired. I realise the time is long past and I hiss through my teeth. We all hope this Harvesting will allow our scientists to genetically strengthen the high-born members of our lifeblood. A high-born would be a choice mate despite their inbreeding. It disgusts me how weak so many of our kind have become trying to keep bloodlines pure. Perhaps, this low-born Desurana will begin the remaking of a strong Arkanian race. With an appalled snarl at my egotistical thoughts I stand, step back from the building's edge and shake my limbs to loosen them. Soon I must begin. The survival of my race depends upon the samples I and other Harvesters collect. I do not wish to live out my life force not knowing a mate, without giving birth to a strong Desurite or Desurana. This drives me forward.

As I run across the tops of buildings a pale moon begins to glimmer above the clouds. I scan the quietening areas below, but few of this planet's inhabitants now remain outside when darkness falls. This ensures harvesting is easier. I'm less likely to be observed. Yet, finding prey becomes harder. These creatures are slow, and I'm usually done before they realise their force is spent. Eventually I find two females together, alone in an open space. I am swift as I deal with the first and silence the second before she can blink. After harvesting the parts required, I set a quiet, leisurely pace and return to the building I was set down upon.

While I'm skimming up its rough surface I suddenly sense something watching me. I finish ascending, then crouch and look down over the edge. My thin armour blends with the colours and textures next to it, but a shaft of light from the moon above would reveal my position.

The dark, narrow passageway below widens slightly at the base of this building where a light is situated, then narrows again. Nothing moves in this space; nothing appears to be present. Hissing quietly, I move backwards as resonant chanting begins a short distance away. I begin to move with its beat. As the sound rises and falls, I glide into its music and dance while clouds mask my movement. The rhythm suits our courting ritual. I point and place my feet, sway my hips, and thread my arms into the ritualistic pattern of desire. As my movement flows into a series of twisting lifts and turns, I raise my arms high, releasing and sheathing the blades hidden in my gloves. My specimen bags swing gently against me and, for a brief moment, this world's moon shines down on my upturned face. As the glow ebbs, a strident sound drowns out the music I was embraced by. This discordance rips apart my ritual calm. Instinctively I unhinge my jaw and scream with it. Subdued by the depths of my emotions, aware I might have been heard, I slowly return to the edge and once again crouch to look down into the area below. There is still no movement, but I do detect a sound. The noise approaches the light and I need to see if it's the right kind of creature. Swiftly, I begin my journey down.

*

After five years Garth finds life as a Private Investigator mundane. Currently he's employed to tail a woman because her husband suspects she's being unfaithful. Unable to completely switch off from his past, Garth's pleased how working as a P.I. allows for the occasional expression of his tendencies and so carries a range of "tools". But self-control is important. Garth wants to live a decent life. Hopefully time will allow him to build a more balanced sense of self. Looking through his camera, he notes the woman's no longer alone. She's chosen to meet her female lover, at night, in a park. That people are being killed doesn't worry Garth, but surely these women have

222

concerns, despite their actions. Obscured by bushes, he begins photo snapping only to find his moonlit pictures capturing the most incredible death sequence he's ever observed. In a matter of seconds their throats are slashed and their bodies dragged onto the ground. The killer is wearing some kind of stealth gear. The individual crouches by the dead women and is doing something but, despite the zoom lens, Garth cannot see what. His view is blocked by the killer's body. Whoever this is, they finish quickly and leave the scene. Garth can now see the bodies have been mutilated. A shiver of excitement runs down his spine. The way the women have been sliced is enthralling. What knife can slice bone so perfectly? He has to follow. What he has just witnessed compels him to do so. Maybe, just maybe, capturing the killer will give him the redemption and sense of belonging he desperately craves. Hiding his equipment in the bushes, he quickly follows.

As they travel across the city, Garth's eyes become accustomed to the way the stealth suit works. When they reach a deserted factory building, the individual swiftly skims up the buildings surface to the roof. Before he can stop himself, Garth gasps. He flattens himself against the factory wall just as the killer spins to check the alley. Garth's mind is reeling but what he has seen only fuels his fascination. When the killer disappears, he thanks God for fire escapes. A rusty one is attached to the factory wall and, quietly, he begins to climb. Reaching the top of the building he hunkers down. Sensing movement to his right, Garth silently slides behind the small building which, in times past, was used by maintenance to gain access to the factory roof. He can hear voices chanting in a nearby street. Carefully, Garth looks around the rooftop entrance.

A glimmer of moonlight breaks through the clouds revealing that the being is dancing in time with the chant. Its movements encompass, yet surpass, the repeated rhythmic phrase. Garth is entranced by the sway of the killer's pelvis, the way its feet strike the roof so precisely. He can see bags swinging from around its hips and his mind briefly returns to the ruined bodies left in the park. Although the chant remains at a constant pace, the being's movements speed up, becoming so fast, Garth finds he's holding his breath. Suddenly, the fullness of breasts beneath the shimmering fabric becomes obvious. The quicker she spins and twists, the harder it becomes for the fabric to keep pace with her movements and more of her form becomes apparent. Garth stares at her lithe body, slender arms and legs, as the dance demonstrates their suppleness and strength. He is mesmerised, enraptured by sudden desire for this creature. When she begins thrusting her hands in the air, revealing the deadly blades sheathed into her gloves, the combination of imminent death and desire sends explosive lust coursing through his body. He has never felt more alive. Moonlight cuts a swathe through the clouds, revealing the killer's face. Garth sees the long planes of her cheekbones, the deep setting of the almond-shaped eyes and the angular shape of her nose. When the curfew's blare rends the air, so does the creature. While Garth looks on, she visibly dislocates her jaw. Her mouth becomes a chasm filled with large, sharp canines and her cry resonates with anguish. Garth can feel the hopelessness and longing in her voice. He understands these emotions only too well.

*

Swallowed up by the dark, Nate hears the curfew as he begins walking through the alley. The soles of his trainers slap the rough, uneven concrete pathway, their sound echoing off the brick walls either side. Nate's sense of relief dissipates. Feeling uneasy, he glances over his shoulder and sees nothing. With a grimace, Nate tells himself to stop being soft. It is just an alley, the streetlights are still on and he can see one ahead. Just past the lamp the space opens up slightly. Glancing across to the disused factory Nate does a double take. He's certain he saw something moving down the wall. His nerves are on edge, that is all. Best to walk on and reach the street just a short distance ahead, before his imagination really runs wild. When Nate takes the next step he hears something land softly on the broken concrete. He picks up pace, refusing to look until the sensation he must overwhelms him. He turns around.

The area behind the factory is empty. A bead of sweat breaks on his brow and runs down into an eye. Blinking it away, Nate looks again. At that moment, moonlight breaks through the clouds revealing the form standing just a few meters away.

It is poised like a child playing a game of statues. The being's figure appears almost human, but its head is long, the jaw larger than normal. It has a slender body with arms which seem to have him in their grasp, despite the distance between them. The outstretched hands have four digits. With the taste of bile in his mouth, Nate turns and flees, running blindly from the thing behind him, striving to reach the end of the alley, to turn the corner and get safely home. Sobbing and pissing himself, Nate stumbles on the uneven path, certain the creature is gaining on him.

*

It is afraid and, it is male; its shape tauter than those I Harvested earlier. I hiss with disdain. He cannot outpace me no matter how fast he runs! I place my body in the killing stance of our people and swiftly follow. As I close the space between us my prey decides to turn. This movement amuses me. It was fast for his kind. I have stilled myself, am barely breathing, but the moon betrays my presence. He sees me. His eyes open wide and travel my body. I could take him now, but no. It will be fun to toy with this one and have his fear feed my senses. So I wait, allow him to see what I am and to know I am strong, fearless. His gaze travels down my arms to my gloved hands and then, only then do his pupils enlarge. I feel his terror and am flooded with glory at having generated such raw emotion. Unsheathing my blades, I grasp his skull and drain him.

This male is a reasonable example of the species. He is young and slim, but fully formed and mature. He is not strong, and I know he was not brave. Unsheathing my instruments I rapidly slice the skull and remove its contents. Then I slice the long cord at its top and base, then pull it free through the uppermost incision. Finally, I farm the seed. As I remove each sample, I place it in a specimen bag which either nurtures or freezes. Once my Harvesting is complete, I give brief thanks to Meridernia. Now it is time to return. As I rise, knowing I've collected a good range of samples, I hear a noise from above. Silently, I unsheathe my blades.

*

Garth is sneaking down the fire escape when the young man reaches the light and stops. Garth wills him to move, to get somewhere safe, when all the while he knows this isn't likely to happen. Then the moon shines and a prequel to death unfolds before his eyes. Like the young man, Garth takes in the female's form. He knows she is playing with the boy, enjoying the moment before the kill. Garth almost chuckles out loud. He knows this scenario, has been through it so many times, especially in his youth. Then fear pervades the air and Garth switches his attention to the lad. Can he save his life? Should he? The youngster hasn't seen such sights as Garth and this alien killer have. He will panic and run. Garth begins to move.

The sound of the young man's feet and his sobbing breath drown out any noise from Garth's rush down the rusty metal stairs. So rapidly is the young man's life over, so high does his blood spray from the slice to his throat, Garth nearly topples himself over the rail in his attempt to stop. She was so quick! The alien and her victim are less than a floor beneath him. One more set of stairs and he would have been there. Yet, instead of feeling remorse for the man's death, Garth admires the kill. Standing directly above the being, he quietens his breathing. She has paid him no attention, clearly doesn't know he's there. Garth has the advantage. He grasps the sharp stiletto he carries. He can kill her instantly. The back of her neck is exposed as she bends over. Instead, he chooses to wait while she processes the corpse.

From his ringside seat, Garth watches as the creature places the lad's brain, spine and testicles into the bags around her hips. Then she utters a strange series of sounds. The hissing and snarls sound like fine gravel stirred by someone's fingers. Garth finds himself strangely moved. The cadence of the sounds, the position of her body, suggest she is giving thanks of some kind. Could she be praying? Garth moves down a step, hoping to get a better view, and the metal stair beneath his feet creaks. She whirls, arms raised like a snake about to strike, an unsheathed blade in each hand.

Ignoring her stance, Garth sheathes his stiletto and walks down the final steps, wondering if he's walking to his death. She snarls a warning, remaining poised. Garth continues, steadily meeting her gaze, stopping within arm's reach. He sees the deep almond eyes move across his shoulders and down to his hips. Sheathing her blades, she steps forward. He stands still as she proceeds to feel the muscles in his arms and legs, then runs her gloved hands down the girth of his body. Her touch feels efficient and she finds each and every weapon Garth is carrying, placing the blades and gun in a line to his left. Sitting back on her heels, she waves a hand indicating his collection whilst looking at him and making a guttural sound. He senses her approval. The patina of her skin glows golden in the moonlight. It is lightly scaled around her eyes.

Noticing his gaze, the alien pulls a glove slightly down, showing him the skin around her wrist. It too is lightly scaled. She repositions her glove as she rises. Then, holding Garth's face with her fingers, she twists his head from side to side. There's strength behind the grip, but her touch is surprisingly gentle.

The young man lies beside them with his slit throat, open skull and soft skin. Garth knows the body is cooling, but blood soaking into the ground reminds him of the moment this creature used her blades. He begins to harden while she runs her fingertips down his face to his throat. Aware she's found the top of an old scar, Garth puts his head to one side, pulls the collar of his jacket down and allows her to examine the fine line across the side of his neck. She grunts, as if in satisfaction, then looks down. The hand which clasps between his legs isn't gentle, but her firm touch arouses him further. Her breathing is rapid. Hooking a hand behind his head, she pulls Garth forward and the thin line of her mouth presses against his. The tongue entering Garth's mouth is forked. Her kiss is hard, her tongue darts and twists around his. The dual ends gently grip and pull, seducing and arousing Garth until he feels as if he's drowning, flooded by desire. Pulling her taut, sinewy body against his, Garth slides his hands down and cups her muscular bottom. Abruptly, she's gone. Garth turns to find her bathed by moonlight at the base of the building. She hisses and points up, then at the fire escape. Garth knows she's asking him to climb, to go with her.

For the first time since he was fourteen Garth is afraid. Yet again, he's been given a choice but, this time, has no idea what it truly means. This creature is a killer, as is he. Garth knows the most satisfaction he gets is at the juncture where blade pieces flesh and blood flows. This is his release, his climax. What would happen if he were to go with her? Would he be her protected lover, a

228

stud, or just a smorgasbord of body parts? Uncertainty taunts him; Garth watches while she nimbly scales the building. Soon, she's out of sight.

He stumbles to the young man's body, drops down beside it. Garth gently closes the opened head, then lifts the body into his lap and cradles it. Tears are streaming down his face. He cries for the boy he was and the man he's become. For the wasted life resting in his lap. He truly is a soulless being who doesn't belong with humanity. As Garth's sobs increase, he recalls the lust aroused by the alien's kiss, the desire expressed in her dance and the hopelessness revealed in the tone of her cry. Garth throws his head back and howls his torment into the night. From the roof above, an answering cry reverberates through the landscape.

TAKING FLIGHT

Julie's younger brother Philip ran across the lawn, his small thin legs working hard to keep up with their father's long, purposeful stride. His golden-brown hair gleamed in the sun, the grass beneath his feet richly green. Dropping the ball she was playing with, Julie followed.

"Daddy! Daddy!" Philip called. Julie saw her father's shoulders twitch, then stiffen.

"Not now, Philip." He sounded cross.

"Daddy!"

Without a further word, Daddy climbed the wooden steps to his newly built pigeon loft, opened the door and stepped inside, closing it firmly behind him. Not once did he look at Philip, who stood by the stump of a recently-cut-down cherry tree a short distance from the loft. Julie reached her brother. He was trembling, his face registering disbelief. From within the loft, Daddy softly spoke to his flock, soothing sounds, dripping with joy, pride and pleasure. Julie felt a wrench in her chest. Wanting to comfort her brother, Julie said, "I'll play with you, Philip."

Philip looked down at the grass. He'd already learnt to hide his tears. Julie held out her hand. She waited so long that her arm began to ache, but when Daddy began to whistle, Philip took her hand. Julie gently led him back to where toys were scattered on the concrete patio between the back door and the lawn. Philip didn't say much, but then the toys Julie had been told she could take outside were not those he liked to play with.

"I'll get your truck," Julie said. Philip's bedroom was the big room at the back whereas Julie had been given the front box room. Envious of the space Philip had, Julie looked for the red truck. It was on the floor near the window. Before picking it up, Julie stood on the tips of her toes to look down the length of the garden, pressing her fingers

231

hard against the windowsill. She couldn't see Philip playing on the concrete, but she could see where the grass began. A side path divided Daddy's vegetable patch from the lawn and the tree stump where Philip had stood. Daddy had cut the tree down because its branches blocked the sky and he needed to be able to see his pigeons returning to their loft. The other cherry tree stood across the lawn, near next-door's fence. Julie was glad he hadn't cut that one down. Its branches were full of yellow-red fruit. They tasted wonderful and Julie hoped Mummy would pick some today. Then she looked at the loft.

It dominated the rear of the garden, hiding the fence behind it; only a small section either side showed. This allowed access to the back gate and the side section where Daddy had a compost heap and lit bonfires. It had taken Daddy three weeks to build and paint the loft. Against the dark blue, white had been used to edge the door and window frames and on the dowels which formed window bars. Light and fresh air could get in, but the pigeons couldn't escape – unless the windows were swung back upon themselves and hooked against the main body of the loft. A wide sill sat below the windows ready for returning racing pigeons. The wooden building was so deep, it ate into the lawn. In the afternoon sun its shadow stretched towards the concrete where her brother played. Julie shivered, grabbed Philip's truck and ran from the room.

*

The summer breeze was stronger on Horsington Hill than it had been in the garden. Julie squinted into the sun. She hoped this time Daddy would let her and Philip run around before they went home. They always got back long before the pigeons. On the ground was a brown wicker basket with even darker brown leather straps holding closed both a small opening, for inserting birds into the basket, and a large one for releasing them into the sky. Inside, the pigeons were rustling, making a throaty noise that seemed to speak of their eagerness for the basket to be opened. Beside her, Daddy said, "I'll undo the straps, Philip, and then the birds can fly out."

Philip crouched on the grass beside the basket. "Can I open it, Daddy? Can I?"

Daddy was smiling, but the smile did not reach his eyes. Julie stepped backwards, wishing Philip had not asked.

"Okay, but make sure you open the whole lid, not the small one."

Philip looked intently at the straps while Julie held her breath. Touching one of them, Philip looked at his father.

"If you think that's the right one, you open it."

Philip's eyes glanced towards her. Julie gave a small nod to say it was okay and he carefully undid the buckle. When Daddy turned to stare at her, Julie looked away. She stood as still as stone.

"Now, undo the next one, but don't look at your sister this time." Out of the corner of her eye, Julie could see unhappiness and uncertainty on Philip's face. He fumbled clumsily with another strap.

"Hurry up. We haven't got all day."

Standing, Philip shook his head. Daddy's face became dark. Pushing Philip to one side, he quickly opened the other straps, then lifted the lid.

Rustling feathers turned into a roar of wings as the pigeons rushed out of the basket, lifting into the breeze. With a cry of alarm, Philip stumbled backwards. He fell onto his bottom, then rolled over pressing his face into the thin, dry grass. Daddy didn't notice. His face was rapturous as the roar steadied into a regular beat and the birds rose high in the sky. Shading his eyes with his hands, Daddy said, "Look, they're beginning to circle, get their bearings."

Copying her father, Julie saw how one broke away. She pointed, "That was quick, Daddy."

He spat on the ground, then looked again at the circling pigeons. "It went the wrong way. I'll wring its neck if it comes back."

*

That year, four-year-old Philip got Lego for Christmas. Julie was given a doll that could drink. Julie longed to play with her brother, to make Lego models with him, but when she went to join in, her mother firmly told her to play with her own toys. Julie hated the doll. Its plastic body felt solid, its hands unyielding; it couldn't hold her hand the way Philip did. She gave the doll water, which ran straight out of a hole in its bottom. Disgusted, Julie said, "Its nappy's wet."

Mummy looked highly amused. "That's what babies do, Julie: they drink and wet their nappies. You'll see, you'll be having babies one day."

*

Every Friday and Saturday was race meeting night. Over time, Julie became used to being scrubbed and dressed in the clothes Mum laid out for her. Julie hated the meetings. The room at the back of the pub had a low ceiling, was badly lit and reeked of spilt booze and stale cigarette smoke. The burnt-orange flock wallpaper was peeling in places. Dad would place his pigeon clock, with its registered times and rubbers, beside the rest while Mum chatted to the other wives. Julie wandered over to the table where Mum was sitting and pulled out a chair, dragging it across the grubby carpet. No one noticed her, they just continued talking. Julie would have asked Mum what the other women were called, but Mum was staring at her drink.

"It would do you good to get more involved, Elaine," a woman with bleached hair was saying. "I know Maureen's had enough of running the race bids and being treasurer. It's easy enough, you just take the money and enter the bets, then work out who gets what after the race results."

"Sounds like a lot of maths to me," Mum said. "And a lot of responsibility." She ran her finger around the rim of her drink. Julie briefly wondered what it was, then recalled Dad asking for a Gin and Tonic at the bar. Mum lifted her glass and sipped.

"You'd be good at it," said a woman wearing black rimmed glasses. She blew cigarette smoke out of pursed lips.

"Yes, you would be," insisted Bleached Hair. She leant towards Mum, saying confidentially, "It'll make your Mark a very happy man if you became more involved."

Mum's face turned red. "I make Mark a happy man by making sure the children don't play near the loft or invite any of their school friends round on a race day. Nor do I hang washing on the line. I come to this club every Friday and Saturday. When he's at work, I feed his pigeons. I'm involved quite enough as it is, thank you."

Julie reached out to hold her Mum's hand. Mum gave her a surprised glance, but gave her hand a squeeze. Bleached Hair shook her head sympathetically. "Each of us does these things for our husbands, Elaine."

"And we've all taken a turn as treasurer, secretary and polishing prizes," Black Glasses continued.

"You're saying it's my turn." Mum's voice was full of defeat.

Bleached Hair smiled. "So that's sorted then, I'll ask Maureen to show you how it's done next week."

As the two women left the table, Julie said, "We don't have to come. We can stay at home - you, me and Philip."

Mum looked at her and gave a smile. "That would be lovely, Julie, but we can't. Your Dad would kill me." She drained her glass and gave it to Julie. "Go ask him to get me another."

To reach her father, Julie had to pass the club notice board where the last week's results were pinned. Julie peered at the chart. Each of his birds had done badly bar one. Overall, he was ranked ninth. Knowing Dad thought he'd done well this week, Julie hoped he was right. He was listening to his friend Bryan as Julie approached.

"I think I've done okay. What about you, got to be better than last week, eh?"

"It had better be, Bryan, or I'll be wringing yet another bird's neck."

Bryan chuckled. "Best not to mess about if they don't make the grade. How's your son getting on? Does he help you in the loft? Jeff's a great help. I can leave him to clean the loft out and he does a good job. He's older than your Philip, mind."

Dad shook his head. "Yeah, well, you're lucky. I tried to get Philip interested but he's scared of the birds. Bloody sissy. If he was a young 'un, I'd send him out on a race and hope he gets lost."

Bryan roared with laughter, but Julie couldn't take another step. She couldn't breathe. Time stopped until someone bumped into her with a careless "Sorry love."

Placing the empty glass on a nearby table, Julie went to find her brother.

*

That Christmas, Philip was given a Meccano set. He tinkered with it all day while Julie sat with her books and a Sindy doll, despite the fact she longed to play with Philip's Meccano herself. Julie didn't mind the doll. Mum had become friends with the lady next door who had made an entire wardrobe for it. The colourful clothing made a difference, but Julie soon found she preferred the books. One was called *The Valley of Dreams*. The story told of a boy who left home to live in a dream world. Julie read it from cover to cover, then read it again, and again.

Eventually Mum took it off her, so Julie began creating a dream world of her own. The next time Dad had one of his moods, she took herself there.

The air was still, grass lush and green, sky a clear blue. The sun glowed a warm, sustaining yellow. Stepping stones formed a path between the lawn and flower beds full of snapdragons, bluebells, roses – but no thorns – there's no place for pain in her dream world. Beyond and around the garden are fields full of golden corn and, in the distance, a wood. Perhaps, one day, she will explore amongst the trees, but for now, sitting on the grass, enjoying being alone in this calm place is enough.

*

From the top of the tree Julie passed cherries down to Philip. He was too scared to climb as high as she did, but the cherries in the uppermost branches were the ripest and juiciest. She was giving Philip the reddest pair she'd found when Dad shouted, "Philip! Get down from there and help me clean the loft."

At the start of spring, Dad had said that it was time he taught Philip how to take care of the pigeons. Now, every few days before he began his homework, her brother was called to assist. Philip's face fell.

"You eat them," he said, "I'd better go."

"I hope they don't peck you today."

Philip was already on the grass when Julie remembered something Dad had said a few days ago; "The latest babies might have hatched," she called.

Unable to get the idea of freshly hatched squabs out of her head, Julie was soon clambering down the tree and into the shade. Once on the ground she hesitated. Dad had made it plain the loft was for men and boys only, but surely he wouldn't mind showing her a baby pigeon. She'd be quiet, approach the loft and peek through the window at the nesting section. If it looked as if some had just hatched, she'd ask. Julie quietly made her way up the steps onto the loft's veranda and crept towards the long white dowels. They were spaced evenly apart with a decent gap between them for Julie to look through. This close, she could hear the squabs squawking and smell the acrid scent of droppings. When she stood on tiptoe and looked in, her view was blocked by Dad's back. He was in front of the hatching boxes with Philip beside him.

"There's a good girl," Dad said. Philip had told her that Dad stroked his pigeons on their breast to soothe them when he wanted to check their eggs or squabs. That must be what he was doing now. He presented Philip with a fleshy pink object that had tufts of yellow down on its body and the start of grey feathers. Its eyes appeared huge and, when closed, its beak reminded Julie of the rubber tip you squeezed to get liquid into a dropper.

"That's good, Philip, check its eyes, spread each wing out and see how they're formed. Check its feet and legs." The squab pecked at Philip as he checked its eyes. He flinched, recovered himself and began checking its wings.

"See how they're formed? They look okay, but a lot depends on how they develop. Now finish the inspection. Let's look at another two: they're a bit further along."

Philip carefully returned the squab to its nest while her father removed and soothed the nursing pigeon. From a different area of the hatching boxes, Dad lifted out a feathered squab who was too young to begin training. Julie could see that Philip was more nervous about handling this one, but he managed. When he spread the first of the bird's wings, Julie almost gasped. Sunlight through the dowels highlighted its symmetry. The blue-grey feathers had a healthy sheen which shimmered like silk. After examining the pigeon, Philip said, "It's got beautiful wings."

Dad smiled, removed the bird and replaced it with another. "What about this one?"

Philip repeated the process, but this time when he spread the bird's wings, it was clear one was slightly malformed. Julie watched in awe as her brother sat the bird on his hand and stroked its softly feathered breast.

"You poor thing," Philip said.

Awe became horror as Julie realised what he meant.

"It's no good for racing. Wring its neck."

Philip shook his head, bringing his free hand up as if to shield the pigeon from harm. "No Dad, I won't."

"It's useless! Wring its neck."

Dad's face darkened, his hands clenching and unclenching. He towered over Philip who was pressed against an inner dividing wall.

"No! You can't make me." He tried to move away when Dad's hands reached towards the bird. The pigeon flapped its wings. It fluttered unevenly off Philip's hand, coming towards the white dowels, blue sky and sunlight. Julie quickly ducked down, hearing rather than seeing Dad catch it. Covering her ears against the forthcoming snap, Julie tried to enter her dream-world before she heard Philip's agonised cry.

*

On her tenth birthday, Julie was given a rabbit. He was black and white with a pink nose and inquisitive green eyes. His whiskers twitched when he sniffed Julie, and he watched her with interest when she fed him. Julie called him Patchwork, which got shortened to Patch. He had a hutch and Dad made him a run from wood and wire. She enjoyed giving him attention, brushing him and cleaning his hutch. Julie spent her pocket money on straw and treats. But Patch was a digger and soon found his way to her father's vegetable plot. Dad placed the hutch on top of the coal bunker and Patch was only allowed in his run under supervision. Julie soon knew Patch had worked out how to open the hutch using his nose. One morning Julie was frogmarched to the car, where Dad placed a box on her lap.

"We're taking your bloody rabbit back to the shop." Dad turned the ignition and pulled out into the road.

"Please Dad, I love Patch, I take good care of him. It's not my fault he can open his hutch. He's clever."

Her father glared at her. "He's going and that's that."

Stunned, Julie sat quietly hugging the cardboard box containing Patch. She felt him move and wished she could hold his warm body against hers one more time. When they reached the pet shop, Dad took the box off her, marched into the shop, coming out a few minutes later stuffing some money into his pocket.

"That'll pay for the vegetables it ate," He said, slamming the car door shut.

Julie entered her dream-world and Patch was there. Part of the flower bed was now a vegetable plot full of carrots, cabbage and lettuce. Patch roamed freely, eating whatever he liked, returning to snuffle Julie and sit beside her, as she lay chewing a stalk of grass. Suddenly Patch thumped both his back feet on the ground. She sat up at the warning and saw the doll she'd been given when she was five sitting on the grass by her feet. Julie snatched the doll up and walked purposefully towards an area of the garden where flowers grew thickly. Quickly, she dismembered the doll, pulling its head away from its body, then its arms and legs. She reached for the small trowel which had appeared on the stepping stone beside her and quickly buried the remains in the loose soil beneath the flowers. Once this was done, she gently arranged the flowers to cover any disturbance. But, when she stood up, they looked dull, as if soured by the object buried beneath.

That autumn, Julie was served rabbit stew for dinner. She looked at her plate and cried. Later that season, Julie was playing in the garden with Philip when Dad dug over his vegetable plot. Dad swore when he unearthed a dismembered doll. That night Julie visited her dream-world. The dull flowers were flourishing.

*

When they walked into the pigeon club, Julie didn't bother checking Dad's position on the notice board. Over time he'd become the top ranking member. Newcomers hastened to talk to him about breeding, training and the best grain to give their birds. Tonight every fancier was buzzing with excitement. An international race was taking place in Europe and members had selected their best birds. Crates of pigeons were stacked in the pub car park, waiting for the lorry that would take them across the Channel. Julie listened to Bryan telling one of the older members how much money he'd won the last time he'd entered a race of this kind. Nearby, Mum rolled her eyes at his boast as she took bids for tomorrow's race, then drank deeply from her glass. Dad was regaling the latest newcomer with one of his racing stories. Wondering where Philip was, Julie stepped through the open door into the pub's garden, walking past where some of the older boys and girls gathered. She found him sitting alone on a bench towards the back. The lights from the nearby car-park didn't quite illuminate the seat.

"You okay?" she asked plonking herself down beside him.

Philip shook his head. "It's my birthday tomorrow and there's a race on."

Julie wanted to hold his hand, comfort him the way she did when he was very young, but if anyone saw, Philip would be embarrassed.

"Mum's got a present for you and there's one from me."

"Dad'll want me to kill a pigeon if it does badly in the race."

"He can't make you kill one, it's your birthday!"

"Yes he can," said Philip. "He made me kill one

241

today. I didn't want to, I said no."

From the way his breath caught, Julie knew he was crying. She moved close so she could see his face.

"How? How did he make you kill it?"

Wiping his eyes with the back of his hands, Philip looked at her and swallowed. His eyes were swollen. "Dad was holding out a pigeon. I said no to killing it. Dad took hold of one of my hands, put it around the bird's neck. He put his hand over mine and forced mine round so its neck broke. I broke its neck, Julie. I felt it snap. I killed it!"

Julie no longer cared who could see them. Her arms went around Philip. His body shook as he sobbed.

"You didn't kill it." Her voice was fierce, "Dad did. Dad killed it, not you."

Something within her tore loose, but Julie didn't know what. All she could see was red.

Julie noticed something different as she entered her dream world. Colour had been drained out of the landscape she'd created. As she stood looking around, a wind sprang up and the fields rippled as if a storm was approaching. Clouds scudded across the sky. As the wind gathered strength, petals were ripped from flowers which had become overblown since her last visit. Softly she called Patch's name. He loped towards her from where the carrots grew. It was reassuring to see him and scratch him behind the ears. Once she'd finished, Patch looked at her, twitched his whiskers then thumped his back legs.

"What is it, Patch?"

Patch could not tell her. All he could do was thump his legs against the ground in warning.

*

Julie was excited for Philip as he prepared the model plane Mum had bought him for his birthday. Today was a family day out to celebrate and Philip would be flying his plane for the first time. They'd travelled to Horsington Hill, devoured the picnic Mum had packed. Even Dad was in a good mood. He stood by Philip, making encouraging comments as the plane took off. Mum beamed as Philip smoothly bought the plane round and back towards them, made it climb and swoop, then level back out. He landed it neatly on the grass. Only then did Julie breathe out.

"That was brilliant, Philip," said Mum.

Julie gave Philip a big thumbs up and grinned at him while bouncing on the grass. She doubted her grin was as big as Philip's.

"Do you want a go, Julie?" Philip held the control out.

Dad snatched it from him. "It isn't for girls. I'll show you how to really fly a plane."

Moments later, the model plane lay in pieces on the ground. Julie got the box it had come in from beside the picnic basket and carried it over to where Philip knelt on the ground. Quietly they began placing pieces of the plane inside it. Behind them, Mum was yelling at Dad.

"You can fix it," Julie said. "You're good at fixing things."

The eyes Philip turned towards her looked dead. "Some things can't be fixed," Philip said, his voice strangely flat.

Julie sat back on her heels. "What do you mean?"

Philip silently shut the box. Julie looked across at their parents. Dad was now trying to put his arms around Mum, but she kept pushing him away. When Mum twisted her body, Julie thought of Philip trapped by Dad's body in the loft, of the pigeon taking flight from his hands and trying to escape. Julie knew that if Mum could fly, she would be taking flight right now. Then Dad caught her, pulled her close, holding her against his body until she relented.

*

Patch is nowhere to be seen. The danger forecast by his thumps has arrived. Lightning ripples across the black sky illuminating a dark presence at the end of her garden, blocking the fields and distant wood from view. Thunder rumbles as Julie moves forward. She needs to know what the presence is, needs another flash of lightning. It comes and she sees the loft. Its dark blue blends into the unnatural darkness, making the loft seem immense. It threatens to crush and destroy all that she is. Another flash lights up the loft's white central door and white barred windows. A mouth and two eyes. She knows that if she steps inside she will have no freedom. The loft swallows you whole and spits out nothing. Dad has created it and used it to trap Philip. The closer she approaches, the more she sees and hears. Pigeons are cooing loudly, flying around the loft and dashing themselves against the white bars. Philip calls, "No, Dad, no! Don't make me kill them."

And Dad replies, "You're useless, I'll wring your bloody neck if you don't!"

The grass is turning brown. The loft is beginning to suck the life out of her dream world. It has no place here, does not belong in her quiet, peaceful domain. The storm rages above and she can see her flowers are dying. Enough! Julie decides. She recalls every time Dad hurt Philip and shapes it into the redness she felt tear free when Philip cried in her arms. She remembers overheard conversations and twists them into sharp, jagged spikes. She vents the pain of Patch being taken from her into a thing even more capable of draining life than that before her. Finally she whirls these forces together and binds them. When lightning strikes behind the loft, as the air immediately shakes in time with a thunderous roar, she throws her creation at the loft.

The red orb has a black centre. The spikes which surround it are barbed. They rip the roof off the loft and throw it back in the same arc that Dad threw the basket open on Horsington Hill. Pigeons take flight, pouring out of the loft into the darkened sky. As they rise into the air, a final lightning flash makes their wings shimmer. The soft blue-grey is glorious. The pigeons are not afraid, they are free to fly when and where they choose. As they gain height, the orb descends into the loft. Julie directs her redness to contain Dad. She won't allow him to hurt Philip again. Her brother is broken, almost gone, and Julie wants him back. The black heart of the orb destroys the loft, sucks the power from it, removes it from her dream-world. The loft withers and decays before her eyes. Paint peels, wood crumbles and finally the garden reclaims itself.

The sky is now the same blue grey as the shimmering pigeon wings. A refreshing rain falls. It revitalises the dead grass and flowers. Patch hops over to her and Julie sits on the damp grass to pet him, glad her dream-world is her own once more.

*

Julie's bare feet slap on the kitchen floor. She rubs sleep from her eyes, wondering why the table is empty of any breakfast things. Steam rises from the boiling kettle which turns itself off and mugs are ready on the work-surface, but Mum isn't there making the tea. The back door is wide open.

"Mum?" Julie calls. When she sees the bottom of the garden, Julie staggers against the door frame. She begins to shake, struggles to breathe, feels her legs giving way. Suddenly Mum is beside her, holding her up saying, "Take deep breaths in through your nose Julie, breathe out through your mouth. Come on now, *in,* one, two, three, four. *Out,* one, two…" Julie concentrates on breathing. Anything rather than look down the garden. When she feels stronger, Julie looks at what remains of the loft, at her Dad on his knees, weeping.

"We don't know what's happened," Mum says, "but the pigeons are gone."

With Mum's arm around her, Julie stumbles over the concrete towards the lawn. She doesn't feel its rough surface, as her feet are numb. What remains of the loft is rotten, blackened. Julie knows if she touches it, the wood will crumble under her fingers. Philip stands by the cherry tree stump, much as he did six years ago. This time, when he looks at her, he isn't full of disbelief and loss.

"Go to your brother," Mum says.

Julie doesn't hesitate. As she approaches, Philip smiles. He wraps his arms around her and holds her tight. Julie holds him just as tightly back, staring at the disintegrating ruin in front of them.

"Let's go and play," says Philip.

WHERE THE TRAIN STOPS

23rd December 1978

Once the guard had checked the doors were slammed shut, he blew his whistle and the overland train to Kenton slowly left London behind. Amy was wedged tightly against a window. The number of passengers returning home in the three carriages was overwhelming. There were no luggage racks, meaning the floor was littered with bags while standing passengers straddled their contents. She could see the Hamleys logo on a number of them. They were bulging with toys that would be wrapped and placed under decorated trees this Christmas Eve.

Amy's sister Becca sat between her and Mummy on the two-seater. Becca nestled against Mummy, one hand toying with the buttons on her emerald green velvet coat. Everything about it was big, the fur-trimmed collar, cuffs and hem, the tightly-cinched belt and buttons. Daddy had bought it for Mummy one Christmas and Amy loved the way it swung around Mummy's knee-high boots, as they'd walked the crowded city streets that evening. Now it was past Becca's bedtime and her thumb was already in her mouth, her eyes slipping shut as the train gathered speed. Those standing swayed in time with the train's motion, clinging to each other or to the hand-holds built into the top of each seat.

Amy rested her forehead against the cool glass once the lights of Euston station faded into darkness. The air on the platform had been bitterly cold but, being so crowded, the carriage was growing warm, the air becoming stale. Amy wriggled her small body in an attempt to get more comfortable and ended up resting her head against the very edge of the seat. She stared at the lit windows of houses the train rushed by, at the jet-black winter sky, hoping that snow clouds were blocking the

247

stars. She longed for a white Christmas. The lights in London would have looked lovely if snow had been falling. Amy had also seen green, red and blue laser beams rising from Oxford Street into the sky. She hadn't thought much of the lasers, but she would never forget the strands of white-gold lights strung above some of the busy roads they'd walked. She wished Daddy could have been there.

Lulled by the rhythm of the train, the repetitive sound of the tracks and by how snug she was, Amy shut her eyes. She recalled walking down Regent Street, looking at the sparkling lights above her and entering the brightly lit paradise that was Hamleys. The excitement of seeing so many toys on display had caused both her and Becca to squeal. Amy was remembering the Pinocchio puppet she'd loved, when the hard train seat beneath her changed.

Her eyes snapped open.

She was lying under a bright light and her hands were resting palm down on what felt like smooth metal.

"Don't worry, Amy, you're safe."

She knew that voice. Pushing herself up onto her elbows, Amy looked at the figure standing at the end of what appeared to be a metal slab. The hairs on the back of her neck rose.

"Daddy?"

He looked perfect. As perfect as the morning before he had the accident which crushed his body and killed him.

*

5th June 2014

"Good morning, Amy, how have you been these past two weeks?"

Amy is tired, so tired she wonders if she can string the words together to answer her therapist's question.

"I've not slept well. Most nights it's as if I'm in a waking nightmare where I'm stuck, paralysed, trying to scream, to move, and my body just doesn't respond."

Lance nods sympathetically. He's maintained eye contact while Amy has been speaking, but Amy can tell he has no idea how terrifying her dreams are.

"Did you try the technique I suggested, of closing your eyes and taking yourself to the safe place you created last time we met?"

"I tried, but couldn't close my eyes," Amy looks away before saying, "It's hard to remove myself when I can see the…figures getting closer."

"What about when you fully woke up?"

"Yes, I visited the bluebell woods afterwards, to calm myself down. That worked a treat."

"Well done, that's really good."

Aware that no condescension was intended, Amy bites back a sharp retort. "Thanks."

A satisfied smile lights the therapist's face, crinkling the corners of his eyes. Lance is about the same age as herself, yet somehow he comes across as grandfatherly. Especially when he smiles over his half-moon glasses in that way.

"I'm really glad you're able to access your safe place easily, even when stressed. It may be useful today."

I didn't say it was easy, thinks Amy, but she keeps quiet.

Moments later, Amy is laying on the therapist's couch in this impersonal room. No photos sit on the desk alongside the monitor which is turned away from prying eyes. She guesses the pale blue walls are intended to be calming, yet light pouring through the solitary window is sharp enough to make her uncomfortable. To Amy's relief, Lance lowers a slatted blind, softening the glare. The two sessions she's already experienced have been straightforward. An exchange of information followed by creating a safe place and a box of things that Amy finds comforting. A Polaroid her father had taken of the bluebell

249

woods near Ruislip Lido is in there.

"Today you're going on a train journey back into the past," Lance says. "You will travel to your earliest memory and then come forward towards the future, stopping at stations along the way. Each station will be an incident which upset or disturbed you."

"I hope you've booked me in for a double session," quips Amy.

"This usually takes a few sessions, so I will bring you back to today if time runs short."

Amy can hear the smile in his voice.

"Are you going to hypnotise me?"

"No, you remain conscious and in control."

"So I can stop if I want to?"

"You can, but the aim is to see if there's something in your past which relates to these night terrors. Now, before your journey begins, I want you to take three deep breaths."

Amy breathes in and out to the rhythm Lance counts. She feels relaxed as he begins to speak.

"Imagine you're standing on a platform and a train is stopping at the station. You open a carriage door, step onboard, then find a seat and sit down. The train departs, taking you back through time. Back you go, the years dropping away until you reach your first memory. The train stops. It is safe to explore this memory at this station in time, for you have control and can return to the present when you choose." After a short pause, Lance asks, "Where are you, Amy, and how old are you?"

Her voice sounds strangely calm as she says, "We're at the lido and I'm four and a half."

*

July 1974

I'm walking past the woods that run alongside the lake with Daddy. We're taking Rudi, his dog, for a walk while Mummy stays at the cafe with Becca. Daddy is ahead of me. I ask him to wait. He tells me to hurry up.

Something flits between the trees. I wonder if it's a fairy, like in the stories. I call Daddy, but he's so far ahead he can't hear me. I know the track ends and he'll have to turn around, so I go into the woods to see if I can find the fairy. The leaves and blossom on the trees break the solid sunshine apart. Birds twitter on the branches and moss clusters around roots. There's no path, so I'm wandering amongst thick trunks on ground that's littered with old leaves and twigs. My eyes slowly adjust to the shadowy dimness the trees create. Where sunlight dapples through, I can see particles lifting off the ground. They swirl as if a breeze catches them.

I notice a figure ahead. It's taller than I thought a fairy would be. I want to run towards it, but feel as if I'm stuck. There's no sound and I can't breathe properly. Then suddenly, I can move and breathe freely, only now it's very dark under the trees and cooler. Much cooler. I don't understand where the sun has gone.

I'm scared. I call out for Mummy, for Daddy. I don't know which way I should go to get back to the lake. Something is rustling nearby and I can tell I'm being watched. I'm sobbing. I want my Daddy. I want to pee, but Mummy will tell me I'm a dirty girl if I wet my pants. A strange hum starts. It unnerves me more than the dark, the rustling. I'm too scared to run, so I sit against a tree, put my hands over my ears, screw my eyes shut and scream. I keep on screaming. Then I hear Rudi barking, and when he presses his damp nose against my face, I open my eyes.

Rudi is guarding me. His hackles are raised and when something rustles behind the tree, he spins round, giving a deep-throated growl. Bares his teeth. The hum fades away and with it the sense of being watched. I stand, grab Rudi's collar and hold on tight. His presence is comforting as he steps forward and he makes me feel safe, but his body is tense and his hackles only drop when we near the edge of the woods. The sun is low and what light remains is ebbing out of the sky. A voice calls out as Rudi brings me towards the lake.

*

5th June 2014

Amy is embarrassed to find she's crying. Lance holds out a box of tissues. Grabbing a handful, she wipes her face and blows her nose.

"I've not thought about Rudi for years," she says, "He wouldn't leave my side after that. Slept on my bed every night until he passed." She gets up and puts the ball of soggy tissues in the bin.

"What type of dog was he?"

"A Red Setter. He was only a year old, still a pup. He made me feel safe."

"Is Rudi there when you take yourself to your safe place?"

"No, he's not."

"Perhaps he should be," Lance says. He looks thoughtful for a moment then asks, "Did you have any bad dreams after that incident."

Amy shakes her head, "No, I didn't. I fell asleep in the car and woke up the next morning with Rudi on my bed."

*

19th June 2014

She is on a train travelling forward from the day in July where Rudi helped her. It stops at a memory station she wishes had never happened.

"Where are you, Amy, and how old are you?"

"I've just got home from school and I'm seven. Mummy is opening the front door." Amy is calmly in the zone, yet she's aware her voice sounds melodic, detached.

*

252

16th March 1977

A policeman comes in the house. I'm told to take Becca upstairs and stay there. We've just started playing when Mummy cries out. It frightens us. I tell Becca the policeman hasn't hurt her, but she wants to see Mummy. We wait at the top of the stairs and look through the bannister. The policeman leaves and Mummy dials the phone in the hallway. She says, "David is dead." It takes me a while to realise that David is Daddy and that Daddy has died. I begin crying. Mummy looks up. Her eyes are swollen. She says to let Grandma in when she arrives.

Becca doesn't understand what's happening so when Mummy goes into the front room and shuts the door, I try to explain. She calls me a liar, runs downstairs and bangs on the closed door, but Mummy won't let her in. "Stay with your sister," is all she says.

Amy gets back on the train to leave this time behind. She travels past the station of her father's funeral as the memory of this day has always felt like ashes in her mouth. Instead she goes to the next station which beckons. Standing on its platform is a memory she pushed to the back of her mind soon after it occurred.

"Where are you now?"

"I'm on a train travelling from Euston to Kenton. It's the Saturday before Christmas and we've been into London to see the lights. I'm nine years old."

*

23rd December 1978

The train is very full and I'm squashed against a window. Becca is sitting between me and Mummy. She's sucking her thumb and falling asleep. My sister's shoes hit my legs as the train jolts forward. The glass is chilly and misting up. I wipe it clean with the palm of my hand, then watch as we leave Euston behind. The movement of the train, the sound of the tracks, is soothing. I rest my head against the edge of the seat and my eyes begin to close…

...then instead of sitting upright, I'm flat on my back.

My body lies on a smooth surface which feels cold at first, but begins to warm under my skin. I'm naked. The clothes I was wearing on the train are gone.

I open my eyes and prop myself up on my elbows, but it's like surfacing after you've swum to the bottom of the deep end of the pool. I'm on a slab and I can see more like it beside me and across the room. There's a strange smell which makes me think of the ward Becca was on when she had a bad chest infection. Above me is a strange curved ceiling which emits a bluish light.

Daddy is at the end of the slab I'm on. He looks perfect, but I know he's dead, so it can't be him, can it?

He says, "Don't worry, Amy. You're safe."

But his face is serious. Too serious. Daddy was always smiling and if I got worried about something, he would say, "Don't worry, Poppet," and tease me.

Plus his lips don't move. I hear his voice in my head.

Thin beings come towards me. A hand reaches towards my shoulder and I see fingers with flat round pads instead of tips. The hand doesn't touch me, but it's as if I'm given a slight push. I can't fight it. All I can do is lie back down.

Something which also looks metallic drops down from a small opening that appears above the slab I'm on. I cry out and Daddy tells me again not to worry. He's standing by my side, but he doesn't look right. I glimpse strange oval eyes. They glisten wetly as the bluish light catches them.

My head goes to one side as if those flat finger pads are moving it and I hear a sound which reminds me of an electric drill Daddy used. My ear lobe is pressed forward and the sound grows louder. I try to move away, but can't.

*

19th June 2014

Amy is gasping for breath. Lance sits before her, telling

Amy to think of her safe place and demonstrating how she should be breathing. Amy feels as if she has left the room and whoever is sitting on the edge of the couch is not her. This trembling wreck of a woman can't be her. But it is. Amy jolts back into the maelstrom of the here and now.

"What the hell was that?"

With a wry smile that belays the concern in his eyes, Lance says, "The start of your sleep paralysis and night terrors."

"But I was on a train, then I went somewhere else!"

"You fell asleep on a train and dreamt you went elsewhere." His voice is firm.

Amy is still shaking. She wants to run home and hide, like she did as a child. A plastic cup of water is pressed into her hands. It's lukewarm. She sips it gratefully all the same.

"Are you feeling better?"

"A bit."

"Now you've found the trigger memory, I want you to examine it once each day until I see you next. Work to remove the fear and terror you felt by revisiting with the realisation it wasn't real. What you experienced on the train journey was a dream. If it gets too much, remove yourself to your safe place and use the breathing technique I've taught you."

"Okay." Amy says, but she's unconvinced.

On the way home, Amy can't shrug off the feeling that she's opened her very own Pandora's box, releasing some truly nasty memories. They occupy her mind as she walks home and are so clear, it's as if she relives them.

*

23rd December 1978

Pain is what registers when Amy first opens her eyes. Pain and fluid trickling down her neck. There's an instant where the other passengers appear frozen, then life clicks back into place. The smell of people crammed together worms

255

into her nostrils along with that of ingrained dirt from the train itself. She puts her fingers behind her right ear and they come away bloodied.

"Mummy!" she cries, holding her hand out.

"Hush, Amy," Mummy says, leaning across Becca to check Amy's hands and neck. "You've scratched your ear while asleep, that's all."

Amy wants to believe her, but can't. What happened is just too fresh, too real. Becca rubs her eyes sleepily while Mummy opens her shoulder bag and takes out a handkerchief. She spits on it then briskly wipes Amy's neck and fingers.

"Stop crying," she says, "You're a big girl and there's no need for a fuss."

When they arrive home, Rudi, who has grown to stand over two feet tall, greets Amy, sniffs her damaged ear and whines. That night, instead of laying at the foot of her bed, Rudi curls his deep chested body with it's long silky hair against her.

Three nights later, she wakes to find Rudi standing over her snapping and snarling at things which slide amongst the shadows of her room.

*

10th July 2014

Sitting in front of her laptop Amy rests her head in her hands and sighs. She's due to see Lance in a week's time but doesn't want to go. She has done her "homework" with due diligence, yet instead of making peace with the "dream", she's become increasingly anxious. Amy is now frightened to go to sleep. The sessions with Lance, the train journeys from past into present are uncovering more incidents.

At the end of her last session, Amy told Lance, "I think there's a damn good reason why I boxed these memories up and shoved them to the back of my mind. I need to be able to function and right now I can't."

In fact, being unable to function has led to Amy being signed off work. Not that she'd been functioning that well before starting therapy. Years of night terrors and sleep paralysis made normal life difficult. It's why she lives alone. The one comfort is how well she now remembers Rudi. So many of the buried memories include him, how he slept on her bed each night, how safe he made her feel. Mum said no to getting another dog after Rudi died, even when Amy's night terrors became so disruptive they prevented her from going to University. Guilt surfaces at how the situation also affected her relationship with Becca during their teenage years.

Pushing thoughts of Becca to the back of her mind, Amy turns her attention to the screen and looks at photos of dogs needing a home. She reads their information while her fingers feel the tiny lump sitting in the soft flesh just below the cartilage of her right ear. Whatever occurred during the train journey from Euston in 1978, Amy is certain it wasn't a dream.

*

17th July 2014

The train reaches a memory Amy had pushed so far down, the platform and station are indistinct as it pulls in.

"I'm seventeen and I'm in bed wishing Rudi was still alive."

*

February 1987

It's dark and my room is freezing, even though January's cold spell is over. I hear movement, look towards the curtains and the window is wide open. Then the door creaks and I feel relieved – I think it's gonna be Mum checking on me, but it's not. It's them. The ones with the flat finger pads. I try to call out, find I can't speak and I'm whimpering from the effort. Two of them come towards the bed. At first they look insubstantial, shadow-like, but the closer they get the clearer they become. I hear more of

257

them coming in through the window. I need to move, try to move. Nothing happens. They crowd around my bed, close their eyes...

...and I'm blinking while laying flat under a bright light.

My arms are by my side, my pyjamas gone.

This time the machine is different. I want to kick out as they move my legs apart. I feel so exposed. But I can't stop them. My flesh crawls as they examine me. Inside I'm screaming, "Leave me alone!" No part of me responds. I make no sound, I'm paralysed.

A voice in my head tells me not to be afraid, that they will be gentle.

It lies. The metal probe they push into me is cold and it hurts. There's a whirring sound and the probe extends, pushing a part of itself deep inside. The pain is awful. I'm mentally pleading with them to stop. Tears are running down my face, I wish I could pass out.

Then it's morning.

I'm in bed, feeling sore and so cold. The curtains are open, the window is wide and there's blood on my pyjama bottoms, on the sheets.

*

17th July 2014

"I don't think I can take much more of this memory train." Amy says once she stops sobbing. The now obligatory cup of water sits untouched in her right hand.

"Are you still experiencing sleep paralysis and night terrors?"

"Yeah. I see them coming into the room and over the years I've woken up with marks on my body. Cuts and bruises and stuff. Sometimes the window is wide open when I wake. Sometimes my feet and sheets are filthy as if I've gone in the garden and not put any shoes on."

"Sleepwalking?"

"I guess." Amy keeps quiet about the fact that her

muddy footsteps led from the bedroom window to her bed.

"How long has this been happening?"

"Years. You're the first person I've told. It doesn't happen often. Mum used to go nuts when she saw the sheets."

"Have the night terrors improved or worsened since you began therapy?"

"Nope. Stayed the same, but I don't think I'm dreaming. When I went into the woods at the lido, I thought I saw a fairy. It was taller than I expected, but to my child's mind, that's what I thought I saw."

Amy looks at Lance. His blue eyes regard her steadily over the top of his half-moon glasses.

"Look, I think it was aliens in the woods. I'm being abducted and experimented on by them, have been ever since that train journey when I was a kid."

Lance sits back in his chair as if to distance himself from her statement. "I can't encourage this type of thinking, Amy. It's not an uncommon 'belief'" – his fingers mark the quotations – "but experience has shown me that night terrors are just non-normal dreams, not abduction experiences." His puffed-up pigeon chest only serves to emphasise the pomposity of his words.

Amy feels the flush rising up her face and tries to keep her voice level as she speaks. "And my research has shown there are many similarities between what people used to report as being taken by the fairies and being abducted by aliens," she retorts, "Also, how do you explain the pain I was in when I was seventeen, the bleeding, the scars on my body?"

"You would have been menstruating at seventeen and this can cause abdominal pain and excessive bleeding. You've just admitted to sleepwalking outside in the garden, so any cuts which occurred could have formed scars." He shakes his head. "I'm sorry, Amy, but there's a logical explanation for every aspect of the alien abduction experience you describe. I think it's important you face that fact, so over the next two weeks…"

*

13th August 2014

Amy puts the kettle on and opens the back door to let Bud, the young rescue dog she's adopted, into the garden. She watches through the kitchen window as he trots around sniffing every plant and flower. It's only been a few days, but this rangy black and tan dog of no particular breed has already bonded with her. Regular mealtimes, walks with treats, plenty of play and affection have done the trick. Bud has slept at the foot of her bed from day one. Amy hopes he will prove to be as loyal and protective of her as Rudi was. There's something in Bud's eyes, an intelligence, that tells her it's likely.

Her last appointment with Lance is tomorrow. Not that he knows this. Amy wouldn't have been so honest with him unless she had a plan. He was so dismissive when she spoke openly. After making her coffee, Amy goes into her lounge, sits on the sofa and takes her mobile out of her sweatpants. There's one call she needs to make while her neighbours aren't home.

"Hello?"

"Hi, Becca, it's me. How are you and the kids?"

"We're okay. Why are you calling, Amy? Shouldn't you be at work?"

"I'm signed off right now. But that's not why I'm calling."

There's a brittle silence before Becca says, "Go on."

"I love you, Becca, more than I can say and this is difficult, but… do you remember the train journey home from London when we were kids? Just before Christmas."

"Yeah. What about it?"

She tells Becca almost everything.

"Jesus," Becca says, "Amy, you had a bad dream

on the train and scratched your ear. Rudi was just a dog and when he died you began having nightmares. Mum always said you were a drama queen, and yes, you are, but this? It's ridiculous!"

"Becca..."

"It's Rebecca! You're no longer a child, although after what you've just said, I do wonder. You don't phone me for months and then, when you do, it's all about you. It's always been about you, even when we were kids. Have you any idea what your night terrors meant for me? Mum was so taken up with looking after you she effectively stopped looking after me. God, she even left you the damn house! Told me I didn't need help because I was married. If you think I'm going to step into her shoes and hold your hand through this latest drama..."

"Becca, please, I just wanted to tell you I'd figured it all out."

"Oh for fuck's sake. You said you're seeing a therapist, right?"

"Yes, but..."

"Then phone him, not me."

The line goes dead. Amy drinks her coffee to give her sister time to simmer down. When she calls Becca's mobile again, her number has been blocked.

*

4am 15th August 2014
Amy is standing naked on a towel before the bathroom mirror. The face looking back at her is very different to the one seen by Lance yesterday. She has cut her shoulder length mid-brown hair short, styled it to have a side fringe that sweeps across her forehead, and dyed it red. The clothes and shoes she recently bought are very different to her normal office skirt and top, or the sweatpants she's lived in since being signed off. What she is taking with her is in the rucksack on her bed alongside her new jeans, low

261

heeled walking boots and waxed cotton jacket.

After putting the plug in the sink and covering the overflow with a damp flannel, Amy picks up a single edged razor blade. She uses her left hand to fold her right ear forward, then feels for the object that sits just below the cartilage where her ear joins her head. The object is incredibly small. Amy is certain it's a tracking device. Not that she's moved around much. She's only lived in this house.

Bud is lying on the mat next to the shower. He opens one eye to check on her, then settles back down. There's no sign that Bud has been tagged. She checked him after the alarm woke them up.

Breathing deep, Amy takes herself to the bluebell woods until her hands stop shaking. Then, hoping she gets it right first time, nicks an opening in the thin flesh. The cut stings and blood begins to trickle. Putting the razor blade down, Amy leans her head over the sink, takes hold of the back of her ear and applies pressure to either side of the object as if she were squeezing a spot.

It chinks on the porcelain.

Blood drips into the sink, covering the object. Amy quickly lifts her head away and cleans herself, applying pressure to the small wound. Next she grabs her tweezers and fishes the object out of the droplets of blood, carefully wipes it clean.

An examination under a magnifying glass shows the object is faceted like a miniature gemstone. Its colour shimmers somewhere between black and blue. After wrapping it in toilet paper, Amy goes into her bedroom. Her ear has already stopped bleeding. Bud pads softly behind her, flopping down on the rug next to her bed. Once dressed, Amy unwraps the object, places it on a small piece of white card and takes a couple of Polaroid photos. Afterwards, she uses sellotape to secure it and rewraps it using tissue paper. Finally, she places the package in a stamped addressed envelope. Amy has given some thought as to where she should send the tracking device. She never doubted she would find one, but two people haven't believed her, downplayed her experiences. The letter she's written indicates what the item is, where it was found and why she has sent it. She seals the envelope, leaving it on the bed while cleaning up, getting rid of the razor, the blood-stained towel and putting the bin out for today's collection. Her destroyed laptop and mobile are already in there.

Before leaving, Amy stands in the kitchen eating a slice of toast and drinking her first coffee of the day. Bud has already demolished his food and is in the garden doing his business. She begins to smile and is still smiling ten minutes later when she shrugs into the rucksack, clips Bud's lead onto his collar.

"Time for a walk," she says.

The night has yet to fade as they leave her home in Totternhoe Close and begin the short walk to Kenton station. Matching his pace to hers, Bud contentedly ambles beside her. Amy absently pats her coat pocket with her free hand. The letter is in there, ready for the postbox they pass on Kenton Road. In the other pocket is an Oyster card Amy will use travelling to and around London today. Any other train tickets she will purchase with cash. The information she found online has given her an idea of where to start looking for the people she seeks. People like her. Hopefully the Polaroid of the tracking device will be her passport into their community.

Even though it's not yet five thirty, Kenton Road is busy with traffic. Amy shields Bud from it as they walk towards the entrance to the station. It's next to a block of flats, with stone steps leading down to the platforms. Once there, she stands with a handful of other early risers, Bud leaning against her whilst they wait. The train that pulls in is very different to the one she caught with Becca and her mother in December 1978. Its doors slide open electronically and seats run down the length of each carriage, leaving a wide corridor in the centre. Bright orange poles and plastic hand straps are ready to assist those standing. Amy sits down, placing her rucksack on the seat next to her. Bud presses his head between her knees. Brown eyes stare into hers with an intensity she already loves. She fondles his ears as the train moves out.

Day breaks with a yellow tinged glow as they approach Queen's Park. Amy welcomes the dawn. It defines the beginning of her new life, one where she has control and isn't terrorised. She is finally free and starting a new journey. Amy can travel to stations she chooses to visit, unhindered by the judgement of those who haven't been abducted. She wonders what Lance will do with the tracking device. She's challenged him to keep it with him and begins to grin as she imagines how he will cope with receiving visitors he doesn't believe exist. Amy's grin grows broader, she starts to laugh and her cheeks begin to ache.

STARLESS AND BIBLE BLACK

"What are you doing?"

Her mother's soft voice in the chill dark causes Marjo's thin frame to jolt. It holds a tremulous edge she's not heard in the seven years since she was born.

"I'm singing, Muumio."

"Who to, hani?"

The quivering tone is still there, despite the gentle question. Marjo realises it is fear. She knows what fear feels like when it clenches your insides. Muumio's must be clenching hard.

"To Karhu," Marjo lies, removing her hand from the frosted gate. She'd been about to unlatch it when her mother spoke. "I wanted to make sure we were safe from the bears." Marjo turns her back on the dense spruce trees which surround all the rear gardens in this cluster of homes with their sharp yet sweet scent. Mummy has her winter coat on over her night clothes, but her shoes are the summer plimsolls she now uses in the house. Marjo is scooped off the ground as if she weighs nothing. Mummy's words come out in a rush as she quickly carries her towards the pool of light spilling from the kitchen door.

"Goodness girl, you're freezing! It's too cold to be singing to Karhu. Let's get you back to bed, get you warm. I'll tell you a story to help you fall asleep, the one about a tonttu who created the first cat in a sauna. You can imagine being in there, cuddling the cat, while you warm up."

*

"Studying hard, I see," says Amber. She sits down after placing a steaming coffee just far enough away from an open book for Marjo to be happy. She smiles before picking the coffee up and blowing on the scorching liquid. A small sip confirms the bitterness that resides in its scent.

265

The noise in the atrium floods her ears. She's been head down since arriving and the place is now full of students. After placing her coffee back down and closing her book, Marjo squeezes Amber's hand.

"Thanks."

The flush that suffuses Amber's cheeks, the smile that lights her face warms Marjo. In a rare show of public affection, she takes Amber's hand and kisses it.

"Now I want to take you over the table."

"Later. You might damage my books." Marjo indicates her coffee. "Mum's got tai chi."

Amber grins, "Later it is then."

Turning to check the atrium clock, Marjo notices a group of students clustered near the television. "What's that all about?"

"There's been another disappearance." Amber's already on her feet, picking up her bag in readiness for her first lecture. "That's four in three months with the same M.O. The police think it's a serial killer."

Marjo shudders.

Soft fingers brush a loose strand of hair away from her face.

"I'll protect you," Amber says.

*

She is walking on the dirt path that leads from the back gate into the forest. Ignoring the pine needles spiking her feet, Marjo walks towards the clearing which lies deep within the woods. The aromatic scent of juniper bushes is in the air. Marjo draws fresh spring air into her lungs and starts to sing. The sound of her small, clear voice is absorbed by the trees. Its melody fills her ears, but isn't reaching as high into the sky as she wants it to. Marjo sings as loud as she can. Notes, which even she recognises as eerie, rebound off trunks and branches. The track widens. She has yet to reach her destination, but even so, Marjo stands for a moment, throws her head

266

back and sings to the stars pinpointed in the midnight sky. Her voice soars into space and there is a moment when she thinks it isn't enough, that she will run out of breath. A small star sings back. Marjo has no words for the overwhelming pleasure which fills her at the sound of the music issuing from the vastness above. Her mother's screaming brings her back to earth. It is then that Marjo realises the soles of her feet have been pierced and are bleeding.

*

Marjo listens to Amber's steady breathing. Moonlight glimmers in the clear night sky softly illuminating the spread of Amber's dark curls upon the pillow. Marjo keeps the curtains open at night. The only time she can clearly see the stars in this built-up area is when a power cut turns the streetlights off. In Finland, it was easy to see them, to hear their call. Here, the bustle of humanity drowns the sound. She can sense their voice on the rare occasions when humanity quietens. When this happens, she feels an urge to leave the suburbs, to seek out somewhere she can join her voice to theirs. Tonight, the impulse to reach the nearest woods is strong, despite the warmth of Amber's body. Once, aged fourteen, she'd borrowed her stepfather's car, but she'd not even reached the road. Since then her mother always sleeps with the car and house keys under her pillow.

Unable to resist moving, Marjo sits up and swings her feet onto the rug beside her bed. Moving silently towards the door, she catches sight of herself in the full-length mirror attached to her wardrobe door. Long white hair glistens and her deep-set eyes, her high cheekbones, look strange in the moon's soft glow. Reminding herself that Amber finds her beautiful, she snatches her dressing gown off the hook on the back of her bedroom door and quickly covers her nakedness. A memory surfaces, of frostbitten feet and hot chocolate while her mother softly tells her a tale of a saunatonttu. It makes her smile. Hopefully she'll be able to sleep with a warm drink inside her. With the ease of someone who is practised at slipping downstairs during the night, Marjo opens her bedroom door without making a sound.

Amber stirs slightly, mutters something, then presses against Marjo as she gets back into bed. Marjo wraps around the curvaceous form beside her. One of the things she loves about Amber is the complete acceptance her girlfriend gives. The reputation Marjo gained at school was one for oddness, for not fitting in. With Amber, there's a sense of belonging. Marjo feels the gentle rise and fall of Amber's chest beneath her hand. Every question she's ever asked Amber has been answered openly. Amber has only ever asked one question in return – a simple one about Marjo's father. She hadn't known how to answer, found the question distressing. There's a lot Marjo hasn't found the courage to share with her. Perhaps she could tell Amber while she sleeps. Marjo isn't ready to rest yet; she still feels the pull of the stars. Or she could leave her body, soar up above the atmosphere and travel back to the forest of her childhood. It's a while since she's done this, but if Amber woke...

"In Finland, my name means *one who has deep inner desires and truths*," she whispers. "It fits me well, for I desire you with my whole being." Marjo strokes Amber's hip. "But when the stars call me, I long to sing with them. Have done since I was a small girl and I think there's a truth, deep inside, in what happens when the call, the urge to sing, gets too strong and I..." Amber stirs slightly. Marjo waits until she settles, then says, "When I lived in Finland..."

*

It's been a week since they arrived in England. Each day rain has pattered on the windowpane. Lifting the net curtain hanging in front of the window over her bed, all

268

Marjo sees is grey cloudy skies above the row of houses across the street. Their bland uniformity is distressing. The front garden consists of a gravelled parking space and the rear one is tiny, a small patch of grass and patio. She misses the forest, the rustle of the trees when the wind blows, the animals and birds that twitched, twittered, and rustled through branches and undergrowth. Instead of breathing the scents of nature, she is choked by the stink of mankind and industry.

Fearing she won't even be able to see the night sky, Marjo stands on her bed, reaches for the wire holding the net curtain in place and unhooks it. There were no nets at the windows in Finland, just curtains to exclude the night, although Marjo kept those in her bedroom open. She takes the net down each day, but her mother keeps putting it back. This time, Marjo's stolen the kitchen scissors. Sitting cross-legged on the floor, she cuts into the mesh-like fabric, then rips.

"Marjo!"

Muumio's voice slices through her as sharply as the scissors snipped the now- ruined net. Shreds of slippery fabric surround her; the scissors lay in her lap. They fall to the floor with a "thunk" as Muumio grabs her arm and pulls her upright.

"What have you done!"

As Muumio's free hand rises Marjo hears the heavy tread of her stepfather's feet rushing up the stairs. He catches Muumio's hand mid swing.

"No, Jaana."

Muumio's face is twisted with anger. "She deserves to be punished. You give her a good home, a home she should be grateful for, and she is deliberately destroying things."

Marjo looks up and meets the eyes of her stepfather. He's older than Muumio, a bit chubby and tries too hard to be nice.

Letting go of Muumio's hand, he says, "The net was there to give you privacy, Marjo. Why did you rip it up?"

"Because I can't see the sky. I need to see the sky."

"There's more houses here than where you lived before, more people. This means there's certain things you need to keep private, like getting dressed in the morning, or ready for bed."

Marjo's only ten, but she's not stupid. "They can see me anyway if the light is on, I know because I can see them."

The deep lines around her new Daddy's eyes crinkle. "You're not supposed to watch," he says, arching an eyebrow at her. Marjo can hear the chuckle in his voice. "Let's do a deal. No net curtain, but when you change your clothing, you draw the big curtains," he points to the heavy blue fabric sitting either side of the white pole above the window, "and open them again afterwards unless it's bedtime."

Marjo shrugs and nods, as if in agreement, but she knows she won't keep them closed at night. How else will she see the stars? She tries not to flinch as he ruffles her hair, then hugs her mother. Muumio doesn't speak or look at Marjo as she picks up the scissors and leaves the room. The set of Muumio's shoulders betrays how angry she still is. Crouching down, Marjo begins clearing the mess she's made into the bin near the door. Her stepfather is trying to make her feel at home. The walls of her bedroom are the colour of fresh grass when the sun warms it, the furniture is new and very white, however the dark green carpet makes her long for the forest Muumio made her leave behind. Her toes sink into it and Marjo's heart hurts so much it feels punctured.

That night, she peers above the streetlights to see the stars. The glow of the city makes this difficult and Marjo longs for the darkness she usually watches them in. She leaves her body, soaring upwards then down to the

270

centre of the forest behind her old home. Although she cannot feel the ground she stands on, she sings to the stars which are now crystal clear. She has the joy of singing, but sadness fills her when there's no response and jolts her back onto her bed. Realisation that she was singing in spirit form while her physical body was adrift, silent, hits. Marjo sobs quietly into her pillow.

*

"Get up. I am taking you to uni today." Marjo's mother announces through the now-open bedroom door.

"We're getting the bus," Marjo mumbles.

"No. Two more people have disappeared. I am taking you in until they catch whoever is doing this."

"Were they together?" Amber sounds sleepy.

"No arguments. Get up. I will make some toast and you can eat it in the car. I cannot be late for work." She begins to go, then calls over her shoulder, "And I will pick you both up."

"Jeez, you'd think we were five, not twenty," Amber mutters.

Marjo's already out of bed. "C'mon, we'll find out what's going on at Uni."

The atmosphere as they enter the atrium is thick with anxiety. A headline replays endlessly across the bottom of the TV screen confirming the news Marjo was woken with. The news reporter's face looks grave; the police inspector she's interviewing has no explanation as to how the disappearances have occurred so far apart during the same night. One of the missing travelled by motorbike, the other appears to have used public transport then walked to the site of his disappearance. Nearby voices murmur: could there be more than one perpetrator – a copycat predator? And still, despite extensive searching, no bodies have been found. Just discarded vehicles, bags, trails of clothing. This time it's Amber who shivers. Marjo squeezes her hand.

The day passes slowly, but October's darkness arrives suddenly as Marjo waits for a text to tell her that mother has arrived. The night air is cold against her face when she leaves the university.

"Where is Amber?"

"She had to go straight to work after her last lecture." Marjo shuts the car door. Her mother quickly manoeuvrers into the flow of traffic. "I don't get why you're so concerned, Mum. We're in a city and people are vanishing in rural areas."

"They might have been taken there, or forced to drive their own car, motorbike, who knows." Agitated hands lift off the steering wheel then grip it tightly. "I don't want you to disappear. Your father did."

"He died of a heart attack, Mum, he didn't disappear."

"Not Michael. Your birth father."

Marjo braces herself for the inevitable verbal slap which has occurred every time she has asked about her birth father. "Then tell me what happened."

Her mother's small and sturdy frame briefly crumples towards the steering wheel. Passing headlights glance off her shoulder length brown hair; highlighting the downturned lines around her mouth, the frown line between her carefully tended eyebrows. To Marjo, her mother's face reflects the meaning of her name, Jaana, for she truly is a sea of bitterness regarding the hand life has dealt her.

"Once we are home," Mother replies.

Marjo waits patiently while they prepare an evening meal together and eat their food. She then clears their plates and makes them coffee. Instead of taking it into the living room, her mother indicates they should remain at the table. After wrapping her hands around the hot mug placed before her, mother takes a deep breath.

"I went with some friends into the forest to celebrate

the summer solstice. We thought it would be fun. We'd camp out, cook food, eat, drink and party. We were in the clearing near to where I found you when you were nine and the soles of your feet were bleeding. A young man sat next to me, one I'd not seen around. He was tall, had almost white hair and deep-set eyes." She pauses, then comments, "You look like your father, move like him." Tears form in her eyes.

Marjo reaches out, gently places her hand on her mother's arm.

"I found him beautiful and when he took my hand…" Her mother looks down, "I wanted him so much, I didn't care when he led me to a smaller, secluded copse away from my friends, the noise they were making. After we made love, I lay there, listening for the sounds of the forest, but it was silent and it was dark, so dark. I looked at the sky and it was completely black. No light from the moon. Starless. I cried out. He held me and sang. The sound was comforting at first, but as he continued singing, it changed, became unearthly. A small star appeared in the dark. It drew close, filled the space we were in with light. The next thing I knew, it was morning, and I was alone."

"Was he with your friends?"

"No, Marjo, and when I asked if they had seen him, they had no idea who I was talking about. It was as if he had never existed. They teased me remorselessly until they found out I was pregnant."

"What happened then?"

"Most became uncomfortable, began drifting away. But your hair, the paleness of your skin and your eyes, gave truth to how I'd described him. When those friends I still had saw you, they fell silent. Afterwards they avoided me."

"Did he tell you his name?"

"No. I didn't ask."

Mother's chair scrapes on the tiled floor, ending the

conversation.

*

It's just past midnight and Marjo is certain her mother and Michael are asleep. The stars tug at her tonight. Desperate to sing with them, Marjo carefully opens her bedroom door and creeps along the landing, down the stairs, avoiding the treads that squeak. The nearest woods are an hour's drive away, but Marjo thinks she can handle Michael's car, knows where he keeps his keys. Unknown to her mother, he's taken her to a local carpark a couple of times and allowed Marjo to drive around. She's not driven at any speed yet, but can change up from first to second gear quite successfully. The pull is just too strong to ignore. She must try, despite the weather.

The keys clink slightly as she lifts them from his coat pocket. The front door bolt makes more noise than Marjo hoped, but soon the door is open. Frost glistens under the streetlights and the endless hum of urban traffic is louder. Her booted feet slip slightly on the icy driveway. Michael always reverses in off the street, so it should be easy to pull out. Marjo winces as the clunk of opening the car door fills her ears, then slides into the driver's seat, adjusting it as Michael has shown her, so she and the car fit together. She starts the engine. The windscreen front and back, also the side windows, are all frosted over. She'll have to sit here, wait until she can see before leaving. Marjo turns the heat up and slowly a small space at the bottom of the windscreen begins to clear. The core of her being presses her forward. She revs the engine a little, hoping to speed the process up.

"Marjo!"

The front door is open. Her mother is shouting then slips when she rushes forward. Marjo panics, slams the car into first gear, releases the handbrake and floors the accelerator. The car lunges forward on the icy drive and slams into one of the twin stone pillars at the end of the driveway.

*

"I'm twenty, Mum, soon to be twenty-one. You can't stop me from going."

"Then I am asking you not to do this. Please, Marjo, stay here where I can keep you safe."

Marjo looks at the stubborn set of her mother's jaw.

"Lock me in, you mean. Lock the doors at night, hide the keys under your pillow. I can't even open the window in my room!"

"It is for your own safety."

"I'm not a child! Amber's parents want to meet me. I'm travelling with Amber and there's not one case of two people disappearing together."

"But they just vanish like your father did, never to return."

"You don't know that, Mum. No-one knows what's going on."

Her mother's face is twisted downwards. The bitterness held within for many years flows out of her eyes. She takes Marjo's hands between her own, gripping them so tightly Marjo feels as if the bones are being forced together.

"Listen to me, Marjo, end this relationship with Amber, before you hurt her so badly she becomes like me. She loves you far more than you love her. Please, for Amber's sake, end it now and stay home."

"Oh that is priceless, Mum. I've been with Amber for almost a year and I love her more than you can possibly have loved a man who fucked you once and left." Turning her back on her mother's tears, Marjo goes upstairs to pack.

The train journey is uneventful and autumn sunshine charts their progress northwards. Marjo is thrilled by the fields and woodlands they pass. Some of the stations the train stops at appear to be in the middle of nowhere. She grabs Amber's hand, talking constantly about what she can see.

"You're so excited!" Amber exclaims. "Have you never been on a train before?"

Amber's father meets them at the station as the sun dips towards the horizon. He hugs his daughter and shakes the hand Marjo holds out to him. Her mother greets them with tea and cake once they are through the door, but she seems agitated as they sit around the pine kitchen table.

"I need to speak with you both before you unpack and get settled." Amber's mother turns her gaze upon Marjo. "Your mother rang, this morning. She told us you sleepwalk, Marjo, said we must lock the doors and windows at night and hide the keys, including the car keys. Under no circumstances are we to let you drive the car. She was very insistent."

A storm stirs deep within. It rises and threatens to break the banks Marjo rapidly builds whilst trying to remain calm.

"She's really overprotective, Mum," Amber declares. "Ridiculously so. Marjo's not allowed to stay with me, I have to go to her home. The house is like Fort Knox at night while Marjo's Mum sleeps with the house and car keys under her pillow. Once people started disappearing more frequently, she insisted on taking us both to and from uni. I'm grateful for the lifts, but I sleep with Marjo most nights and she's never sleepwalked. Not once."

The storm subsides and Marjo finds she's crying. Amber's mother gets up, walks around the table and puts her arms around Marjo. Warmth and the smell of baking exudes from her clothing. Marjo leans in, finding she's crying in earnest while Amber's mother strokes her back saying, "Let it out, hon, let it out."

The days pass without incident and the late October nights are wonderful – clear and crisp. Amber takes the net curtain in her room down as soon as they get in there. The small town her parents live in is quiet at night, the streetlights sparse. They sit gazing at the night sky together, while Marjo points out and names the stars they see, the constellations. The freedom Marjo feels in this household combined with the love Amber shows towards her is a heady mix. The stars pull strongly at every fibre of her body but, for the first time in her life, Marjo finds it easier to resist. If this becomes a struggle, she wakes Amber up, asks to be held until the sensation stops. Now she tells Amber her story while they're both awake and is relieved by the understanding Amber shows, despite the strangeness of the tale. Often Amber does more than just hold her. She takes Marjo's mind elsewhere using assertive, knowing fingers and a gentle tongue. Marjo wishes they could stay: she's the most at ease and happiest she's ever been, but the remainder of the term beckons.

Marjo's heart sinks as they wave Amber's parents goodbye through the steamed and dirty glass.

"They really liked you, Marjo."

"And I them." Marjo sits down. "It feels strange to be going home. I daresay Mum will be waiting for us at the station."

"Move out. We can get a place together."

The idea is liberating.

"Okay, let's do it."

Amber snuggles in, rests her head on Marjo's shoulder as the train gathers pace. The clocks turned back by an hour that morning and pale sun shines obliquely through the carriage window.

Two hours later, the train stops just outside a station. A voice over the intercom tells them an earlier train has broken down and there will be a delay. Free coffee and snacks are made available, and people start complaining. Marjo and Amber pass the time reading. Hours pass. The sun becomes red and lowering; the sky is scarlet. Marjo can feel the trees on either side of the track crowding in. By the time the train moves, scattered stars are gleaming, and the waning crescent of the moon traverses a dark sky. The pull to get out of the train is there, in the pit of her belly. It increases as the train continues its journey, stopping at station after station set in the middle of nowhere. When the train slows towards yet another isolated platform, Marjo finds herself on her feet, at the carriage door, hand poised over the button which opens it once the train is stationary.

"What are you doing?"

"I must get off." The urge is so powerful, Marjo's poised to run.

"Are you feeling ill? I'll grab our bags."

"No, Amber, you can't come with me. I…I've got to go."

Realisation dawns on Amber's face.

"It's the stars, isn't it. They're calling you."

Marjo can only nod. The call is so strong. It's urging her to push Amber aside.

"Don't do this, Marjo. Let's sit down, I'll hold you until it passes." Amber takes her hand and begins guiding her away from the door.

Marjo tries, she really tries to put one foot in front of the other. She wants to allow Amber to take her back to their seats, but then the train door hisses open and Marjo knows it is hopeless. The call of the stars is just too strong, and the woods are so close. She stops and when Amber turns around, Marjo kisses her. Amber responds with the passion Marjo knows so well.

"Remember I love you," Marjo says, breaking away. Giving Amber a gentle push backwards, she leaps out of the open carriage door just before it closes. The train moves forward and Marjo runs. She doesn't look back, but senses Amber screaming her name, hammering on the

278

murky windows as the train gathers speed.

The station is unstaffed. Marjo leaves it behind and begins searching for a way into the woods situated just behind the small brick houses lining the street. As if drawn to it, she finds a stile, climbs over and follows the thin track leading between the trees. Their scent is different to that of the spruces she walked between in Finland. Damp air and a moss-like earthiness fills her nostrils when she places a hand upon the coarse bark of the closest tree, breathing the woodland in, listening to the noises made by those that reside there. A fierce tug in Marjo's core leads her onwards. It acts like a compass needle, spinning her this way and that until her feet walk upon a wider pathway leading towards what she knows is her destination. Her throat and mouth start to form the shapes of the notes she's been longing to sing for oh, so long. In the periphery of her mind, Marjo registers removing her coat, prising off shoes with first one foot, then the other. She has to stand still to take her jeans and socks off, then continues down the path. Twigs snap sharply and the earth feels hard beneath her bare feet. The force which pulls her towards it has been with her throughout her life, yet somehow, she's doing what she's always desired. Her blouse is open. Marjo doesn't recall undoing the buttons. She focuses on singing, drops it to the ground. Around her, the woods fall silent.

Standing on the boundary of a man-made clearing, Marjo removes her pants and bra. Surrounding the cleared space are carefully piled logs and chainsawed roots. Thin trunks raise bare branches to the night. Throwing her head back, she sings to the stars. The notes are pure, sweet, their pitch is perfect. Her voice projects upwards as the waning moon struggles to prick the bible-black sky. Marjo stands tall, arms held out from her sides, singing loud and clear. Her voice fills the starless expanse above and she can no longer see the moon.

A small star in the dark draws close. It sings with her. Their duet is timeless, relentless, unyielding. Marjo is drawn to the centre of the clearing. The solitary star is now above her head as they sing. The sound is beautiful and Marjo is filled with an overwhelming pleasure she recalls from childhood. A column of light from the star glints off something metallic then encircles her. Marjo's back arches as her feet lift off the ground. Her voice and that of the star become one.

Marjo ascends.

ACKNOWLEDGEMENTS

The support I've received from the horror/sci-fi/fantasy community since I began this journey has been amazing. Some of you I know better than others, but each and every one of you counts.

I'd especially like to thank:

Gary Couzens – you got what I was doing from the first story of mine you critiqued and have helped me to improve my writing skills through numerous beta and proof readings. You're a great mentor and a valued friend.

Trevor Denyer – for your belief and faith in my ability to tell a story. Working with you on this collection has been brilliant.

Ralph Robert Moore – praise and encouragement from a writer like yourself means the world. I hope to meet you in person one day.

Kate Probert – the painting you created for the cover so perfectly reflects my story, "Starless and Bible Black". Your support for this project and my writing has been solid and meaningful. You quietly banished my self-doubt.

Allen Ashley – for your constant encouragement that I get my stories out there. Also for taking the time and trouble to read this collection and comment on my work.

Finally, C.C. Adams, Phil Sloman, Pippa and Myk Pilgrim, for the stories you have beta-read and given feedback on.

When it comes to family and friends outside of the horror/sci-fi community:

My son, Ben. You visited pretty much every book fair Trevor and/or I had a stall at. It's a privilege to have you in my life.

Sarah Crome and Marion Kirby – you've both supported my desire to write for around twenty years.

Sarah, you and Paul Hunter understand the urge to create.

Susan – my American friend. The support and help you've given me has been much needed. I'm glad to have you as a friend and a day together watching films is long overdue!

Salim, Marc-André and Damien – however long I've been a member of Belle Sakura Salon is the length of time each of you has supported my efforts as a writer. Long live the Renegades of the Internet.

Mum – It took a little while for you to realise I was serious about writing, but once you did, you were on board and supported me all the way. An avid reader, your comments and insights were always helpful, but I miss you for far more than just this.

My friends and the community on Absolute Write – many of the stories in this collection are the result of the Winter Solstice and Summer Sisyphus. These events ensure I write two short stories each year. Long may they continue.

When I was fourteen, my English teacher read an early version of "Survival" in class. Afterwards, she took me to one side and told me I had an ability. She said I must keep on writing stories and do something with them. Hopefully, this collection is what she meant.

STORY NOTES

A Cup of Tea

I watched a war report from the Green Line on *Channel 4 News*. The reporter was so fired up, so alive. I wondered how someone who thrived in a war-front environment, would cope once they were home in the UK.

Time To Go

In my early twenties, I travelled to the Hebridean Islands by motorcycle (the bike I owned the longest was a Kawasaki Z440) and camped there. This story was inspired by the small sandy bay with bright-blue sea you could see through, along with the tiny church at the top of the cliffs, on the Isle of Harris. I wrote the first draft when I was twenty-four.

A Gambling Man

A programme called *The Unexplained*, hosted by William Shatner, discussed the disappearance of the Anasazi people. It mentioned a number of potential causes including an extended period of drought, well over 100 years – which transformed the landscape of Colorado and other areas – and a "Gambling God". I decided there was a story to tell, but by goodness a huge amount of research was needed. Fortunately, Ralph Robert Moore knows the area and the ruins where I set my story. He also knew the pip in chokecherries was poisonous which saved me from making a mistake.

The Little Lighter Girl

I enjoy retelling fairy tales and myths. For this one, I decided to switch London for Mumbai, cold for heat. Oh, and the person who wanted a retelling of a fairy tale that Winter Solstice Sisyphus, also wanted tardigrades.

Justica

Yet another Sisyphus story which retells a fairy tale. I placed the central character on another planet so she wasn't human, introduced sci-fi elements and upped the horror.

Handfuls of Nothing

The accident on the escalator actually happened. For some reason, I saw a foreshadowing of this as I approached it. There was no opportunity to say anything before Mum had put me in front of her on the steps. Yes, I lifted my hand off the rail as soon as it went backwards, yes the people behind me copied this action and yes, I caught the woman who then knocked me backwards. I have a cyst where the edge of the metal step bashed my back. I also wanted to explore how a misconception of an action could affect a family relationship. This idea became the story which dovetailed best with the horror of what occurred at Victoria Station.

Lightning Jim Bowie

I wrote this in the hope of taking part in a workshop at Worldcon 2014. It won me a place, introduced me to

Story Notes

Martin Owton and the T Party Writers' Group (since renamed, Gravity's Angels). I met Gary Couzens through attending meetings held in London. I wanted to write a time-travel story with a difference. Decided on a dog. Should be fun – right? I think this turned into one of the saddest stories I've ever written, but it seems to resonate with people. I hope it did with you too.

Happy Birthday

I started a Humanities Degree when I was thirty-seven. In the second year, a number of us fought for Creative Writing to be re-included in the program. We won; the university brought in a lecturer from Hull to run a series of evening seminars. "Happy Birthday" is based upon an incident which occurred in the market town I lived in during my second year. The only difference is that the girl survived; she was spotted by a couple driving past the park. The whole incident shocked me to such a degree, I had to write this.

Gaia's Breath

Trevor Denyer was looking for futuristic and horror stories based on the "strange days" we were living in. My mind kept returning to a futuristic novel I was writing, to the characters peopling its pages. As I couldn't break away from the society I'd already created, I decided to go with it and focus on a section of that society which has an independent role in the novel itself.

Rhapsody

Well, the Sisyphus prompt I received wanted an end of the world scenario which hadn't been done before. I went for full-blown horror on this occasion. Plus, shadow people and night terrors interest me. Luckily, my daughter Naomi was a fully trained paramedic. The detail in the opening section of this story is down to her.

To Have and To Hold

The aim here was to update a well-known myth so it reflected aspects of modern society together with the self-love narcissism embraces. I also wanted there to be a sense of an older world underneath that which was modern. There are many versions of the Narcissus myth, but I researched to find one close to the source material.

Death on the Mary Celeste

I had an absolute blast writing this. It came about from a submission requesting a "big" structure in space. My brain went "Theme Park!". I thought it would be fun to have a few deaths on a "mystery" ride and, well you've not long read the rest. There wasn't time to complete the story for the submission deadline, but I'm glad Trevor has included it in this collection.

Remembrance Day

Remembrance Day was the result of a Sisyphus story prompt which wanted a Tolkien elf in a situation where they didn't belong. This was fun to write, despite the horror of

286

the first World War. Hopefully I've reflected this horror in an appropriate manner. I needed to do lots of research for this and am grateful for the help I received from fellow Sisyphus participant and friend, Norman Mjadwesch who has written a novel set during World War One.

Survival

The first version I wrote, when aged fourteen, featured a woman stalked by a killer and a mouse stalked by a cat. I switched between the two viewpoints and showed the cat killing the mouse. It has seen many re-writes since then. This version I wrote for an Odysseus on-line writing course about point of view.

Taking Flight

The Valley of Dreams by A Polillo is an actual book. It was given to me by my parents for Christmas when I was seven. It made me want to be a writer.

Where The Train Stops

Alien abduction fascinates me. One of the things Jacques F. Vallée explores in *Passport to Magonia* is the similarities in accounts of being taken by fairies and abducted by aliens. I blended this with my own experience of Cognative Behavioural Therapy to produce a story which Trevor accepted for Railroad Tales.

Starless and Bible Black

The last story in my collection is the result of yet another Sisyphus prompt. I think a lot of people know what it is to not feel quite at one with the world we live in; to feel trapped in a specific place, or role, by a controlling individual. When acceptance is found and we feel understood, it's an amazing feeling. But, what if we were constantly compelled to move in an alternative direction? This is the crux of Marjo's story.

Printed in Great Britain
by Amazon

25687052R00165